THE TIN ANGEL

THE TIN ANGEL

BY PAUL PINES

William Morrow and Company, Inc.
New York   1983

4/1984
gen'l

*To Mike, Lisa and Chris, who know there is more
to the story than words can tell:
To José, who showed me that words were clues
to what we really know:
To Lynn and Fred, whose love and friendship helped
find this book a way into the world.*

ACKNOWLEDGMENTS

*The author would also like to express his gratitude to the
MacDowell Colony, the Ossabaw Island Project and the Virginia Center
for the Arts, where most of this novel was written.*

CONTENTS

I SLOW VAMP WITH FREEZE

II THE CATBIRD

III NERVE ENDINGS

The real surrounding is a medium
more than man can will, despoil, or even reckon with.

—WILLIAM BRONK

I

SLOW VAMP WITH FREEZE

AFTER-HOURS

When Lloyd McNeill piped the vamp to a tune by the Brazilian pianist, Dom Salvador, the conversation level dropped to a low hum. Diamond Jim moved behind the bar in time to the music, improvising on his own keyboard: martini, bell, wine, champagne, cordial and brandy glasses that hung by their stems from dowels like notes waiting to be struck. There was standing room only now, with tables full in the main room and in both cafés. I walked slowly from the rear, nodding to regulars, keeping a casual if proprietary eye on the waitresses and my doorman, Noah. Stepping into the Bowery Café, I glimpsed a shadow malingering outside and knew immediately it belonged to a pisser.

"Need me, boss?" asked Noah as I rushed past.

"If I do, I'll call you."

My adrenaline started to pump. When I catch a pisser assaulting the fitted wooden panels of my cafés, something inside of me snaps. Even the chill of the February night failed to cool me down. I rushed to the far end of the Bowery Café a minute too late to stop him. A big black man, he had already unpacked his fat dork. Reeling with Tiger Rose, he'd begun relieving himself when I grabbed him by the shoulders and pushed him into a neighboring doorway. He fell squirting into the wind.

"Wha' the fuck," he muttered in disbelief.

"Don't ever piss on my café again!"

The hip, well-dressed room full of jazz folk sat safely inside as the drama on the street unwound just beyond the compass of reflected light. I could hear Dom Salvador's piano tinkling like a full moon over the Caribbean as the pisser rose unsteadily to his gargantuan height and lunged at me. It took place in slow motion. Hours passed between the time he started for me and the time he covered the few feet that separated us. He mumbled something as I sidestepped him, and a tremendous weariness descended on me when he smashed into the fender of Rodeo Jim's Plymouth Duster.

My jazz club, the Tin Angel, sat on the corner of Bowery and Second Street, an oasis in badlands that stretched between Fourteenth and Canal. I had spent the last five years of my life defending it against the pissers, hawks, drifters and winos who spilled out of the men's shelter on Third Street. At times it felt like I'd been doing it all my life.

Most things aged quickly here. The panels of the cafés that ran along Bowery and Second already had the seasoned look of antiquity; their lattice windows, filled with hanging pots of Swedish ivy, were topped by awnings that had been bright red but were turning orange. Only the small panes of shatterproof glass covered by red-and-white calico curtains separated my customers from the street.

The big pisser moaned, tried to raise himself against the fender, then fell back to the curb. I left him there and walked to the corner where the two cafés converged around the set of carved oak doors Ponce and I had appropriated from an abandoned Hoboken townhouse late one summer night in '71. They opened into a vestibule that ramped up to another set of doors, on the other side of which Noah, perched on a bar stool, collected a two-dollar admission.

"What's up?"

"Just another pisser."

But it was the accumulation of little things gone awry that made me shake with battle fatigue. Tonight had been particularly nerve-racking. I'd spent most of it stationed by the ladies room praying that the toilet I'd just plunged into submission wouldn't back up again. But no sooner had I resumed my post than the bossa strains of Lloyd's flute were eclipsed by the roar of the thunderbox, and a stream of water trickled out beneath the door. And there I sat, Pablo Waitz, helpless at the controls. Finally, I prevailed upon Noah, whose plumber's tools were in the basement. He gave me a sharky grin full of little white teeth, followed by an expression that read: *What would you do without me?*

"What would I do without you?"

"Sometimes I wonder."

He had blond ringlets, rosy cheeks and a pair of shoulders like an oak beam. My Horatious at the bridge, he also had a drinking problem. I took the money and assumed Noah's position at the door.

I faced the stage where Lloyd's quintet presided over a dining area of wooden tables. They started to empty as the final set drew to a close. Bordering the dining area was a dark-grain banister we had salvaged from the fallen Broadway Central Hotel. But the real jewel, the prize surpassing any other, ran parallel to the banister against a brick wall: a forty-foot art deco bar made of pine, rosewood and mahogany.

My favorite spot was the last stool by the service end. It was my catbird seat. From it I could keep a weather eye on the bar, which was where trouble usually brewed. If I caught it quickly, I had a chance of stopping it before it turned ugly. I always tried to sweetheart trouble out the door.

My other catbird seat was in the section known as Watts, because for some unknown reason it was most attractive to our black customers, and only our black waitresses made out well there in tips. This section, where the room narrowed to the left of the stage, had deep booths along both walls. Beyond the booths were the bathrooms and the entrance to the kitchen.

From the first booth in Watts I had a clear view of the floor, but, more important, I could keep an eye on the bathroom traffic. More than one jazz club had perished because its bathrooms became places to score hard drugs. Slugg's Saloon, for instance. I had watched the junkie shades gather by its men's room through the sixties until Lee Morgan got shot and died with the mouthpiece of his horn still hot from his lips while his old lady stood there with a smoking gun.

It wasn't going to end that way at the Tin Angel!

Slugg's stayed open a year or so after that, death-rattling into the early seventies, when it expelled its last breath. Diamond Jim, who'd been tending bar there, drifted West, like the expired soul of that great club. Now he stood at my service end, as vigilant as I was; he had no desire to return to limbo, however moving the music there.

Lloyd was ending his final set with "You Don't Know What Love Is" in a moody Latin tempo, making his flute sob in the lower registers. I handed the door money to Diamond Jim behind the bar and descended to the basement through a trap in the kitchen.

Noah stood between Ponce's office and the supporting stone wall, holding a wire snake under an exposed pipe. His coveralls were spattered with the waste that had backed up behind a pacifier wrapped in a silk stocking: a message some disgruntled woman had flushed into my world. Noah held it up for my inspection as though it were the Kimberly Diamond.

"I know. What would I do without you?"

Smelling of eau-de-sewage, my doorman followed me upstairs, where the after-hours regulars had already started gathering in a back booth under the hanging lights. There was Big Baldy, who had a head like a porcelain doorknob and worked the Five Spot on weekends; Pepe Nero, who trod the duckboards of a basement saloon on the West Side, bore living testimony to the fact that it was harder to throw a customer up a flight of stairs than down one; Junius Brown, a small black man, wrote lyrics and drove a cab. Brown was staring at Diamond Jim, a lean, curly-headed man with a moon face who was making white lines on the table.

"I wish you'd hurry up with that!"

"Easy, Brown." Pepe tugged at his organ-grinder's mustache. "It's the only White Lady you're gonna get tonight, and you might as well take your time."

"And he's not even going to be the first," Diamond Jim smiled, pleased with the symmetry of his lines. "Boss, you wanna open your nose?"

"That could be dangerous."

"I thought I smelled something." Big Baldy's nostrils quivered.

They all stared at Noah, who was sipping Wild Turkey in a booth of his own on the other side of the aisle.

"The toilet backed up. What do you think runs in a toilet?" Noah toasted them.

"Sheeeit," drawled Brown.

Rodeo Jim used his gravity knife to cut a swizzle stick, which he handed me. The other half of the bartending duo known collectively as "The James Boys," he was a quick man with a square jaw and a shy smile. I vacuumed up a couple of arteries, then put some on my gums for the freeze. Mel, a lean man whose gray beard brushed the top of his bib overalls, removed his chef's hat and started passing joints. Lisa of the hazel eyes, tired after a long night on the floor, let her head rest on Rodeo Jim's shoulder. The tuner was set on WRVR, where Roland Kirk was blowing "Bright Moments."

The night's receipts, together with the take from the door, were stacked in a metal cash box at the service end. I opened it, checked the tapes, then counted the cash. Savoring a sweet crystal rush, I hardly felt the pain of ending with only $200 and change after subtracting the day's pay-outs.

It had been a mild February evening, the room mostly full of people moving to the hypnotic Brazilian jazz; hard to believe we'd made no more than this. At one time, I could judge a night's take by the feel of the house, almost to the penny. No longer. The last six months of recession had changed everything. Gerald Ford had put on a W.I.N. button and told us to "whip inflation now." We were trying. My high-rolling partner was wearing last year's lambskin coat, and I thought twice every time I hailed a cab.

Someone started banging on the kitchen door. Ronald Perry, the dishwasher, was sweeping the floor and stacking chairs. He put down his broom.

"I'll get it, Pablo."

Ronald had suffered a perforated eardrum doing underwater demolition in Nam, but he could hear a pin drop if he wanted to. He returned, followed by Christ in a tan bomber jacket. I closed the cash box.

"Pablo."

He was breathing heavily, but his face was white, bloodless. A street cop who blended into the East Village scene with chameleon ability, Christ had shaggy blond hair that curled over his collar, a beard that was more an advanced case of stubble and a gold stud in his left ear. It wasn't difficult to hear the sirens going off inside him. They screamed behind his watery blue eyes.

"Can I talk to you . . . alone?"

"As soon as I bring the cash down."

"Now, Pablo."

"This isn't a raid, is it?"

"Please!"

Butterflies fluttered in my solar plexus. By the time I walked back to Watts, where the air was thick with Oaxacan grass, the after-hours crew were already putting on their coats.

"What's up?" Diamond Jim bent over me. His long body became a question mark.

"You need help?" Rodeo Jim set his square jaw firmly. He'd spent years powdering his bones on the backs of Brahma bulls.

"I dunno. But I gotta ask you to leave."

Mel scraped a small mountain of grass back into a tobacco

pouch as Brown licked the last ghostly traces of coke from his dark fingertips.

"Anyone for Chinatown?" called Pepe.

"We could drop a few bucks at the Gaming Club," suggested Big Baldy.

"Let's march!" yelled dishwasher Perry, leading the troops through the kitchen where he opened the steel door.

"See you tomorrow, boss." Diamond Jim touched my shoulder.

"If you need me, call," said Rodeo Jim.

"Good night, Pablo."

Lisa kissed me on the cheek. Her expression these days was one of startled expectation, a reflection of her feelings about Rodeo Jim. It stayed on her face even when she smiled.

Christ sat at the bar. In front of him there was now a bottle of Canadian Club and a water glass nearly half full with neat whiskey. I took down a clean snifter, poured myself a double shot of Fundador, sipped. By the time I made it to a bar stool I was feeling the booze; velvet arms caught me on my way down from the coke.

His voice was thick. His hand trembled. "When did you last see your partner?"

"Ponce?"

"How many partners do you have?"

"This morning."

"When?"

"Around eleven, give or take a few minutes. I didn't actually see him. We talked on the phone."

"About?"

"Business. We're on the phone together three, maybe four times a day, depending. This morning he called me here, when I opened. We had a big argument."

"Go on."

"We argued about our chili."

"So?"

"No big secret. We make our chili from scratch, starting right with the raw bean. Ponce thinks we're losing money on it because Mel makes it by the barrel and it goes bad. Ponce's on this economy kick. He told me he wanted to start doctoring the chili from cans. I told him he was being penny-wise. What separates us from the place up the street is the fact that we start right from the bean."

"Is that all you discussed?"

"It wasn't a discussion, it was an argument. We're business partners. We don't talk. We argue."

He took another belt, waited.

"You tell me how a guy can drop a hundred bucks in ten minutes at the blackjack table, then get his balls in an uproar over a five-cent savings on a portion of beans. Why the third degree? Did Ponce go out and hijack a truckload of canned chili?"

I felt the brandy rise in my gorge. Christ glared at me with veins popping out of his orbs.

"Dammit! What is it, man! Is he in trouble? Hurt?"

"Neither. He's dead."

He dropped it and let it lay there. A fist closed around my Adam's apple. I gasped. There was no oxygen in my lungs, just nausea rising from a vacuum in my stomach.

"For God's sake! No!"

Although it came from inside, it sounded like someone else's voice. The world turned liquid for a moment. When I focused again, Christ's expression was unchanged.

"Tell me what you know."

"*What I know!* What a minute. You come in and lay this on me, and, and . . . what's going on!"

"He didn't die of old age."

"How?"

"He was shot, along with two others, both cops."

"Ponce didn't own a gun."

"He wasn't the shooter."

"I can't believe . . ."

"Those cops were my friends, Pablo. Bill was my partner for three years when I first hit the street."

The corners of his mouth dropped into a scowl that went beyond anger to wretchedness.

"Oh, man!"

"Right now half the cops and detectives in Manhattan South are canvassing door-to-door from Avenue B to the Drive."

"Where?"

"It happened on B and Tenth. . . ."

"I'm sick," I told him. "I'm going to the bathroom."

B and Tenth, Avenue Boo, Alphabet City. I turned on the cold water, thinking, as it ran over my wrists, about the winter of '62, my twenty-first, in a sixth-floor walk-up without heat or hot water. *Avenue Boo, shame on you.* I keep the stove burning, sleep beside it. There's been a rat decomposing in the wall by the tub since late fall. Gawd, how it stinks! Then, one day, it stops, becomes nothing. Most of the winter I've hustled chicken hearts from the kosher butcher on Avenue C, some leftover soup from a place called the Little Rose, but due to an increasing local demand, the chicken hearts and old soup have run dry. I've budgeted myself for a bowl of cabbage soup a day at one of the Ukrainian restaurants across Tompkins Square Park: Paul's or Leshko's on Avenue A. Alphabet City, DP camp of the U.S.A., where a bowl of *kapusta* and two pieces of black bread cost twenty-five cents. I've lived on it for over a month, pausing daily on my way across the park to hear fat Lionel Mitchel lecturing to no one in particular on negritude from a bench by the dog-run. Finally, at the end of my re-sources, I enter a dark saloon on Avenue B called the Annex where the hip blacks hang out: Bob Thompson, the Walker brothers, Ishmael Reed, David Henderson, high-voiced Ray

Taylor, loud Mike Bramble, a loosely wrapped package of nitroglycerine named H. Rap Brown. King Pleasure is singing "My Little Red Top" on the box. A bowl of beef stew costs thirty-five cents and a mug of beer fifteen cents, and there are as many peanuts as you can eat, gratis, in a large barrel in the middle of a floor covered with peanut shells. I scoop a bowl from the barrel, put my last half-dollar on the bar and order a beer and a beef stew. The Nuyorican bartender with an Afro and tango dancer's mustache does a double take and, smelling hard times, pushes the money back at me. After I empty the mug and bowl of stew, he refills them. Before he can refill them again, I rush into the street to puke; my stomach has grown unused to so much solid food at one sitting.

That was how I met Miguel Ponce! And his woman, Hattie, her strong hands on my shoulders, lifting me, leading me to the bathroom where I rinse the vomit from my mouth. Over ten years ago. I'd been a casualty. Ponce had taken me under his wing, maybe saved my life. Now he was gone, and here I was again gargling deep in my throat trying to wash away the taste of bile.

I splashed cold water on my face. The image staring back at me hadn't changed much over the course of time. I'd learned to accept the brown eyes that were too large, the face that was too long, the ridged nose of my Sephardic ancestors, the thin brown hair and high forehead that made me appear more vulnerable than I would have wished.

I can always tell what's going on in you, Pablo, which is why we can be partners; you give yourself away, said my fast-talking, card-playing partner, Miguel Ponce, ladies' man, masked man, dead man! Gone!

Removing a folded bill from my wallet, I opened it, poured a tiny mountain of white crystal on my hand between my thumb and forefinger. The sharp bite in my nostrils, the peppermint taste down the back of my throat steadied me. In about thirty seconds the tired engine knocks started to disappear; my heart idled, a motor timed slightly fast, but smooth. Cocaine numbed the pain as it produced a brittle sense of power known only to hopheads.

"Eddie Marovitch and Bill Greene spotted this '69 Dodge with a broken blinker making a left from Tenth onto B. They motioned for it to pull over. Something was fishy, must've been, because Bill radioed the license in as soon as they spotted it."

Christ cleared his throat. His voice still sounded as if it were coming through a handkerchief.

"They knew something was dicey, but they didn't follow procedure."

"How do you know?"

"Because they were caught flat-footed with their guns still in their holsters. If they'd followed the book, they'd have stood back, guns ready, and asked the driver to step out; that way, if someone in the car is a shooter, at least you've got a chance. But neither of them was ready when this guy at the wheel jumped out and unloaded a sawed-off twelve-gauge."

"You've got the weapon?"

"No. We found the cartridges. Scumbags like that don't clean up after themselves. It would've had to be a pump or an automatic to catch both of them; the shooter didn't have time to break the chamber and reload."

"Ponce hated guns, wouldn't have one on the premises here, though we certainly have reason."

"There were two passengers, Ponce and a woman. She was in the middle. After the first blast ripped through Eddie's chest, Ponce jumped out. Maybe he was trying to help the woman, but it looked like he was reaching for something. Greene had managed to get his gun out by that time. He caught Ponce through the back with a heart shot. Next second, he took one in the stomach at no more than ten feet. Left a hole the size of a softball."

"The shooter?"

"Got away. So did the woman. But if they're anywhere within ten blocks of the scene, we'll find them."

"Witnesses?"

"A couple of junkies, an old Russian woman who went into shock and now has enough tranquilizers in her to keep her airborne until spring. No description worth a shit. The woman wore a muffler and a hat, the shooter wore a peajacket and a watch cap."

"Right where the Annex used to be."

"Ponce died instantly. We had a patrol car at the scene five minutes after it went down, before the morgue wagon arrived. They put Marovitch in the backseat, managed to get part of the story out of him before he died at the entrance to Bellevue. Halfway back, they passed the morgue wagon. Bill Greene had rolled under the suspects' car and bled to death."

I stared past him into the room Ponce and I had built.

"The only thing here when we walked in was the burned-out shell of an old wino bar. A few local boys ran a craps and Sneaky Pete concession against the Second Street wall. We moved them, gutted the place, beat back a street full of hawks and jack-rollers to end up with a club people come to from all over. Hell, they know us in Europe!"

"Drink up."

"You remember Avenue B in the sixties?"

"Towards the end, when hard drugs came in."

"No-man's-land. Harlem and Bohemia nose to nose, and everyone was hungry. We were the new immigrants."

"Bill Greene was my partner. He left a wife and two kids behind."

Christ slid his palm along the bar. It made a squeaking sound.

My mind flashed on a quiet Christmas Eve at the Annex with Ponce, Black Hattie, Maria, sipping brandy, laughing; unlike the other lost souls at the bar, we'd had each other. . . .

"Maria! Has anyone contacted her?"

"She's probably at the Ninth right now."

"Maybe nobody reached her."

I dialed Ponce's sister. No answer.

"She's at the station, where we should be, unless there's something you want to say for my ears only."

"Let's go."

I switched off the circuit breakers, leaving on the track lights above the bar. Suddenly a shudder passed through me, a chill from scrotum to forehead, followed by a notion that had haunted me all my life.

"What is it, Pablo?"

"Nothing."

"Bullshit!"

"It doesn't make sense, but I'll tell you anyway if you want to know."

"I do."

"Sometimes I think that things keep happening, you know, like Hannibal is still crossing the Alps as Billie Holiday sings "There Is No Greater Love" at the old Five Spot."

OYSTER EYES

As we turned up Second Avenue, the wind tore through the lining of my old leather jacket, tunneled into my bones. Even the young jack-rollers who came all the way over from Alphabet City to prey on drunken pensioners had called it quits and gone home. A group of quiffs who hadn't made it into the men's shelter before the eleven o'clock curfew writhed in the doorway of an apartment house on Third Street, groping each other. On Fourth we threaded through a herd of transvestites spilling out of the Club 82 in bouffant wigs, costume jewelry and phony mink. Their spike heels clattered on the pavement as they called out in loud falsettos, fell in line with the hookers waiting for truckers to pull over and invite them into the darkness of their big rigs.

"What was Ponce into these days?"

Christ paused on the corner to light a Lucky, cupping his hands against the wind.

"When you have a business like the Tin Angel, you don't have time for much else."

"As I see it, you do most of the actual running of the store."

"Ponce handled the outside stuff: licenses; payroll; taxes; insurance; health, fire and building inspectors; the physical plant; things you don't see."

"I didn't see much of him at the store."

After several matches, his cigarette held a light. He took a long draw, then continued walking.

"We worked it that way, Mr. Inside and Mr. Outside. It helped us deal with creditors."

"The stall?"

"We're playing for time. Business is way off. He wrote the checks but was never visible."

"Nice."

"Come on, you guys play it all the time. Good guy, bad guy; you invented the game."

On the opposite corner of Fourth, we passed the Last Supper Deli. It remained open round the clock. Benson Supper, a wiry pipe wrench of a man with a set of gray muttonchops, gave us a tired wave from behind the counter. After half a century on the planet, he was showing signs of wear and tear. He could've packed a knish and several hot-dogs-to-go in each of the bags under his eyes.

"Give me something, Pablo, a wild guess, a hunch, *anything*! What would place Ponce in that car?"

"Listen . . ."

"No, you listen. Two men got killed tonight besides your partner, two cops. The guys are mad, and when they're mad they get nasty. If they suspect for a second that you're not playing straight with them, they'll make your life miserable."

"It's already miserable."

"It can get worse. They'll follow you into pay toilets, bug your soup."

"I get the idea."

We waited for the light to change on Fifth; in the glow of his ash, his eyes were shattered glass.

"Pablo, I don't want to see you get hurt. Bill Greene was my friend, like Ponce was yours. I just want to find out what happened."

"Me, too."

There is a fine line between friendship and self-preservation. I found myself walking it.

East Fifth Street flickered with flashing lights as radio cars, parked on a diagonal, pulled in and out; the red-and-white patterns they made against the buildings were leaping flames of a ghostly fire. Uniformed cops rushed around the gray stone precinct in a way that left no doubt that there was panic in the beehive.

Inside, men milled about the high front desk to my left as I entered. Phones rang. A teletype spat out information in a cordoned-off area against the wall to my right as a uniformed cop approached us. He was heavy, with dark curly hair, a bright red sweater showing beneath an open coat that flapped as he walked. He touched Christ's arm.

"Sorry."

"Yeah, Rizzuti."

We proceeded to a narrow stairway and were halfway to the second floor when we met two men in plainclothes on their way down; the tall black man's shoulder holster looked like a prosthetic device against his white turtleneck, while his buddy, a broad white man with silver-gray hair, wore a shiny blue sport coat that all but hid the gun on his hip.

"Too bad." The black detective faced Christ on the same step. "You and Greene were partners once, weren't you?"

Christ nodded.

"Don't worry, we're going to get that scumbag!" The white detective used his palm to smooth back his wavy hair. "We can't let them take us out like sitting ducks."

"Anything new?" Christ asked.

"Nothing yet. We're going for coffee. Want something from the deli?"

The black detective allowed his hand to remain on Christ's shoulder for a second. Christ looked at me.

"From the Last Supper Deli?" I inquired.

"Nothing else is open, Pablo."

"Who's this?"

The white detective nodded in my direction. I held his eye as Christ introduced us. It made him uncomfortable.

"The business partner of the deceased, Miguel Ponce. And a friend."

"What's your name?"

The black detective leaned toward me. He smelled like Old Spice.

"Waitz. Pablo Waitz."

"You Puerto Rican?" snapped the white detective.

"No."

"But that's a spi ... an *Hispanic* name, isn't it?"

The white detective glanced at the black one, whose lips were compressed in unspoken disapproval.

"My mother played the cello. She liked Pablo Casals."

"What about your last name?"

"I'm a Sephardic Jew. One of the chosen among the Chosen People."

"Chosen for what? To do time?"

"No, to suffer fools."

The way his head jerked back, you'd think I had cold-cocked him.

"You callin' ..."

"Come on, Toomey," the black man coaxed his partner down the stairs. "Let's get some coffee."

"See *you* later."

Toomey made it clear just whom he meant to see later with the coldest stare his gray eyes could produce.

"He's not a bad guy when you get to know him," said Christ. "He and Marovitch were next-door neighbors. Toomey broke it to Eddie's wife."

Down a narrow hallway on the second floor, the detectives' office was packed with men in baggy jackets, shirt-sleeves and shoulder holsters. Some stood, while others sat around a row of desks against a wall. A white-haired woman with the high cheekbones and narrow eyes of the Russian steppes stared vacantly at a book of mug shots. The lines webbing her brow and temples deepened when she shook her head. A carrot-top chewing an unlit cigar instructed Christ to take me to a room on the other side of the "bull pen," by which he meant the cubicle to the right of a small holding cell. I gathered that the

Latinos in the cell were the two junkie witnesses they had decided to squeeze for information.

The interrogation room I entered was even smaller than
the bull pen; no larger than five by ten, it contained a wooden
table with three chairs and a large mirror on one wall I'd bet
worked like a window from the other side.

"It's Grand Central out there."

"Well, you've got at least twenty men from Homicide,
Manhattan South, plus our own guys."

"Where is Maria?"

"I'll check. Be back in a minute." He paused at the door.
"This is your last chance if there's anything you want to tell
me. Once they start on you, you're on your own."

"Let Maria know I'm here, OK?"

"Sure."

He left the room without looking back.

Of course, Christ knew I was sitting on something. Ponce
was always into shit, even when he was standing around with
his hands in his pockets. He schemed to keep himself together,
to make life bearable. Ten days ago he had paced back and
forth in my office guaranteeing double our money back, plus
enough interest in cocaine to make our world a silver frost for
the rest of the winter.

Nieve pura.

*No, not the thirty-five we've got in the bank. Ponce, that's
our cushion! If we blow it, we've got nothing to fall back on.*

*Trust me, Pablo. I'll drop seventy in front of you, right on
the desk, enough to pay debts and sail through bad times. With
what we've got, we watch it shrink until we're hanging by our
thumbs from week to week. Don't pass this up!*

With his hands in his pockets, pacing and shaking his
head, *Trust me, trust me.*

I always did. It was Miguel Ponce asking, the man who
had fed me when I was hungry.

When I thought about it, there had been something
slightly off, an edge to his behavior for several weeks preceding

the deal. I hadn't considered it at length, ascribed it to the downward turn of our receipts at the Tin Angel, or to the new girl friend he was seeing, Julie Fine.

Julie was one of the few lady drummers in the business who worked steadily. And it seemed that she had gotten under Ponce's skin in a way unique in my experience of him. His love affairs usually moved quickly through the same revolving door. Not this last one. But how could I start to understand the feelings of a man no longer around to talk about them?

Instantly, Ponce became a total stranger. His image receded in my mind as though dollying back for a fade-out in a low-budget film.

It may've been ten minutes, no more, before Christ returned carrying a brown paper bag. He took out a container of coffee, a hot bagel drowning in butter substitute, and placed them in front of me.

"Maria's fine. She knows you're here."

"How can she be *fine*! Her brother's just been killed."

"She's conscious and coherent, which means *fine* in my book."

"You guys are too much."

I was working through my first bite of radioactive dough from the Last Supper's radar range when a troop of detectives entered. Among them I recognized the two who had stopped us on the stairs. The room became an arena, at the center of which I sat abusing my digestion. The carrot-top with the unlit cigar sat on the table in front of me.

"Will this take long?"

His cigar moved from one side of his mouth to the other without the help of either hand.

"That depends on you, Mr. Waitz."

Then it began.

It was all very polite, very "Yes, Mr. Waitz," and "Do you recall, Mr. Waitz." The redheaded detective, who had introduced himself to me as McGrath, did most of the questioning.

No funny games, no good-guy/bad-guy stuff, just straight repetition. Who was Ponce to me? How long had I known him? Did I have any idea what he'd been doing in that car? Who'd been with him? Who were his friends? Did any of them own shotguns? Did Ponce have girl friends? What were their names? When had I last seen him? Could I recount his movements over the past week? Over the last two days? Anything unusual? Times, places, people? Again, Mr. Waitz, let's take it from the top. Was he in debt? We know he gambled. Were the loan sharks after him? Was he the type to commit armed robbery? What could be the target at that time of night? A card game? A numbers bank?

They had active imaginations.

I chewed and swallowed the same bagel a dozen times as they tried to put together a case for armed robbery, a foiled attempt, based on what they had: a hot car and a couple of shells from a twelve-gauge shot gun. They wanted the names and addresses of every woman Ponce had flirted with, as well as the people we employed.

"Do you own a gun, Mr. Waitz?"

"No."

"Did your partner?"

"I've already told you, he hated guns."

"Who might've been the shooter, Mr. Waitz? Any guesses?"

Over and over until I was seeing double.

"OK, Mr. Waitz, that's it for now."

McGrath's skin was translucent under the overhead light.

"We have to ask you not to go anywhere; you know, out of town. And we're going to want to talk to you again, say, Monday morning at ten, all right? Good. Who knows? We may come up with something that will jog your memory."

Maria was slumped over a desk in the detectives' office. The first thing I saw when I wobbled out of the interrogation room was the top of her head resting on her arms. She looked up as I approached, her eyes deep wells in her face. Her black hair had been cut short, permed; she was a Latin Topsy with gold hoops in her ears. When she stood, it was only to fall into my arms. I could feel her tremble with a chill working its way out from inside.

"Pablo."

"I know. I know."

The last time I'd held her this way those seashell ears had been hidden under long tresses. But the line of her back, the firmness of her breasts were familiar. It had been six, no, seven years! We'd talked politely on the phone. Once or twice she'd breezed through the Tin Angel behind Ponce, always trailing her brother. A swell of anger broke, then receded. Even back then, for the brief period Maria and I had been lovers, Ponce's shadow had fallen between us.

"Stay with me."

Her cheek was damp against mine.

"We want the next of kin to make a positive ID." Christ stood behind her. "It'll only take a second. We'd like to do it before the autopsy."

Maria spun on her heels. The muscles that had been soft in her arms were now taut with anger.

"Why! Why cut him open! Pablo, why?"

"It's the law."

Color flooded her golden skin, then washed away as her full lips turned in a scowl.

"He was shot. You know how he died, why butcher his insides!"

"They have to," Christ whispered. "Whenever death occurs in any way other than by natural causes, the law demands an autopsy."

"You know where you can stick your law."

"What if he'd been drugged, shot up with speed? You'd want to know, wouldn't you?"

She'd been holding my hand all this time. She let it drop.
"What possible difference would it make?"

Her eyes met Christ's, then she took a tissue out of her
handbag on the desk, blew her nose.

"Let's go," she said.

We hitched a ride up First Avenue in a patrol car. The
rising sun was turning the windows of Kips Bay Plaza a shim-
mering rose as we approached the medical examiner's building, a symphony in blue ceramic face-brick, glass and stainless
steel. We followed Christ past the front, down a sloping driveway that separated the building from Bellevue to a basement
entrance where the morgue wagons were parked. Behind doors
that swung inward, a Hindu in a white lab coat sat inside a
glass-walled room. He shoved a book at Christ that reminded
me of a hotel registry. Christ put down his name, rank and the
name of the deceased.

"Follow me," said the Hindu.

"Wait. Just a second, please."

Maria had started shaking violently on my arm. For a
moment her ankles buckled and I gripped her around the
waist.

"Take your time."

"I'll be all right. Give me a moment."

I kept a supporting arm around her as we entered a room
lit by white fluorescent bulbs. The walls and floors were white
porcelain tile, except for the wall facing us, which was a fifty-
foot expanse of refrigerated vaults. Four tiers of them.

Our Hindu attendant led us to a vault in the middle of the
second row. He opened the stainless-steel door. I closed my
eyes for a second when he pulled out the tray. Christ turned
back the sheet. A deep animal sob came from Maria, then she
buried her face in my neck. I assumed it was sufficient for a
positive identification and held her head until the Hindu
volunteered to guide her back to his office.

Christ turned the sheet down still further. Ponce didn't care. They hadn't even bothered to close his eyes. He didn't care about that, either, just stared at me with orbs that were a muddle of pupil and iris, oyster meat. There was a bruise on his forehead where he had probably hit the ground. It was swollen and blue. The face had a greenish cast, bluish around the lips as though he'd stayed too long in a cold pool. Against this pallor, the familiar mole on the cheek, the thin tango dancer's mustache, the deep cocaine circles under the eyes might as well have been painted on rubber to compose a mask. My friend wasn't even behind it. *Se fue!*

"That's the exit wound. You want to see where the bullet went in?"

"No thanks."

Christ was gazing at a red hole, about the size of a half-dollar, under the left nipple of Ponce's nearly hairless chest. It was craterlike, ragged, the frayed ends of an old cloth.

"Hardly any blood."

"Never is with a heart shot. The pump just shuts down with all the blood still in it."

I'd never realized Ponce was so thin. I could count his ribs. The corpse wasn't hard to look at. On the contrary, it mocked my former hesitation by insisting that we were all flotsam in space. It was a papier-mâché puppet, a piece of theatrical exaggeration. But no sooner had I thought this than a wave of grief broke over me, receded into a sense of irreversible loss.

Was it possible for flotsam to grieve for flotsam?

Christ let his eyes play between me and the corpse.

"They're working on the premise this was a robbery that went sour."

"I know."

"They're reasoning from evidence to motive. But I think it was something else."

"What?"

"Drugs. We both know Ponce wasn't a stickup man."

"Find anything?"

"Not even a roach."

I pulled the sheet up, folded it around my dead partner. You win, I told him. I'll stop making the chili from scratch. Mel will doctor it up from cans, like you wanted. We'll even list it on the menu as "Ponce's Gourmet Chili." How's that?

"Tell me when you're ready," said Christ.

"I'm ready."

"WHEN THE DOG BITES,
WHEN THE BEE STINGS . . ."

After filling my nose in the men's room, I found Maria outside the clerk's office. She handed me a folded piece of paper with a message from Christ. It said that if there was anything I wanted to discuss, I could reach him later at home.

Maria asked the Hindu in the lab coat about the autopsy. He assured her in delicate language that in this case it would be quick; the body could be picked up by a funeral parlor tomorrow, late afternoon, or anytime thereafter. The way she thanked him worried me. Her eyes were dry and her voice controlled.

"Are you OK?"

"No, I'm not," she snapped.

We walked up the driveway to First Avenue. The streets were full of taxis fresh out of the garage. We hailed one. She sat in silence until our cabbie threw the meter, then turned on me.

"You look like you're half in the bag."

Instead of returning with some sharp answer, I closed my eyes, allowed my mind to drift: I was with my brother, Zach, in a Boston whaler on the Sound trolling for mackerel, pulling them in three and four at a clip, their quicksilver bodies flickering. Zach was manning the outboard, I was seated in the bow. Just as I was about to let my line back into the water, I heard Maria's voice.

"We're here."

The cab stopped a few doors east of Avenue A in front of a row of old townhouses that face Tompkins Square Park on Tenth Street. These houses might as easily have been in the chic seventies off Central Park West. In fact, they were several blocks away from the tenement where Maria and Ponce had grown up, just around the corner from where he had been gunned down.

I followed her up stone steps and into a carpeted vestibule where she fumbled with her keys. She opened the vestibule door, then proceeded down a hallway to the right of a restored Victorian staircase. We entered a semidark room where two curtained windows facing Tenth Streeet trapped some indirect morning light. I hit the switch by the door. The room turned white. It had high ceilings, elaborate moldings and, over a parquet floor, a wine-red Persian rug full of birds and flowers.

"Very nice."

She took my jacket and threw it on a couch with her own.

"Not bad for the *barrio*. I even have a patio in the rear."

She indicated a chair at a round butcher-block table. The shadows of ivy vines twisted in the blue curtains.

"Coffee?"

"Thanks. Uh, Maria?"

"Yes?"

"Are you angry with me?"

She clenched her fists, pressed them to her temples and closed her eyes. After a moment she spoke, pausing after each word.

"I'm . . . just . . . trying . . . to . . . hold . . . myself . . . together."

Then she walked into the kitchen.

Facing me was an impressive wall of books. On the opposite wall hung two prints. In one of them a woman in a slip sat on a bed alone in a room full of shadows. It was inscribed by the artist in a fine wavy hand: "To Maria, Raphael Soyer."

"Do you like it?"

She stood framed in the archway holding a tray. Behind

her I could see wooden cabinets, Formica shelves, an electric oven.

"I don't know."

"I spent a year as his assistant."

"It's sad."

As she put the tray on the table, I examined the other picture. It was a large, brightly colored poster of three arms raised, white, black and yellow, against a bright red field; a fist at the end of each arm closed on a bunch of grapes, the juice of which oozed like blood along the wrists. A legend at the top read: BOYCOTT CALIFORNIA GRAPES.

"Would you believe that the League of Advertising Artists gave me an award for it?"

"I would."

"They got two for the price of one, a token woman and an Hispanic, too."

"It's very strong, Maria, like this place, very much your own."

"I keep forgetting you've never been here," she said as I sat at the table. "Cream and sugar?"

"Just cream."

She poured the coffee.

"You haven't changed, Pablo. You don't even look any different. The same ragged jeans, coat with torn pockets ..."

"It's the way I'm comfortable."

Her voice turned brittle and she rattled her cup in its saucer.

"Potholes for eyes ..." She dropped the cup, and coffee spilled over the table onto the floor. Quickly, she grabbed a handful of napkins from a holder and started to blot it up, speaking frantically as she moved. "Don't you think I've seen eyes like that before! I'm Miguel Ponce's sister."

"Maria."

She raised her voice to keep it from breaking.

"Whenever he or any of his friends came into this house with a head full of blow, I saw those eyes!"

"If you want me to go, I will."

She sat behind a pile of wet napkins, put her face in her hands and shook her head. When she spoke, it was with a child's voice, small, pinched, scared of the dark.

"Talk to me, Pablo. Remind me of something good."

"I have some memories, Maria."

"What?"

"It's a May afternoon, we're walking along the East River; there's a tug pulling an oil barge towards Long Island City, kids riding bikes, sea gulls, and time is our friend. Tonight maybe we'll eat spareribs at the New Garden, or . . ."

"It was short and sweet."

"Both."

"What happened, Pablo?"

"I got restless . . . thought I could go away and come back again."

"And find little Maria waiting like an orphan of the storm?"

"For another orphan of the storm."

She paused. Tears started to run down her cheeks.

"I watched him grow up, saw what happened to him as a child. I knew what was going on in him when he ran through women, one after the other. And when they went sour, he filled the emptiness with booze, drugs, cards, anything to make him feel like he wasn't dying inside. But he was, all the time."

"Maria."

"No, let me talk. Earlier tonight, after I got the news, I was thinking of ways to kill myself. Pills. Gas. When I realized I had an electric oven, it struck me so funny I gave up the idea of suicide. I also understood that Miguel wasn't killed by a bullet. The Miguel I loved had been dying for years."

The floodgates opened. Her body began to jerk with spasmodic sobbing. I stood at the back of her chair with one hand on her shoulder, stroking her head with the other. It must've taken her five minutes to empty herself. When she had, she wiped both eyes with the backs of her hands, blew her nose and took a deep breath. I poured two more cups of coffee from the pot.

"Perhaps this isn't the right time to discuss this, but, you know, with Ponce gone, you now have a half-interest in the finest semibankrupt jazz club in town."

"Oh, no . . . I can't. I've got my own life. Do you realize that I'm one of the few commercial artists who could open her own agency and be making money from day one if I wanted to go into business?"

"Who's talking about making money? We've an outstanding loan with Chemical for thirty thousand against our personal guarantees."

"And the assets?"

"Ponce took them to buy dope."

"And you let him!"

"We worked that way."

"Oh, Pablo."

She shook her head. I felt like a fool, the object of pity. It embarrassed me and made me furious.

"I'm going to get the money back."

"How do you plan to do that?" She knit her brow.

"Nothing was recovered, which means that the money is still out there, either in coke or in cash. I want it back."

"You don't even know . . ."

"No. But I have ways of finding out."

"How?"

"Same way the cops do. Talk to people, call in favors, squeeze where I can."

"Please, don't! It's too dangerous. Three people have been killed . . . promise . . ."

She stood and I could see once again she was shaking. Then I held her, smelled her lemony fragrance, felt her heart beat.

"I'll be all right."

"Please. We can raise money, I have . . ."

I held her shoulders and disengaged.

"Maria, trust me. I know what I'm doing."

"I wish . . ."

But she never completed her wish, at least not aloud.

"Now I think I'd better go."

She nodded. Moving slowly, she picked my jacket from the couch, held it as I struggled to find my sleeve in a torn lining.

"Pablo, be careful."

"Try and sleep. I'll call you when I wake up."

She kissed me lightly on the lips and let me out.

I crawled into bed at noon. The sun was a smudge in the gunmetal sky that arched over my rooftop apartment on lower Second Avenue. As I closed my eyes, Ponce sat up on his stainless-steel tray, cautioned me against too much spice in the chili, shook his head and lay back down. When the telephone rang, I was almost grateful, until I heard my mother's voice.

"So, you're still in one piece."

"Yes, Mom. As far as I can tell."

"Don't you think you should've called to let me know? Do you have any idea how I felt when I read about you in the *Post*?"

"You what?"

"I was in the luncheonette having breakfast, reading the horoscope, "Dear Abby," then I turn the page and see . . ."

"Mom, I had no idea."

"The shock, Pablo. I'm still vital and strong, but I'm not as young as I used to be."

"You're ageless."

"If I open the paper one morning and read that you've been shot, I swear, my heart will stop."

I had a vision of Carlotta clutching at her toasted English as she rolled off her stool at the counter.

"Ponce was shot, not me."

"Here I am, *in public*, having breakfast, when suddenly I see my son's name in black and white linked to that crook...."

"He wasn't a crook. He was my best friend."

"Crooks get killed in gun duels with the police."

"It's been a nightmare for me, Carlotta. Please don't put me through the wringer."

"You! What about *me! I'm your mother!"*

I wanted to scream, *Carlotta, get off this fucking phone and leave me in peace!* I wanted to remind her that she'd given up her right to haunt me when she had run off to seek her fortune and left Zach and me with our father before we'd hit puberty. Instead, I noticed that it had begun to snow. The Twin Towers were barely visible through a fog that hung over the Battery.

"I'm really not up to this."

"How do you think I feel when I learn my son is mixed up with known criminals?"

"I'm not ..."

"Right here in black and white, for all the world to see. What will my friends say? Not to mention my clients."

"Your friends will understand because they're your friends. Your clients only know you by your maiden name."

"They'll find out. Take my word for it. In twenty-four hours everyone will know."

"Frankly, Mom, I don't give a shit."

"Of course you don't."

"You expect me to get worked up about a possible blemish on your reputation when a man who was like a brother ..."

"What about your real brother?"

"What about him?"

"Your real brother is a respectable young man in a fine profession. How do you think this will affect him?"

"He'll be the toast of Albert Einstein. How many bacteriologists can boast a brother in organized crime?"

"I don't want to fight with you, Pablo."

"Then why are you doing it?"

"All I want to know is, why are you always holding the shit end of the stick?"

"Who says?"

"I do. You opened a restaurant on the Bowery, didn't you?"

"It's where I live."

"Exactly!"

"I've lived here for fifteen years, since Pop died and I was a kid with no place to go. Remember that?"

I hoped a little guilt would stop her, but in my heart of hearts, I knew better.

"How could I forget?"

"Is that a question?"

"Don't be a smartass. You know I was fighting for my own life. Would you have preferred me to be a little woman in an apron baking pies?"

"The very image staggers me."

"Wise guy. Don't you think it hurt me to think of you living in a slum with bedbugs? So? Didn't I come down by subway with a mop and bucket and disinfect that pigsty?"

Whenever she wanted to enlist sympathy, Carlotta pictured herself on the subway. The fact of the matter was, she'd never learned to drive a car.

"All right. You don't have to take a subway anyplace on my account. What I need from you now is what I needed then."

"Tell me. With you, I never know."

"Support, not *Mr. Clean.*"

"You want support also for those pimps and addicts who parade across your stage with hot instruments?"

"You're amazing."

"I wasn't born yesterday."

"My mother, the original liberated woman."

"You bet your ass. I won't be modest. The last few years

have been good to me. I guess you could say I'm one of the more sought-after theatrical agents in town."

"Mazeltov."

"Listen, if you really want my support, I'll help you get started in another part of the city. I can get you quality acts. Vegas talent."

"Forget it."

"You don't really want my support."

"I'm not interested in a choir of honky violins, that's all."

"Don't be stupid. I'm a musician myself."

"You were a very good one. But when was the last time you picked up your cello?"

"Furthermore, let me remind you that *you* are a honky. Worse, you're a Jewish honky!"

"Didn't Jolson sing in blackface, and he was a cantor's son. And Gershwin, he wrote *Porgy and Bess!*"

"And Sam, he made the pants too long."

"Jews have always loved black music."

"You're not a Jolson."

"Let's drop it. I've got to make arrangements for Ponce."

"Where is his mother?"

"Frying bananas in Puerto Rico. We'll fly him down there."

"Tears your heart out. Poor woman."

"Maria will fly down with him."

"Who?"

"Maria."

"His wife?"

"His sister."

"Are you sleeping with her?"

"None of your business. Good-bye, I've got to shower."

"Think about my offer, will you?"

"Good-bye, Carlotta."

I walked out on the roof in my underwear. Usually, I was able to see a panorama that swept the eastern half of Manhattan from Wall Street to the Chrysler Building. Not today. The snow was blinding. I braced myself against the wind-driven pellets stinging me awake. My apartment, actually a little four-room house, was distinct from the other units in a building that had been a hotel for actors in the heyday of Yiddish theater. It looked more like a houseboat moored in a sooty sea than an apartment. I returned indoors just as the phone rang again.

"It's Zach, Pablo. What's going on?"

"You talked to Carlotta?"

"A moment ago."

"Then you know I'm in league with the Cosa Nostra?"

"She mentioned it."

"I can't tell you much, Zach. Ponce got involved in a coke deal with all our money and came out dead."

"You've got to get out of there."

"Come on, Zach."

"You could be in danger."

"Every time I cross the street."

"You can sleep on my couch. I'll cook you chicken cutlets."

"I'm allergic to your cat. Besides, all those boutiques up there make me nervous."

"It wasn't always this way," Zach sighed. "When I first moved here it was just another grubby neighborhood. Columbus Avenue was a sewer. Anyway, better boutiques than bullets!"

"Stop trying to change my life."

"I know, you think I'm a pussy, don't you?"

"How can you say that? I've watched you pull up those big blues."

"By the way, the mackerel are coming. They're steaming up through the Gulf towards Miami."

"OK, bro. I've gotta get off."

"Stay alert."

"Sure. Keep your surgical mask on."

The phone didn't stop ringing. In the space of an hour I spoke with Big Baldy, the James Boys, Pepe Nero, Noah, Lisa, Eddie Jefferson, Richie Cole, Lloyd McNiell, Monty Waters and Joe Lee Wilson. They all wanted to know if I needed anything.

Maria hadn't been able to sleep, either. When I met her under the green awning of the Ortiz Funeral Home, with the hood of her long black coat covering her head, she was the very picture of a medieval nun who had just undergone unspeakable austerities. Her eyes looked as though they'd been gouged into her head.

The mortician, a smiling little Latin in a dark pinstripe, informed Maria that she would have to meet him at the ME's to secure the death certificate, then led us to a showroom full of coffins. He might've been showing us a line of cars, the way he gave us the price and particular features of each model. We chose a simple wooden casket with brass fittings. I gave him a check drawn on our business account for $1,852.33, which included transportation and embalming, as well as an afternoon in a carpeted room for those who wished to pay their respects to the deceased. Considering a hearse to Kennedy and a one-way ticket to Puerto Rico came with the package, I thought it not at all a bad deal. I just hoped the check would clear. The mortician said he would reserve a seat for Maria on the same flight, though she was responsible for her own fare.

I slept all day Friday.

On Saturday, the day of the reception, I kept my nose full of cocaine, put my feelings on ice, so to speak. Many years ago, when my father died, I learned that grief is a time capsule in the body that releases itself at intervals according to an individual's tolerance.

Maria huddled close, her gold-olive skin flushed of color.

Only once did she mention that my orbs looked like marbles; that was as we stood shaking the hands of those who filed past the closed coffin. She made no mention at all of my black-and-brown herringbone suit, though it was obviously from another era with its narrow lapels and cuffed trousers.

Sunday, when I awoke, I was visibly struck by the effects of my body's effort to sustain the drug-induced roller-coaster ride; the ascents were getting slower, the descents, faster and dizzier. The wrinkles in my herringbone were repeated in my face. As I locked the door behind me, I resolved to put my life in order. One day in the not-too-distant future, I'd stop freezing my brain and buy some new clothes at Barney's.

Maria was waiting in front of her building in the same black coat, even paler than yesterday. Her eyes were so swollen, I wished she had worn a veil. She got in the cab and patted my knee.

"Don't worry, Pablo. I'm hanging together."

Her hand rested on my thigh. I covered it with my own hand.

Leaving the Lower East Side is emerging from the bowels of the earth. The water along the FDR was slate-gray with ribbons of white. Gulls nattered and wheeled around the United Nations as though trying, vainly, to reconcile vital issues of their own. The remains of two World Fairs in Flushing Meadow Park loomed on the horizon. We made it to the Eastern Airlines ticket counter with twenty minutes to spare.

After a tall blonde in a blue jacket with silver wings on her lapel confirmed Maria's ticket, we filed through the X-ray apparatus to a row of plastic chairs in front of a window facing the runway, where a ground crew was servicing a 747. Both of us tensed when a hearse drove onto the field and stopped under the fuselage. Two men in black overcoats opened the rear of the hearse, removed the coffin, then waited until members of the ground crew helped them hoist it into the airplane's belly.

Maria shuddered.

A few minutes after the hearse drove away, the plane taxied to the open end of an umbilical corridor attached to our
gate.

"Pablo." She held my arm.

"See you in a couple of days."

She hugged me hard.

BLUE NOTES

Wino Rose, a perfectly square bull dyke who walked with a limp and had a voice like Moms Mabley, crossed in front of me on her way to the men's shelter, her gaggle of quiffs in tow. Periodically, Rose and her retinue of black drag queens entered the Tin Angel and asked to use the bathroom. When I'd answer "No!" she'd spend a couple of menacing seconds at the door, then leave. She hoped to wear me down, catch me off-guard and turn my bathroom into a nest for street hawks.

Ponce had hung floodlights on the exterior wall above the Bowery Café to wash the street with light. There was nothing hawks, quiffs or jack-rollers hated more than light. As I got out of my cab, I noticed a group of hawks from the Kenton Hotel. They clustered on the dark side of the boundary our floodlights made, just beyond the café. But my sense of mastery disappeared when I saw a coven of pissers in the shadows of the other café, the one on Second Street. Ponce hadn't gotten around to illuminating that side.

There must have been eight or ten of them surrounding another of their clan. By the time I broke through their ranks, he was shaking off the last few drops. A small bubbling stream ran down my panels to pool between the roots of a newly planted elm at the curb. I grabbed the pisser by his shoulder and threw him against the fender of Rodeo Jim's Plymouth Duster.

"Hey, man! You shouldn't do that!" He rose, steadying himself against the tree. "I mean, it was too late to stop me. Ain't you got no *respect!*"

No sooner did he invoke the first commandment of street law than we became plaintiff and defendant arguing a case before the Street Court.

"*Respect?* How can you use that word after pissing on my restaurant, and my baby elm!"

"I didn't do anything to no elm."

"No? Look at those little roots, they're going to shrivel up and die."

"The man is *correct,*" the jury rendered their verdict after weighing the evidence.

"You don't own the street." The guilty pisser made one final stab at the court's sympathy. "And you ain't got no business with this tree."

"You ain't got no business pissing on it like a dog. What do you think, the whole world is your bathroom?"

"You're right," they told me, "and he's wrong." Their decision stood firm.

"I don't give a damn! Just get out of here, and stop pissing on my place!"

The man in front of me explained to Noah that he had paid the admission earlier this evening. My doorman asked him to put his left hand under a gooseneck lamp with an ultraviolet bulb; an imprint that read *paid* glowed above the man's wrist. Noah let him pass.

I saw another radiant glow, this one in my bouncer's eyes. It read: *Wild Turkey.* Blond ringlets fell around his broad forehead as he lurched on his stool.

"Doan worry, Pablo ... everythinsunda control."

"We made a deal about drinking during working hours. Remember?"

"I thought I might take the liberty on thisoccaishun. Wha' everyone's having a drink to old Ponce, toashtin him, you know?"

He smiled and turned into Harpo Marx.

"Just when I need all the help I can get."

I should have known. Pissers were omens; they were barometers of stress, increased sunspot activity, new cosmic viruses in our atmosphere. Well, at least the room was full.

"You can count on me, Bosh."

Onstage, Sheila Jordan was singing "God Bless the Child."

"Know what your problem is, Noah?"

"I drink too much."

"No, that's a symptom. Your root problem is that you have the soul of Audrey Hepburn in the body of Arnold Schwarzenegger."

At a glance, I saw many of the musicians who had played at the Tin Angel. I gathered they had come to pay their respects. The jazz community is like that about death. But I searched in vain for the pale skin and honeyhair of Julie Fine. Ponce had taken a look at her performance one night, and his eyes never left her until the set was over. She was one of the few people who might be able to tell me something. Maybe that's why she wasn't here.

There were a few hard-core regulars at the bar. The Laughing Budweiser chuckled at his own reflection, and there was Arty Whiffle with his raven-haired girl friend, both skunked.

"Arty, your cuffs and gun are hanging out, would you pull your jacket over them?"

"Sure. Sure."

"When your piece is showing like that, anyone could rip it off."

"Dammit, you're right!"

Arty was the only probation officer I knew who carried a gun. He moonlighted two nights a week as a security guard. One day a shadow would startle him and he'd shoot himself in the foot.

I ran the gauntlet of musicians who gave me their condolences. By the time I finished, I was imagining Ponce in a white robe surrounded by a heavenly big band welcoming him home. The picture dissolved when I caught sight of Rodolfo Colon.

He was standing by the jukebox talking to Pepe Nero. This sometime-actor who made his money dealing blackjack at the Gaming Club was also a drop for Black Hattie. If anyone knew what Ponce had been into, or could find out, it was Hattie. She'd been Ponce's girl friend in the old Annex days.

I looked past Rodolfo. No sign of Black Hattie. He was about to leave when I caught him at the door.

"Hey, Rodolfo."

"Pablo, man, just stopped by to pay my respects, man."

"Thanks."

"*Nada,* man. Ponce was my friend."

His eyes darted right and left, his large Adam's apple bobbed in his throat. Rodolfo had quick hands that had allowed him to make a living dealing cards and a brown face with high cheekbones that had disarmed many women.

"Do you know about what went down?"

"Only what I read in the papers, man." He fidgeted.

"Nothing about who he was with?"

"That's the jackpot question. You answer that and you get the prize."

Rodolfo gave me a close-lipped smile.

"And what's that?"

"What?"

"The prize."

"Hey, man, don't ask me! But knowing Ponce, you know, there must've been one."

"How about Black Hattie?"

"Hattie's out of town, been gone about a month."

"A buy?"

"You got it. In Brazil."

"I didn't know that."

"Sure, man. If she was in town, don't you think she'd be here right now, man! She and Ponce was tight."

"We were all tight."

"I'm hip."

Nobody had an ear to the wall of the coke trade like Black Hattie. It had taken her out of the Lower East Side, allowed her to prosper. She would know where to search, what rocks to turn over.

"When will she be back?"

"Could be anytime."

"Tell her I want to talk to her, OK?"

"*Claro*. She be right here with you, man, when she hears what happen to Ponce."

He gave me a power handshake.

"Later, Rodolfo."

"*Te veo*, Pablo."

He spun on his pointy shoes and walked out. I never trusted him. How could you trust a guy who'd grown up dealing three-card monte on Lexington Avenue?

"Telephone, Pablo."

Diamond Jim handed me the receiver across the service end. I heard the soft Brooklynese of Ken Brown, who managed Phebe's Place up the street. Two guys who might be purse snatchers were heading my way. They'd split when Ken had spotted them. One was black, balding, in a long leather coat. The other, in his early twenties, was white, dirty blond and wore a black-and-orange baseball blazer with GIANTS on the back.

"The kid probably doesn't even know who Bobby Thompson was," Ken added before signing off.

I passed the description to both James Boys but decided to leave Noah out of the play. He was perched precariously enough already. But who should I spy through the ebb and flow of customers after several minutes of vigilance? None other than Carlotta! I felt my eyes bug out; panic fluttered in my chest. I recalled her last appearance, months ago, when she had chucked both James Boys under the chin, then announced to the cocktail-hour crowd that her son owned the bar. The owner had nearly shit in his pants.

Carlotta caught my eye, blew me a kiss. Perversely, I imagined Ezio Pinza singing "Some Enchanted Evening" with phlegm in his throat, but Ezio evaporated as she led her party in an assault on table number three against the Second Street wall. Bertie, her boyfriend, waved briefly before helping her off with her coat. My mother looked like one of the Gabor sisters in her blond wig.

"Paaaaaaaablo."

Faces turned. I made it to the table in record time lest she cry out again.

"Hi, Mom. Bertie."

"Good to see you in one piece," she said.

"How many did you expect?"

"You look terrible," she whispered when I gave her the obligatory peck on the cheek. "Have you been sleeping in that suit?"

"No. We have twin beds."

"Sorry to hear about your partner, Pablo. I know how you feel."

Bertie's clean-shaven features twisted in a grimace of sympathy. With his long red hair, prominent nose and cheekbones, decked out in a snappy blue leisure suit, he looked more like Danny Kaye as Hans Christian Andersen than a cop.

"Thanks."

"If there's anything I can do . . ."

"I'll let you know. How's life in the Bed-Stuy?"

"The same. But they're kicking me upstairs. Next week I'm going to be attached to a special gambling division."

"Watch out. Another promotion and you'll be working with the clean shirts."

"Beats chasing muggers up and down stairs in a bullet-proof vest."

I recalled that the Cornerstone Baptist Church, where they held services for Bill Greene, wasn't too far from his precinct.

"Were you at the ceremony today?"

"No, I used to go to all the cop funerals, but I finally stopped." He took out his wallet and showed me his shield; it had a piece of black elastic around it. "Whenever a cop gets killed we're supposed to wear the black band for three days following burial. I got tired of taking it on and off, so now I leave it on."

He closed his wallet, put it back in his breast pocket.

"Bertie gave a good-bye speech before the school board," chimed Carlotta. "They presented him with a little plaque with his name on it, didn't they, Bertie?"

His face turned the color of the rose wedged into the deep cleavage of her black lace blouse. He started to squirm.

"No big deal. I was the community liaison."

"They really appreciated him."

I respected Bertie's stamina. He was the youngest and most adoring of all Carlotta's lovers and had managed to hang in with her where others had dropped away.

"Do you know everyone else?"

Carlotta's party of client-friends had arranged themselves around her like apostles at the Last Supper.

"You remember Steve." She nodded at a young man who could've been a double for the young Rock Hudson. One of Carlotta's oldest clients, he was a prodigy who played solo violin on cruise ships and places like the Palm Room. He worked the rich-widow circuit.

"How's it goin', Steve?"

"Condolences, Pablo."

"This is Lillian."

"Hello, Lillian."

"Hi," squeaked a girlish woman in a white cardigan.

"Lillian is a songwriter. She has something on the charts right now, don't you, Lilly?"

"Twenty-eight this week," she beamed. "It's called 'Love Juice.'"

"Have you met Jake? Jake owns a few clubs in the Dallas-Fort Worth area."

Jake was a short bald man on her left. He extended a damp hand.

"Nice place you have here. What do you recommend for dinner?"

Jake gave the menu a professional glance.

"Ponce's Gourmet Chili," I told him.

Sheila Jordan was singing "My Favorite Things":

> Girls in white dresses
> with blue satin sashes,
> snowflakes that stay
> on my nose and eyelashes . . .

"Give Lillian a little attention," Carlotta whispered in my ear. "She's just gone through a bitter divorce from a guy who turned out to be a fag. She needs to feel attractive."

It was with a sudden sense of relief that I straightened up to see a black man, resembling Ken Brown's description of one of the purse snatchers, hand Noah the two-dollar admission.

"If you'll excuse me, I've got to see everything is working as it should."

"We understand," said Jake.

"Hurry back, Pablo," Carlotta called through puckered lips.

The black man made his way to the bar, a leather coat draped over his shoulder, cape-fashion. A minute later, his partner entered. They wound up standing shoulder to shoulder behind a well-dressed uptown couple seated on stools close to the service end. Every time the black man raised his arm to signal the bartender, his coat fanned out, hid the lady's purse, which hung on the back of her stool. It also covered the white man's left arm, leaving it free to work undercover.

I jostled between them and tapped the shoulder of a woman with a pixie haircut and a face to match. She was wrapped in bassist Harvey Swartz' solo in "I'll Remember April."

"Excuse me, but would you check your purse to make sure you have all your valuables, then keep it on your lap."

"Yes . . . yes . . . of course," she muttered, confused by the interruption.

Shaking her head like one awakened from a deep sleep by a sudden noise, she went through it.

"Everything's here." She closed her purse and put it on her lap.

I'd made it in time.

Suddenly she cocked her head as if trying to recall a vague discomfort, an awkward pressure, then turned to face the men who had pressed against her stool. They backed away. The older one glanced right and left to find both James Boys focusing on him. And Bertie! How had he gotten into the act? A cop's nose. Bertie gave the purse snatcher a no-shit smile.

The younger one drained his bottle of Heineken and took off. His confederate carried a rocks glass full of amber liquid back to Watts, where he leaned against the wall next to the ladies' room. I leaned on the wall a few feet away.

"You should mind your own business." His voice was low and full of gravel.

"This is my business."

"We all gotta make out, you know?"

"Not in my place, you don't. And don't bother with CBGB's down the street. The bouncing there is done by Hell's Angels. Why don't you go back to the West Side?"

"Can I get my money back at the door?"

"You must be kidding."

I glimpsed Carlotta across the room in one of those unguarded moments when her gaze turned inward. She wasn't simply listening to the music, she was engaged in an internal conversation which must have been important, judging by the way she nodded her head in assent. I remembered that inward gaze, had seen it often as a child when I lay on the living room floor and listened to her play the cello. She'd been softer, more secretive, almost another woman. I was trying to recall her when I saw something that made my heart stop for the second time tonight. Babar.

Babar made Noah look like Rebecca of Sunnybrook Farm. He was six by six, with a head that sat on his body like a small cube on a big cube; no neck, all thorax. He had piggy eyes, yellow-putty skin and shiny black hair that fell over the collar of a navy-blue raincoat. When he wasn't acting as muscle for Black Hattie, Babar did restaurant work. He was currently out of a job, which was why, I guessed, he had come to see me. As he approached, the crowd parted for him the way the Red Sea parted for the Children of Israel.

"Can I speak widyuh a minute?"

"Sure, Babar. Go ahead."

"In private."

"Let's go downstairs."

In the kitchen, Mel was ticking off the number of hamburgers he'd made with marks on the fire wall above the friolator. They were the kind of marks a prisoner makes counting the days to his release. Leonard Dandy, my swing-shift cook, would come in tomorrow and complain that Mel kept the place a shithouse. Babar was fascinated by Maggie, a jittery waitress who was all elbows and long brown hair. She was sniffing empty Redi-Whip cans. There were half a dozen of them lined up on the ice-cream freezer. She did her best work high on Freon.

"You run a tight ship," said the Elephant Man.

It wasn't nearly as tight as his fit through the trap. After he'd squeezed himself into the basement, I led him to my office. Ponce's office held the files, adding machine, checkbook and payroll sheets. Mine was large enough for a small desk, cot, lamp and an easy chair. In addition to the offices, the liquor room, pantry and walk-in freezer were also down below, built into existing coal vaults in the supporting wall. Through the Sheetrock I could hear the beat of our compressor, the pumping heart that drove our refrigerators.

"What's up, Babar?"

He lingered in the doorway, filled it. I sat at my desk feeling trapped. Slowly, he reached into his back pocket, removed a wallet and from the wallet a folded dollar bill. Just as slowly, he laid it on the desk, then pulled up a chair.

"Take a crack at that."

I unfolded it. George Washington's face peeked at me through a cluster of white crystal.

"Looks good."

"*Good!* It ain't hardly been stepped on."

"What the hell."

It was a tactical mistake to accept Babar's coke. I knew it even as the small pile I poured on my hand winked up at me between thumb and forefinger. I inhaled.

"Where did you get that suit?"

Babar grinned. His teeth were small and square. I filled my other nostril.

"Yuh get it at Sig Klein's second-hand store for fat men?"

I stifled the urge to quip back.

"You didn't come here to discuss my tailor."

"Right about that. I came to tell yuh that yer partner got a tough break."

"Very nice of you."

"And to ask yuh fer a job."

"I see."

"The place I was workin' closed. I been lookin' around, but no one will hire me."

"I'm full at the moment. I can put you down as backup on the door if Noah is ill."

"He looks ill to me right now."

"It's been a hard day."

"No, I donwanna work no door. I'm tired 'a bein' a heavy. I wansomethin' nice, in the kitchen or behind the bar. Go on, take some more blow."

"Thanks."

"I donwanna get personal widyuh, but those two guys yuh got behind the stick, I seen better in Coney Island."

"I don't agree. I'm happy with my staff."

The coke was bolstering my courage. He held up his hands like a fighter playing rope-a-dope.

"OK, OK. I donwanna tell yuh how to run yer store. If anything comes free, I wannabe the first to know."

"All right, Babar."

I refolded the bill and passed it back to him. For a second our eyes met. I wondered if he could read my thoughts and began to sweat. No, the only thing he could read was fear; it was the knothole through which he viewed the world.

"Remember like I remember. Yuh know why they call me Babar, don't yuh? Cause I don't ferget."

"Maybe you can do me a favor."

"Maybe."

"I have to talk to Black Hattie."

When his forehead creased, his eyes nearly disappeared under a thickening ridge of flesh along his brow.

"What do yuh want with Hattie?"

"It's personal."

"Yeah, to me, too."

Babar adored her, followed her with a childlike devotion mixed with pathological jealousy. He stared at me, then pulled his chair so close only the corner of the desk prevented our knees from touching.

"Come on, give."

"She can help me find out what happened to Ponce."

"So can I. He got shot."

"I mean, the whole story."

His breath smelled like a sausage hero.

"Yuh got it all wrong. She can't tell yuh nuttin'. Hattie ain't even been around."

"She'd know who to talk to."

"Didnanyone ever tell yuh what happens to guys who stick their noses in other people's business?"

"This is between friends, Babar."

"They lose 'em."

"What?"

"Their noses. They lose their noses."

He used the quarter-inch dowel he took out of his coat pocket to scratch his head. It was only about six inches long, but he loved to warn people how much damage he could do with it.

"I'm sorry you feel that way."

"I was in Brooklyn the other day, over on Cropsey Avenue, yuh know where that is?"

"I was born in Brooklyn."

"Well, I saw this guy in the gutter with his nose tore right off his face. An' you now what he woulda said if he coulda talked?"

"No."

"He woulda said, 'Tell everybody it ain't no fun bein' noseless.' "

I'd heard enough. My heart was in my mouth, but I got up and pushed past him. Didn't want him to see the fear in my eyes.

"I've got to get upstairs."

He rose and followed me out.

"I'll be in touch widyuh again next week. An' remember, nobody likes a noseless guy."

Babar's huge body twisted sideways to make it through the trap. He exited without so much as glancing at my bouncer, who was defying the laws of gravity from his bar stool.

"I think what we've got on our hands is a waxing gibbous moon," suggested Diamond Jim.

* * *

"I'm not criticizing what you've done, Pablo. I know it wasn't easy to take a dump and turn it into a going concern." Carlotta's eyes moved around the table, pulling out nods and grunts of general agreement.

"Helluva job," said Jake. "Helluva good chili, too. How do you make it?"

"Dash of this, pinch of that."

"Wonderful, wonderful." Steve drummed on the table with his violin fingers.

"I'll be back." Lillian batted her long lashes.

"*But,* no matter what you do, you can't turn a piece of *drek* into a bar of gold," my mother concluded. "The Bowery is the Bowery. On the other hand, Pablo, with your knowledge and my contacts, we could really put something together."

"Imagine that," gasped Lillian.

In my mind's eye I saw a marquee with flashing bulbs that spelled CARLOTTA'S PLACE.

"Get some rest, Pablo. You could use it."

Bertie put on his camel's hair coat, then helped Carlotta into her sealskin.

The musicians were packing up their instruments. It had been a long night, and I was anxious for the room to clear.

"Perhaps one day you'll see the light." Carlotta reached out to pat my cheek.

"*Don't do that!*" My rage was spontaneous, uncontrolled. "Oh ..."

She uttered a little cry. For a second her fingers trembled in the air.

"I'm a naturally affectionate person, Pablo. I can't help it if that makes you uncomfortable."

Carlotta pressed her lips together and walked to the door. Bertie was right behind her, stroking her back with the palm of his hand.

AN EVENING'S EPILOGUE

It took me longer than usual to count the money. Babar, Carlotta and my deceased partner kept breaking my concentration. As I finally made my calculations, Christ came through the kitchen, pulled up a stool and accepted a tumbler with several ounces of Canadian Club in it.

"Maria get off?"

Fine, I told him. Had he gone to Bill Greene's funeral? Just the services, he said. His watery eyes were still red and angry. I couldn't see mine, though it was clear we looked out at the same landscape from different sides of the fence.

The moon had been waxing gibbous at the Ninth Precinct, too, he told me. A woman had come in to complain that aliens were trying to suck her into their spaceship through a large Hygeia Sipper, and the desk sergeant had patiently explained that complaints against aliens were useless; the best thing she could do was go home and wrap her head in tinfoil.

Again he asked me if there was anything more I'd like to tell him, to which I responded that if there was he wouldn't have to come to me, I'd find him. He reminded me of my appointment tomorrow, no, today, in less than six hours at the precinct, finished his drink and left.

Alone at the register, I thought about Maria. I wanted to feel her softness, curl up in the nest of her arms and sleep. No, I'd have to be careful about that. I had already hurt her once. I couldn't trust myself not to do it again.

With the cash box under my arm, I proceeded down to the

basement where I stuck it in the hiding place, a hole in the brick wall behind Ponce's office. By the time I returned, the after-hours crowd was already passing the swizzle.

"Jesus!" yelled Pepe, taking a noseful. "This saloon life will get you in the end."

"It's not a bad way to go," offered Diamond Jim.

"What do you know?" challenged Big Baldy.

"I know the difference between school and saloons, Baldy. In school, all the answers are possible."

"Amen." Brown snatched the swizzle from Pepe.

When I pulled up a chair, they fell silent, waiting for me to say something. I couldn't think of a way to begin. Most of them, I knew, had already been questioned by the cops. Those who hadn't, would be. That made it tough. But weren't they my friends, these people with whom I shared the adrenaline nights? At last I was able to break the silence.

"I don't know how things will come out in the end, but I need some answers."

"What?" asked Brown.

"Who was with Ponce when he got shot?"

"Careful, Pab," cautioned Pepe.

Big Baldy took a quick pull on a joint, then let out the smoke.

"The stakes are homicide. That's touchy."

"Regardless, if you hear something, please let me know."

"Listen to them," said Lisa. "They're making sense."

They all seemed to be moving away from me as though I had a contagious disease.

"Hey, Pablo." Junius Brown touched my shoulder. "You gotta keep something in mind."

"Tell me."

"You may be Clark Kent, but you sure as shit ain't Superman."

SPREADING THE NET

It was a few minutes after 11:00 A.M., Monday, when I approached the saloon doors of the Ninth, otherwise known as the "Kojak Precinct" because it was used for exterior shots in the TV series. Above the entrance a heavy black-and-purple wreath with two streamers draped around the lintel reminded everyone who passed this was a house of mourning. The usual banter between the men lounging on the steps was absent. They parted silently to let me by.

Inside, also, it was deathly quiet, except for the telephones, papers being shuffled, the mechanical noises of teletype and computer. Inspector Borden's door was closed, but that wasn't unusual for a man whose low visibility had become standard operating procedure. I pictured him, a nervous, graying fifty with a quick hemorrhoidal smile. I had found him at his desk, once, years ago when I'd come to introduce myself as the owner of the Tin Angel and request that he beef up patrols along the Bowery. We needed help. The look on his face had been both pained and apologetic, explaining that he already had to cope with junkies and fences along Houston; pimps, porn palaces and methadone on Fourteenth Street; and every act of cruelty, despair and desperation imaginable between Broadway and the East River.

"Can I help you?"

A beefy desk sergeant stood behind the high platform like a helmsman on the bridge of a ship, a black elastic band around his shield. When I told him who I was, he directed me upstairs to the detectives' office.

I passed men in civilian clothes and in uniform, all walking slowly, talking in muted tones. Greene and Marovitch had been of their number. In uniform, each was a facsimile of the other, and this heightened everyone's sense of his own mortality. I wondered what it would be like to spend twenty years inside these gray walls thinking about a pension.

At the top of the stairs, I made a left and knocked at the door at the end of the corridor.

"Come in!"

I wasn't overjoyed to discover the detective who had given me a hard time last week sitting behind the desk. He was alone in the room, except for two Nuyoricans and a muscular black man in a torn T-shirt huddled in the bull pen.

"Good of you to be so punctual, Mr. Waitz. Have a chair."

"Thank you."

I sat in the one by the side of his desk. He was in shirtsleeves, a black band around the gold shield hanging from his pocket. I had the impression he was on his best behavior. He glanced at his watch.

"I'd like to wait for Harris, my partner. I'm Detective Toomey."

"Will he be long?"

"He's taking a crap. Mr. Punctual. Got a gut like a Bulova, takes a crap every morning after breakfast. Someone could be getting mugged, but if Harris had just finished breakfast he'd have to take his crap first."

"Some people are lucky."

"No joke. I envy him. I got a gut full of iron, can't ever tell when the urge will hit me. I go for a day, maybe two or three, never more than a week; but my doctor tells me not to worry, says I've got a sluggish colon. *Sluggish colon!* I've heard of weird things in my life, but how can a colon be sluggish? Smoke, Mr. Waitz?"

"No, thanks. I'm trying to stop."

"You picked a helluva time."

Toomey removed a small notebook from the inside pocket of his sharkskin jacket hanging over the back of his chair. As he flipped through its pages, he shook his head.

"Stopped cold turkey, huh? And from what we've been able to gather, your business is in rough shape. Helluva time to stop."

"Talking with my creditors?"

"Not all of them, just a few locals: Square Jack Carbonero, your butcher; Jimmy Iglesias, your liquor salesman. From what we can piece together about your business, and the circumstances of your partner's death, I'd say . . . you picked a helluva time to stop smoking."

"I was up to three packs a day."

Toomey lit a Camel.

"Fucking miserable habit. Did your partner carry any life insurance?"

"I don't believe he did."

"How about a will?"

"None that I know of."

"Harris hasn't touched a cigarette in two years, since we teamed up and he started jogging. He quit cold turkey, too. When we first teamed up, he farted every time he stepped on the brake. Then he started jogging, became a health nut, a spade with nerves of steel. He carries sunflower seeds in one pocket and bean sprouts in the other."

"Sounds like a hard guy to live with."

"I mean, I wish he'd fart once in a while, or eat a hot dog."

"They're full of nitrates."

"Waitz, how could I give up smoking with a sluggish colon?"

"I don't know."

"I'd blow up like the Goodyear Blimp."

Detective Harris entered. He had a soft baritone.

"Sorry to keep you waiting. Give me a minute to get set."

Harris, also, was in shirt-sleeves; on the vest of his three-piece brown suit, the banded shield. He rummaged through papers on his blotter until he located a note pad, then ransacked his drawer for a pen.

"What are you doing, Harris?"

"My gold pen. Did you return it to me, Toomey?"

"I could swear I gave it back." He patted his pockets. "Use one of mine."

"I loan you my goddamn gold graduation pen and you give me this piece of shit, a nineteen-cent Bic?"

"He went through John Jay on 'open admissions.' " Toomey winked at me. "It's a virgin, Harris, you got to break the seal."

"I swear . . ."

Harris scrawled on his pad until the ink flowed, then cleared his throat and started asking questions. It was like being interrogated by Billy Eckstein. The questions hadn't changed. How long had I known Ponce? Did I have any idea who the shooter might be? Who were his other associates? Recount his movements the day before the shooting. Who had he been with? I made up my mind to tell them no more than was necessary to keep me on the right side of cooperation when Harris turned the direction of the questioning.

"We know he dealt drugs."

His voice was matter-of-fact. Both detectives watched me for some physical response.

"You knew that, didn't you?" echoed Toomey.

"Everyone in this part of town passes a drug now and then."

"We're under the impression the deceased did it more than 'now and then,' " pressed Harris.

"How do you know?"

"We have our sources."

Christ. He had decided to open up the investigation. I'd been hoping that they would continue looking for an armed robber, but Christ wouldn't allow that to happen.

"I can't tell you how frequently Miguel Ponce passed a drug, but I'd guess it was seldom, and then only a bit of grass. We had our hands full running a business. We both saw what hard drugs did to Slugg's in the late sixties—tore it apart. We'd made up our minds the Tin Angel wasn't going to be another Slugg's. We kept it clean."

"I wish you wouldn't do that with my pen," said Toomey.

"What?"

"Stick it in your ear."

Harris took the dry end of the pen out of his ear, paused before speaking.

"Mr. Waitz, do you have any idea what the deceased was doing in that car, who was with him?"

"No I've told you already."

"We want the scumbag with the shotgun." Toomey's eyes narrowed.

"I hope you get him."

"You should. The two on the run have a double homicide on their minds, two cops! Maybe they're not sure what your partner told you, how much you know. As far as they're concerned, maybe you could finger them, and they're itchy enough to wanna make sure you don't."

"You're a hot item," said Harris. "It would be a smart move to play ball with us."

"If I find anything, I'll let you know."

"Do that, OK? Anything else, Harris?"

"Not for now. Oh, where is the deceased's sister, Maria Ponce? We can't reach her."

"In Puerto Rico, burying her brother. She'll be back tonight."

"Tell her to get in touch with us?"

"Sure."

"And we're going to want to see you again," smiled Toomey. "Same time, Friday?"

"How often am I going to have to go through this with you guys?"

Harris closed his notebook.

"As often as we think necessary. It's as much for your protection as for anything else."

"We want to be close by in case someone takes a shot at you," whispered Toomey.

Suddenly it struck me—what was so familiar about the wavy hair, sharp nose and sharkskin suit.

"Toomey, has anybody told you that you resemble Spiro Agnew?"

"Yeah, all the time." He flinched.

"Spiro Agnew! Spiro Agnew!"

The two Nuyorican kids in the bull pen grew animated. The fatter of the two slapped his knee and began to sing to a salsa beat: "Spiro Agnew is a *pato.*"

"Enough out of you, scumbag!"

"Don't you think he look like Spiro Agnew, man?" The fat Latino turned to the black man in the corner of the cell.

"Yeah, he do."

"Quack! Quack!"

"If you scumbags don't can it, I'm gonna stick your heads in the toilet and flush. I don't have to tell you what the toilet's going to be full of, either, do I?"

Across the street, kids were bobbing and weaving in the schoolyard. A few played basketball, others touch football and a half-dozen more were swiping at a hockey puck. Keeping your own game separate when so many others were constantly running through it wasn't easy. It was one of the ways you developed rhythm in the ghetto.

A crisp, sunny afternoon. I left a note in Maria's vestibule saying that I'd return, was anxious to see her, before walking down Avenue B to Ali's *bodega.*

The soft-spoken Palestinian Arab had been making book, fencing hot stereos and milking the fire-and-flood clause of his insurance policies for as long as I could remember.

Once upon a time, when Ali had owned the deli on

Fourth Street, he'd hired elderly Jews to sit around, talk Yiddish and call him "Moishe." The wily Arab had also owned two other *bodegas,* a block apart, on the opposite side of Second Avenue. A few weeks before the city started digging up the street to put in a subway, both *bodegas* burned down. A year later, after the city decided it didn't want to put in a subway and started filling in the trench, he sold the deli to Benson Supper and pulled back to Avenue B, where he had kept a profile almost as low as Inspector Borden's.

Beside a smattering of Yiddish, he was fluent in Arabic, Spanish and English. People loved to talk to him, often told him more than they realized. In spite of the fact he had made himself scarce, his antennae reached everywhere. He had also been close to Ponce, almost a father to the fatherless boy.

Ali's *bodega* was a cavernous room on the shady side of the street, with a musty smell, like a grotto. A plump Puerto Rican woman in a green dress that threatened to split like a pea pod if she inhaled stood behind an old, cast-iron cash register.

"Ali no here," she said.

"*Importante, emergencia . . . comprende?* Tell him it's Pablo, OK?"

"*Quién?*"

"*Dile, Pablito. El me conoce, somos amigos, señora.*"

"*Puertoriqueño?*"

"*Yo? No, señora, pero soy amigo.*"

"Okey-dokey," she grinned. "Wait here, make sure nobody run away with my money."

"*Gracias, señora.*"

She disappeared through a curtained door at the far end of the counter. Sparsely stocked, as usual, there was canned ravioli, different kinds of Goya beans and soups, some old cheese in the cabinet beside a sad pepperoni and, on the counter, plastic containers of macaroons and *crema de leche.*

"Okey-dokey, *señor.* You go *allá.*" She pointed to the curtained doorway.

"Gracias . . ."

"Me llamo, China."

"Gracias, China."

She grinned and wriggled by me.

Lit by an overhead bulb, the room behind the curtain was furnished with two overstuffed chairs, a couch and a refrigerator with a TV on top of it tuned to a Spanish soap. Ali sat at a bridge table scribbling in a ledger, surrounded by stacks of bills in rubber bands. He gave me a slow, wistful smile as I settled on a metal folding chair across from him.

"Aye, Pablo, Pablo."

"Hey, Ali."

"We've lost our Ponce."

"He's gone."

Ali shrugged.

He didn't even look like an Arab, no proboscis parting a burnoose. He had a button nose and burnished copper skin. I couldn't figure his age, except to say that he had to be on the far side of fifty, but there was something ageless in his appearance, a youth preserved in vinegar like a pickled pig's foot.

"Drugs, Pablo . . . bad business. I take numbers, bet the horses, the *fútbol,* anything like that, but drugs, never! Drugs are poison."

"It was a coke deal, I think."

"Here, in America, there's no reason to do that if you have a brain in your head."

"Easy money, Ali."

"Look, if you take away from me everything I got today, I'm still gonna make out. You know why? Because I know the value of things. I can tell you how much is worth an antique, a diamond, a rug. If someone gimme a broken toaster, I can fix it. I can buy and sell. Why do I have to dirty my hands with drugs when I can use my head?"

"What have you heard, Ali?"

"You want something, Pablo?"

"Who was he with?"

"*Que lástima!* Shame and pity, that's what I hear when I listen. You know the poet, he say, '*La vida es dura, amarga y pesa.* . . .' Since Miguel was a child he know that if he come to me I have a job for him so he can make a little money, get candy or food. His papa, *se fue.* I always try to tell him the right thing to do, like a papa."

"You meant a lot to him."

Ali scowled.

"I always tell him, 'Stay away from drugs, they only hurt you'!"

"Not everyone's as smart as you."

"Anybody can learn. *Anybody!*"

"Ali . . ."

"I treat Miguel like my own son, but I know what he do. I know someday he's gonna break everybody's heart. I see. I got eyes."

He pointed to his right eye.

Suddenly I noticed he was wearing a red woolen watch cap, with no hair showing around his ears or the back of his neck. I couldn't stop staring.

"Are you all right?"

"You mean my head?"

He wiped his mouth with the back of his hand, paused, then pulled off his cap. Except for a few wisps of hair here and there, his dome was full of flaking skin.

"I have what they call lymphoma."

"Jesus, Ali!"

"Don't worry, it's under control. They give me chemicals and radiotherapy. I don't drink alcohol no more, no more cigarettes. I don't eat no red meat, lots of fresh vegetables, only the best food, and carrot juice."

He put his cap back on his head. It made him look more like one of Santa's helpers than a bookie.

"You have a good doctor?"

"Up at the VA Hospital, in the Bronx. They treat me good."

"Please, Ali, if you hear . . ."

"No, Pablo. I know what you want. I did what I could for the living; now, I wash my hands of the dead."

He rubbed his palms together.

"It's important."

"Be smart. Do the same. Wash your hands, keep them clean."

"How can I?"

On the opposite side of Avenue B and Sixth, Geraldo and Papo came out of Benny's candy store, walked past the closed storefront that was Pop Farkas' Fishing Club, where the card game never ends. Papo cupped his hand against the wind to light a cigarette. I waved, caught their eyes and walked over.

The caramel youngster who used to sit in the first-floor window of my old tenement, Geraldo, had blown up to resemble his older brother, Meatball. But if his features had thickened under a mop of curly black hair, a hint of the cherub lingered in his smile.

"Pablo, what's hap'nin'?"

"Geraldo."

"See who it is, Papo?"

Papo held out his hand. He was thinner than his cousin, with darting eyes, hair as disheveled as the grass in Tompkin's Square.

"Hey, man. Long time."

"Wanna make me feel like an old man?"

"No, Pablo. You still look the same."

"How's Meatball?"

"Good," said Geraldo. "He works moving furniture."

"What about you? Why aren't you in school?"

"I don' go no more. The only thing in school is trouble, everybody hangin' out, smokin' dope an' fightin' an' shit . . . an' they don' teach you nuthin'."

Papo cupped his hands around his cigarette and puffed.

"Hey, man. I'm cold. Less go inside."

I followed them into the tenement vestibule. The smoke from Papo's cigarette filled the space.

"You guys hear about Ponce?"

They nodded.

"Shot 'em in the back," spat Papo. "Just like the pigs." Papo's blue denim jacket had the colors of the Dynamite Brothers stitched on the back, a gang of Lower East Side Latinos from fourteen to forty, most of them high-school dropouts like Papo and, it appeared, Geraldo.

"Somebody else started the shooting. Both cops were killed."

"Ponce was unarmed, man!"

"Right. But when someone takes a shot at you and the guy next to him jumps, you're going to move fast, too."

"That's true," Geraldo nodded.

"Whose side you on?"

"The right side, Papo. Whichever way that falls. I just want to get it straight."

"Ponce was a good guy."

He dropped his butt and crushed it under a sneakered heel, then lit another. I decided it was time to call in a favor Papo owed me.

About a year ago, after a pirogi dinner at Leshko's on Avenue A, I walked out to hear a man's voice screaming for help on Seventh Street. Backed against the fence around the park, he was attempting to hold off the young jack-rollers who swarmed over him like ants. Before I had time to think, I found myself beside him, under a broken street lamp, pulling one of the thugs off. I pinned the thin arms of the young punk from behind as the wailing of a siren grew louder. Just as the flashing lights turned the corner, the boy in my grip twisted to see who was holding him, his face flickering with desperation. Papo! In the darkness I recognized him. Again, without thinking, I let him go.

"Would you do me a favor, Papo?"

"Name it."

"Very carefully, you hear me? *Carefully,* ask around, use your connections in the Dynamite Brothers to find out what you can about who was with Ponce when he got it."

"OK."

"Don't come on like Gangbusters, man! *Suave,* huh?"

"You think I been out on the street all this time and I don't know the story?"

"No way."

He knew the story. Even though kids like Papo dropped out of school before they could read and write, they knew the story.

We small-talked. Geraldo complained that the current cutbacks had cost him his summer job with the Department of Parks. I told him to come see me at the Tin Angel when he was ready to work.

"Thanks, Pablo."

"Later, fellas. Say hello to Meatball."

"*Te veo,* Pablo."

"Yeah, *te veo.*"

Leonard Dandy, our swing-shift cook, lived on the corner of Eleventh and B. He had been sick all week so I hadn't talked to him since Ponce's death, but he was a longtime resident of Alphabet City and might be able to help me. Moreover, in his own way, he had loved Ponce.

Passing what had been the Annex, I paused. A spectral juke played King Pleasure singing Eddie Jefferson's classic lyrics to "Moody's Mood":

> There I go, there I go
> theeer I go. Pretty baby
> you're the soul
> that snaps my control. . . .

Not even in my wildest fantasies could I have imagined Eddie would one day sing those words from my stage. The ghostly music stopped. There was nothing here now except an empty room with a padlock on its doors.

My eyes scanned the sidewalk and gutter for signs of last week's massacre. Those stains under the litter and grime, were they blood, or oil leaks from cars? Alphabet City. The whole place was burning down, slowly, slowly; what we saw as rust was actually invisible flame licking at the fire escapes and garbage cans. It was Ponce who told me rust was slow fire.

Leonard Dandy once described himself as "the onriest faggot in town." He had peanut-butter skin, a small mustache, a trim waist and a faint touch of gray in his hair. The only other thing that marked his age was his heart: it had attacked him twice. But this didn't dampen his taste for bourbon, cocaine and young men. I climbed to the sixth floor, knocked at the maroon door. An eye stared out the peeper.

"Hey, baby, come on in."

Leonard was wearing a wine-colored robe over yellow pajamas. Standing at the center of his kitchen full of potted ferns, he held my hand, shook his head sadly. When he finally spoke, his voice cracked.

"Today's the first day I've been able to get out of bed, sweetheart, or you know I would've been over to see you."

"I know."

"This Hong Kong flu is a bitch. Come and meet some folks."

We walked towards muffled voices in the front room. Several teenagers, street kids Leonard referred to as his "sweet meat," his "tender chickens," sprawled on the couch, lay back in one of the two great Victorian chairs. Bimbi and José were Latin. The third, John, a blond Anglo, explained that he had wandered into New York a few days ago from Mendocino and wound up here trying to score.

Bimbi offered me a can of Schaefer from a six-pack. I thanked him, popped the lid.

"How's Maria?"

"She took him back to P.R., should be returning tonight."

"Never should've taken him down there. He didn't like it down there, you know? Whenever he had to go on a visit, he pissed and moaned. Funny he should end up buried there."

Leonard explained to his guests that I was the owner of the Tin Angel, that our friend, my partner, had been killed last week in a shoot-out just down the street. Dandy had such class; he might've been a grande dame introducing a distinguished visitor at one of her *vendredis*.

The thin, nervous Bimbi became still. José sat back in his chair, closed his heavy lips. Only John, the wanderer, leaned forward, intrigued by the scraps of our conversation. He watched Dandy, standing in front of the window with his hands clasped behind his back.

"Things like this go down all the time. Only the cat that usually gets it is someone you'd expect to find in a garbage can or empty lot sooner or later. Ponce had his ways, but I never ..."

Leonard let the thought trail off. I addressed the two Latins.

"Either of you guys heard anything? Talk on the street?"

They shook their heads.

"Nuthin', man," said José.

Bimbi stared at his beer can.

"OK, Leonard, I'm going."

"Sorry, baby."

"Listen, if you do hear anything, Leonard knows where to reach me. I'll be very appreciative."

They all stood, shook my hand, but the blankness in the eyes of Bimbi and José let me know that their lips were sealed. Not that they knew anything, except that the man they had just met wasn't safe.

Vagabond John wished me luck.

FLOATING EYEBALLS

When I stopped back at Maria's my note was gone, but her lights were out and nobody answered the bell. On the stoop, I tried to peek through a crack in the blue curtains but saw only darkness. If she had returned, she wasn't inside. I started across Avenue A, had barely reached the other side when someone called my name.

"Waitz! Pablo Waitz!"

The voice came from a black Continental parked in front of the ice-cream parlor facing Tompkin's Square. Above the half-open smoked window, I saw the thin blond hair and patchy red skin of Ralph Ford, my old friend Danny Mac's partner.

"Ralph, what the fuck you doing here?"

"Passing through. Danny Mac would cut my cock off if I didn't bring you back. How about it? Come on, hop in."

"I wouldn't want you to lose your pecker."

In a tan suit with vented jacket, a dark overcoat folded on his lap, Ralph sat like a semiprecious stone in a blue setting. The world I entered was thoroughly upholstered: powder blue seats, dark blue floors and walls. There was a row of buttons on Ralph's armrest that controlled the blue smoked windows, and a clear one that opened and closed between us and the driver. After instructing the driver, he closed it and we were soundproof.

I sat facing my host in one of two chairs on either side of a small bar.

"How long's it been?"

"Two years, thereabouts. Drink?"

"I'll pass."

"I think I'll have one. You don't look any the worse for wear, Pablo."

Ralph poured himself six fingers of Jack, sat back and sipped it neat.

"I owe it all to my tailor. You're as natty as ever."

"Feeling OK. Except I could use more exercise, get rid of this spare tire. This doesn't help."

He took a huge swallow.

Ford was an ideal front man, a WASP with a business degree from Wharton. His appearance was that of a middle-rank government official, State Department or international trade, rather than an administrator in the distribution of drugs. He gave me an ambassadorial nod.

"You're one of Danny's favorite people. He talks about you all the time."

"We've had some good times together. Say, where we going?"

"South Street. We're tied up there."

"Tied up?"

"We travel mostly by water these days, Pablo. We have a boat, *The Aphrodite*."

"Nice way to move around, Mr. Ford."

"People think so. I grew up around yacht clubs, never could stand the water."

We fell silent as the Continental turned left on Houston towards the FDR Drive. I thought about Danny Mac, proud descendant of warrior-chief Robert Bruce who decided the destiny of his clan one day in a cave watching a spider dangle from a thread. Danny had been slightly looped when he told me about his ancestor. We'd finished closing down Hannigan's, an Upper West Side saloon we worked together weekend nights. The cash had been locked in the safe, and those gray-green eyes that kept his end of the bar full of women twinkled with Remy. But there was another side of Danny Mac, a dark one I glimpsed, also after-hours, getting high in the empty room. His voice had grown deeper, more halting as he described leading a small group of men on reconnaissance through the jungles of Nam. He had always tried to lead them away from the enemy, to places where they could wait out their mission in safety. On one such occasion, he took the wrong turn. There was a deafening explosion, the sensation of his body rising and falling; when he came to, the first thing he saw was that his buddy's head had been blown off. It stared at him from a crater in the road.

I told him I had spent the better part of a year there myself, as a merchant seaman. It had changed my life. He nodded, but we never talked about it again. After that, he showed me the face he showed everyone else; it held the genial smile of a man who lived every day as though it were his last.

His was a Gatsby story, only instead of hooch it was grass, everything from commercial Mexican to primo Hawaiian. Someone who had seen a front-runner in Danny Mac had set him up to handle deals involving heavy weight. Along the way, he teamed up with Ralph Ford, quit the bar and began turning up in white linen suits with foxy women on his arm.

When I opened the Tin Angel, first night, he was there, buying everyone champagne, always the gentleman, a man Robert Bruce would have been proud to call his own. A measure of his popularity was that nobody envied his good fortune. Then, quietly, he had dropped out of sight. It had been two years, at least, and I found myself excited by the prospect of seeing him.

We exited the FDR, continued along South Street under the elevated highway; finally, we pulled up opposite the Seaport Museum, facing the river, before a wire fence.

Ralph pointed to a white yacht tied up at a pier beyond the fence.

"There she is. *The Aphrodite.*"

She couldn't have been less than 120 feet, a fresh coat of white paint on her hull and ample housing midship with quarterdeck and flying bridge. It would take a half-dozen men to crew her, and she could sleep a dozen more with comfort. Ralph led me through the gate.

"What do you think?"

"I'm impressed."

Her registry, in bold black letters on her stern, was Fall River, Massachusetts. She had twin screws, said Ralph, and could cruise at twenty knots.

A huge bear of a man greeted us from his watch at the deck end of a gangway. Greeted, perhaps, is an exaggeration. He gave us a bearded nod.

"Fred, this is an old friend. Pablo, our chief mate."

His hand swallowed mine, ground it and let it go before we proceeded along the fine teak deck. Our steps echoed on it until they were muffled in a carpeted cabin out of the pages of *Playboy.* My feet sank into a thick, sea-blue pile; there were black leather couches and chairs, a mirrored bar, modular shelves containing books, records and stereo components. A huge color TV on a swivel had a table of its own in a sunken corner of the cabin, laced with pillows and feather beds.

"Make yourself at home. I'm going to tell Danny Mac you're here. Will he be surprised!"

The gentle twitching of this tethered giant against the dock started my stomach gurgling, a discomfort deep in my gut.

"Pablo? Jesus, man, I can't believe it!"

Danny Mac's voice preceded him. He stepped into the cabin wearing white ducks and a black silk shirt. Gold dripped from his neck, fingers, wrists; he still wore a small gold stud in his left ear. Wind and sun had darkened his skin, made it coarser, and there were hints of gray in his chestnut hair. When we embraced, he slapped me on the back.

"My God, Pablo, how the hell are yuh?"

"Hey, Danny."

" 'Hey'? It's been too long, man. Let me look at you."

There were tittering sounds in the companionway. Danny's grin broadened.

"Girls, come in and meet an old friend, someone dear to my heart."

There were three of them; blonde, brunette and redhead. They all wore bikini bottoms. Two had covered their torsos with skimpy white T-shirts emblazoned with silk-screen pictures of the ship and her name; but the real Aphrodite, the dark-haired woman close to six feet without shoes, wore no top at all. There was an oriental quality, a suggestion of the Eurasian about her eyes; her firm breasts blossomed into dark, velvety flowers. Danny Mac was delighted by my fascination.

"Her name is Peony; Dutch father, Chinese mother. Beautiful? And this is Jan, and Sherry."

I exchanged smiles with Peony and Sherry, but Jan, the redhead was pouting. She kept thrusting her chest in Ralph's direction, while he seemed to notice only blond Sherry, whose breasts fell just short of being a burden.

"Sherry, will you pour us all some Cordon Bleu for the occasion?"

I sat down, tried to relax.

"Just a taste for me, Danny."

Sherry switched her hips in staccato movements to the bar, as Peony draped herself over the chair beside Danny Mac. The deep gold tones of her skin were luminous against the black leather. Jan busied herself flipping through record albums. She selected one, put it on. Billie Holiday sang "Hush Now, Don't Explain."

"You're doing well, Danny Mac."

He passed me a cherry-wood box.

"No complaints. No, not true. One. I miss my friends. When you're always on the move, friends are one of the things you lose. Everything in life is a trade-off, and, as you see,

I've done well. But even with all this, I miss friends like you."

The old Danny Mac would never have talked about trade-offs; he had wanted it all. I opened the cherry-wood box. My face stared back from a mirror on the inside lid. The box contained a golden spoon on a bed of snow.

"Help yourself, Pablo."

"Thanks, Danny, but I'd better not."

I didn't want to meet Maria with eyes lit like pinball bumpers.

"It's *puro,* my friend. Go ahead."

"Try it, you'll like it," said Ralph.

It had, to say the least, been a frustrating afternoon. Of course, I didn't want to upset Maria, but on the other hand . . .

"Maybe just a little."

Hating myself, I delved with the golden spoon.

"Water or soda behind this, Pablo?"

"Nothing, thanks."

Sherry's breasts swung towards me beneath her T-shirt as she bent to put a snifter of amber liquid on the table. I sipped, relishing the liquid over the crystal freeze; the moment was a shameless touch of heaven, and I clung to it.

"That's the way."

"*Salud,* Danny Mac."

"*Cienan!*"

He raised his glass, sipped, stared into it for a moment before asking: "How's Ponce?"

"Dead."

I filled my nose and watched him.

"What?" He smiled. "That bad?"

"No, Danny Mac, no joke. He's dead, stiff, buried."

I filled the other nostril.

"You're kidding."

His expression wavered between humor and surprise.

"A cop shot him, last Wednesday, trying to run some of this white stuff up Avenue Boo."

Danny's mouth dropped open. Ralph, who had been gazing out the porthole, turned and looked at me with a poker
face. Jan and Sherry sat on my right, still as statuary lawn
pieces. Billie Holiday was singing, "Give Me a Pig's Foot and a
Bottle of Beer."

Why had I dropped it on him that way, without any cushion? Had I been testing him? Or perhaps I resented his freedom
to untie the lines that bound him to shore and sail away on his
seagoing harem.

"Sorry, Danny, I didn't mean to lay it on you that way."

"What happened?"

"Ponce took thirty-five grand from the business to buy
coke; one of the people he was with on the delivery opened fire
when two cops pulled the car over. Ponce caught a bullet in the
lung, the cops got blown away and the others escaped. That's
all I know so far."

"Did Ponce have a piece?"

"You know better than that."

"Who was he with?"

"Can't tell you. But I'm going to find out."

"Why?"

"Because there was no dope found, and my thirty-five
grand is still out there. I'd also like to know who the asshole
was."

I sipped my Cordon Bleu, filled my nose again before
passing the box to Danny Mac.

"Want my advice, Pablo? Let it go. Call it a business loss."

"You can afford to give that advice, man. I can't afford to
take it."

"The name of the game, my friend, is *survival*."

Was that really the bottom line? We fell silent.

"Is there something I can do?" he asked.

"You can dig around, canvass your people, see if they
know anything."

"Not likely, Pablo. I spend most of my time between

ports. I'm out of touch with the street. Hey, how 'bout you come along with us? Right now. Get someone to watch the store for a couple of weeks and come down to the Grenadines. We have to make a stop in Miami, but it will be mostly fucking and fishing."

"It pains me to refuse an offer like that."

There was a buzz over the intercom. Ralph inclined his head.

"Danny Mac."

"I've got to go topside for a minute, but you wait here. Sherry, stay with Pablo; use all your powers of persuasion to keep him aboard. We'll shanghai you yet."

Sherry gave him a mock salute.

"Aye, aye, *mon capitaine.*"

When the others left, she knelt in front of me, a kittenish smile on her face. Her soft breasts molded themselves around my knees. She rubbed them slowly back and forth, arousing herself as she stroked my thighs. She rose on her haunches, leaned toward me. I could see her nipples had grown hard underneath the thin shirt. She started to knead my groin.

"Sherry, listen . . ."

"Yes?"

She pressed closer, her lips on my ear.

"You're lovely and . . ."

She took my hand, ran her tongue over my palm. I squirmed with pleasure. Then she placed my moist palm under her shirt until it filled with the warmth of her swollen flesh. She fiddled with my fly.

"Maybe some other time, some other place . . ."

I forced myself up, the bulge in my pants an incongruous counterpoint to my words.

"What's the matter? Don't you like me?"

Breathing heavily, she looked up, hazel eyes half closed with desire.

"Of course I like you."

She pulled her shirt over her head. I stared, dumbstruck by her opulence.

"Come to Mama," she purred.

"Sherry, listen, I've got a girl . . . I'm in love. . . ."

I backed towards the door.

"Oh."

Her face underwent a sea change. She closed her eyes, composed herself, then gave me an appraising once-over.

"Don't think for a moment I . . ."

"It's all right," she conceded. "I can dig it."

"Tell Danny Mac I said good-bye."

"Hey, don't go! I'm gonna catch it if you're not here when he comes back."

I was already on deck, walking as fast as I could towards the gangway. Fred gave me another bearded nod. Filling my lungs with cold air, I returned through the wire fence.

Walking uptown on South Street, I replayed what had just happened. Why had I passed up a willing, unbridled piece of ass? I'd said I was in love, that I had a girl friend. It had come out before I knew what I was saying.

Did I love Maria? I didn't know. But she was the only one who could touch me now.

Under the Williamsburg Bridge, I paused at the handball courts where Ponce, Maria and I had played in days gone by. Ten years of days. They had grown up playing handball here and beat me easily. A bitter thought chilled me. Even on the handball court, the real action had been between the two of them, with me looking on.

I had a splitting headache, a throbber, up front above my left temple. Maria shrugged, sadly, before disappearing into the kitchen. In a minute she was back with two Tylenol and a glass of water.

"Those eyes are about to pop out of their sockets. You won't be happy until you blow your head off."

She wore a dark blue woolen sweater and jeans, and two gold hoops in her tiny ears. Most of all, she was tired. The circles under her eyes were as deep as any carved out by cocaine. She described Ponce's funeral, how they drove the coffin to Aquadilla in back of her uncle's pickup, said a mass and put him in the ground behind the hen house on her uncle's farm.

I told her about all the musicians who showed up to pay their respects. Then I made the mistake of describing my tour of Alphabet City, trying to squeeze some juice from the grapevine. Pablo, she said, I beg of you, let it die with Miguel, let it lie under the earth.

"When I threw in that handful of dirt, I told myself I was burying my past sorrows. Why do you want to dig them up?"

It was a question without an answer. Instead, I related my run-in with Ralph, the visit with Danny Mac aboard *The Aphrodite*, everything except my encounter with Sherry. I did tell her about the way I'd dropped the news of Ponce's death and fled with such a mixture of anger and regret my head had started pounding.

"The Danny Mac you saw today wasn't the same person you used to call your friend, no matter how much you both would've wished it so."

"I could've at least said good-bye."

"He died for you as sure as Miguel did."

"The ground is sand under my feet, Maria."

"Stop trying to hold on! Let them sail away, all of them, the hustlers, the dope dealers, the slick professionals in their big yachts, stop holding on to them!"

She stood up and came over to me, took my head in both her hands and pressed it against her belly.

"Make love to me, Pablo."

"I want to, but I'm scared."

"Of what?"

"Hurting you."

"Stop being responsible for everyone. I'm a big girl, I can take care of myself."

She knelt, held my face.

"If we made love tonight and you never wanted to touch me again, I'd survive. Do you understand?"

It was no longer clear to me who I was protecting, her or myself. I wanted to tell her that I wasn't sure *I'd* survive, but before I could she pressed her lips against mine. Suddenly I was crying, swift, silent tears. Maria just held me, and I realized that this was what I'd been afraid of, what I needed more than the proffered sex aboard *The Aphrodite*. Clearly, the events we'd shared bound us to each other in ways we could hardly understand, no less give them a name.

We took off our clothes in the bedroom and lay down, holding each other, caressing as if every part were tender. She breathed once, deeply, when I entered her, took me in, held me, moved slowly, pressing and withdrawing until I stopped her to let the tension subside. My hands moved over her breasts, down her narrow waist to raise her underneath by her buttocks, lips pressed, understanding all the while just how we were alone together in the world. We built again, quietly at first, her tongue filling my mouth as our movements grew shorter, quicker, harder and her breath came in tiny spurts; she moaned, softly, louder, louder, erupting into a deep animal cry from the pit of her stomach that shook her entire body. She was all pulse and current as I exploded with the pain and frustration of my days and nights, with the fear of death, of life, with a hunger that ebbed now for a moment.

II

THE CATBIRD

THE TOOTH OF LOVE

A little more than two weeks after Ponce's death, Maria handed me a key to the apartment her brother rented under the name of Juan Pollo. Officially, he resided in the same apartment he'd occupied from childhood, overlooking an airshaft on Twelfth Street. For his own reasons, he'd kept the fact of his place on Second Avenue quiet, and I wanted to look through it before the cops turned it inside out. I didn't have much time. It was Tuesday evening. Tomorrow, I'd have to turn the key in at the Ninth.

On my way over, I recalled that the Hip Bartenders' Consciousness-Raising Group was meeting tonight in Pepe Nero's place on the sixth floor of the same building and decided to stop by. My partner had been a member. Perhaps he had said something there that would give me a clue, at least to his emotional state.

Ponce was an even less likely consciousness-raising type than the other hip bartenders who composed the group. It had been born one reefer-high night when Pepe suggested that if the women were getting together to raise their consciousness, why shouldn't the men? Not just ordinary guys, either, but men who tended hip bars, whose lives were led at the center of a continual party.

Ponce had assured me that they took it very seriously. It wasn't just another boys'-night-out. Would I care to join? The James Boys were members; Brown, Big Baldy and his buddy Mensch Mednick who worked the stick at Spring Street would be there. No, I told him; if my consciousness were any higher, I'd have to walk around on tiptoes.

At ten past eight I entered the walk-up on the corner of Second Avenue and Houston and decided to stop at the meeting first. As I climbed the stairs, I wondered why most of my friends with no elevators lived on the sixth floor.

The door was ajar. They were already in the front room of Pepe's railroad flat screaming at each other. Nor did the screaming stop when I came in and found an empty seat by the window. The others sprawled on a double bed or twisted in folding chairs.

Rodeo Jim put both hands on his knees and leaned forward.

"Come off it, Mensch. Don't tell me you never considered marrying again."

Mensch was short, thin, with a trim mustache and hair parted on the left; early George Brent. He jumped up, took a few steps, sat back down on the bed.

"Never! I'm telling you, *never!* My sexual relationship with my wife was one continual act of vengeance. It's bad enough that most of the time I will crawl into the sack and feel like I'm fucking my wife."

"Part of the compulsive fucking syndrome," said Pepe. "I have a problem with that, too."

"That's a problem?" inquired Big Baldy.

"Sure is," Pepe continued. "I'm seeing this brilliant, beautiful lady; she leaves town for a few days to visit her parents in Sacramento and suddenly I'm in a different lady's bed every night, for no reason."

Big Baldy shook his head.

"You need a reason? How about, *it feels good?*"

"It didn't even feel that good."

"It felt bad?"

"Baldy, one day you may discover that fucking can be a shameful pattern of self-destruction."

"I hope so."

Mensch's face turned red.

"You guys aren't even scratching the surface."

"Did you ever believe in love?" Diamond Jim challenged him.

"You bet. Love and childhood were two experiences I was lucky to recover from."

"Jesus!"

"You guys, it's disgusting . . . you're all supposed to know better, but you keep expecting it to come up roses, candlelight and violins. Ah, but way down deep you know what it's about as well as I do."

"What's that?" they chorused.

"*Combat!* You heard me. I said, *combat!*"

"The male of the species is a rogue elephant," declared Big Baldy.

"I ain't no elephant," chimed in Brown. "Leastways, I ain't no *white* elephant."

Mensch slammed his fist into his palm.

"Forget this male-female shit. Take it back where it belongs, where it started. Not once have any of you suggested discussing our relationship with our parents. For instance, I hate my mother! Does anyone else here hate his mother?"

My tongue knotted in my mouth.

"Whenever I fuck a woman," continued Mensch, "I'm not only still fucking my ex-wife, but I'm also getting back at my mother for what she did to me. Tell the truth, you guys, has anyone in this room ever wanted to fuck his mother?"

There was a stunned silence.

"Come on. We're supposed to be letting it all hang out, aren't we?"

"Wow!" said Pepe.

"Could we talk about something else?" said Brown.

"Brown, your people invented motherfucking."

"Let's talk about why you mothafuckers is so *prejudiced.* That's what interests me."

"You get that way working saloons," responded Big Baldy.

"Pepe," Brown folded his hands, "if Israel invaded Harlem, do you think I could still sleep with Jewish girls?"

"Some consciousness-raising group," put in Diamond Jim. "A black guy asking an Italian if he can sleep with Jewish girls."

When I got up and walked to the door, Pepe grabbed my wrist.

"Hey, Pab, you leaving?"

"I'll be downstairs at Ponce's."

"Shit, poor Ponce," said Mensch, as if taken by surprise.

"Poor mothafucker," echoed Brown.

The first thing I did after turning on the lights was open the windows. Everything had been shut for so long the place smelled like the inside of an old sweat sock.

It was laid out like Pepe's place: a front door that opened into a kitchen with a bathtub; a large bedroom in front; a smaller room Ponce used as a study in the rear. His toilet was in the hall. But the walls were painted white, the floors had been taken down to the wood and finished with a clear seal and the furnishings were tasteful. Because he was a builder, he'd erected a loft bed and a system of shelves and closets that gave the place more useful space than it would have had otherwise. One wall had been taken down to the brick. On it hung a picture of Julie Fine. It was a promotional shot of her, a glossy eight-by-ten, which caught the rapture in her face when she rode high above her drums. I'd been calling her every day, only to have her machine announce that she wasn't in and ask me to leave a message after the beep, which followed ten seconds of percussion. I had. Either she was out of town or avoiding me.

I'd never realized he had so many shirts. They were folded

neatly in a dresser. A few suits, a selection of leather jackets, an array of dress shirts and four pairs of shoes waited for no one in a closet. He'd also been a fastidious housekeeper. There wasn't a piece of scrap paper, an old matchbook to be found anywhere. This wouldn't be the case after the guys at the Ninth went through it. They'd tear out the insides of the upholstery, remove the seams in his clothes. But for the moment, at least, it was almost as though nobody had lived there.

Except for the study.

I found his files in the drawer of a metal office desk. In a few minutes I'd gathered his telephone bills for the last six months, his bank statements for the same period and his checkbook with its personal record of checks written. I also found a UNICEF engagement book with a picture of dancers from Bhutan on the cover.

Scanning Ponce's records, I noticed he had written monthly checks to one Heather Moore for amounts that varied between $150 and $300. Her name also appeared twice on his engagement calendar during January, surrounded by numerous dates with Julie. There was a notation about the chili! And a number: #1501. It could be a street address, post office box, locker or room number. It was entered a week before his death, on the sixteenth. The twenty-fourth to the twenty-eighth was filled by a sketch for the rigging of floodlights along the Second Street wall. I put everything into a garbage bag I found under the sink. Later, I would study them.

By the time I got back to Pepe's, the Hip Bartenders were striking yet another blow for consciousness. They had broken out the booze and drugs, but continued with pieces of their former discussions. Mensch handed me a roach.

"All these guys want to talk about is pussy, pussy, pussy. What's so great about pussy?"

"You have to ask?" answered Nero.

"If I didn't, I wouldn't be here."

"What about Ponce?" I directed my question to Mensch. "Why did he come here?"

"He was pretty quiet. We'd argue and fight, he'd mostly listen."

"That's not true," said Rodeo Jim. "He thought he was in love with this lady drummer. He talked about that."

"What did he say?"

"He admitted to being scared," said Pepe. "Which is pretty good for a macho dude like he was. Yeah, and he also said that for the first time in his life he didn't want any other pussy."

"Things was changing for him," was Brown's comment.

"Did he ever talk about a lady named Heather Moore?"

They shook their heads.

"Uh, what kind of questions did he raise? You know, were there certain things that interested him more than other things?"

"Not really," said Baldy.

"Think. The last meeting he attended, what did he talk about?"

They all sat lost in thought until Mensch spoke.

"He asked me about my boy, how he was. I sometimes talk about him here."

"What did you tell him?"

"About my kid's first date. He's fourteen and had never been in that kind of situation before. He took this girl to the movies, came home and told me he'd kissed her, touched her tits and put his finger in her pussy. Then he asked me—dig it—he asked why, after doing all this, he and the girl were still strangers!"

"A good question," said Pepe.

"Ponce wanted to know what I told him. He seemed really interested in my relationship with my kid."

"What did you tell him?"

"My kid? How could I tell him anything? I'm still asking the same question. I just tried to let him know that there was nothing wrong with feeling the way he did, that he was a good boy and to me he was a blessing."

* * *

The only Heather Moore in all five boroughs resided at Five Montague Terrace, in Brooklyn. After setting up the register bank for Thursday, I taxied there from the Tin Angel, arriving a few minutes after eleven, a civilized hour for an unannounced social call.

Montague Terrace was a small tree-lined street that ran parallel to the Promenade at the end of Montague Street. Across the water, Manhattan's skyline stood chiseled in the stark gray light of the late winter sky. A tramp, leaving one of the piers below, steamed towards the Narrows. A couple of joggers in his-and-hers matching green sweat suits entered the bench-lined walk and turned north. The houses abutting the Promenade were mostly individual brownstones with small gardens in the rear. They were covered by ivy. Heather Moore lived in one of the smaller attached buildings across the street; more modest, but also "old Brooklyn." In a small vestibule I found her mailbox and pressed the buzzer. In about thirty seconds, someone buzzed me in.

In spite of the fact that the walls needed a paint job, touches of elegance showed through, like the slight scalloped curve of the staircase, the carved moldings and door frames. I knocked on Three A, which had a sticker on it asking the visitor to support the United Way. No answer. I knocked again.

"Use your key." Her voice was deep and clear.

"I don't have a key."

There was a pause, then footsteps shuffled to the door; it cracked and sky-blue eyes peered at me over the taut chain lock.

"I thought you were someone else. Is there something I can do for you?"

"Yes. My name is Pablo Waitz, I'm a friend of Miguel Ponce's."

The deep voice that had been warm, almost lyrical, became slightly shrill.

"You'll have to come back another time, Mr. Waitz. I'm

getting dressed for an appointment and I'm running late. Call first, will you? Good-bye."

I already had my foot in the door. Literally.

"Miss Moore, I won't take much of your time. You know Miguel Ponce was killed a few weeks ago."

"Please, I know. But I can't discuss it with you now."

"I have two years' worth of canceled checks made out to you, Miss Moore. I can turn them over to the police."

"Please take your foot out of the door, Mr. Waitz."

I did. The door closed. I heard the chain lock slide and drop before it opened again, and I walked into a room with white walls and a beige shag throw rug.

"As you can see, I am getting ready for an appointment. Do you mind if I dress as we talk?"

"Not at all."

Heather Moore wore slippers and a green housecoat. She was a small woman, with an extraordinarily well-shaped head. Her blond hair was cut short, parted on the side and combed forward in a boyish way. Her nose was strong, no cute ski slope, so was the line of her jaw; but it was the full lips that softened her expression, gave her the same provocative quality I'd heard in her voice.

An ironing board stood next to the couch. She picked up the iron and proceeded to smooth the wrinkles out of a paisley blouse. I sat down.

"Who are you, Mr. Waitz?"

"I'll tell you if you'll tell me who you are."

She nodded. I told her, then pointed out it was her turn.

"It's a long story, Mr. Waitz. One that goes back to a time before you knew him, when I was a younger and somewhat naive girl who thought she knew a lot more than she actually did."

"No crime in that."

"Depends on what you mean by crime. But that's not important. You didn't come here to find out about my emotional life, did you? You want to know why Miguel Ponce sent me money. Do you have any idea?"

"No. Love? Blackmail?"

She smiled.

"Neither, Mr. Waitz. In all your years associated with Miguel, he never mentioned me to you? Or Garret?"

I told her that neither of those names had come up between us. She shifted the blouse and walked to the bookshelf. I couldn't help but notice she moved with an efficiency that bordered on grace. She removed something from a shelf and handed it to me. It was a framed photo montage.

I studied it.

"That's Garret."

"Yes. I see. Your son?"

"Mine, and Miguel's."

She didn't miss a beat. Cool as a winter's afternoon, Heather Moore finished ironing her blouse while the first wave of shock passed through my system.

"He was the father only in a biological sense, you understand. He never did take any real interest in the child. Garret hardly knows him. Calls him Uncle Mike. Excuse me for a minute while I put myself together."

She left me muttering and studying the photographs. They were a quick survey of mother and son's journey from his infancy to the present. In what I judged to be the most recent snapshots, they stood at the rail of the Promenade on a warm day; neither wore a coat. He was as tall as his mother, had her coloring, except his eyes were brown, his face narrower than Heather's and he had Ponce's delicate thin lips. By the time she reappeared in her freshly pressed blouse, a dark wool skirt and high heels, I'd had time to absorb the information and collect myself.

"He'll be thirteen on his next birthday, that's only two months away. God, how fast it goes!"

After folding up the ironing board, she sat next to me, lit a cigarette, and told me how she'd come from a small town in Washington County and met Miguel at the opening of the sixties at the old Stanley's, a hip bar on Avenue B. She'd been twenty-two. Ponce had sweet-talked her, shown her a side of the city that she never could have seen with anybody else. For almost a year things were fine. Then she discovered she was two and a half months into a pregnancy. But she got scared and didn't say anything for several more weeks, after which abortion had become risky.

"He was nervous about having a child and took me to see his mother. She was considered a *bruja,* you know? Well, I went along with it."

Heather put her hand to her forehead and shook her head, as if to shake the visual memory from her mind.

"I found myself naked in the bathtub with the old lady. She was douching me with alum, trying to start contractions. After a while it began to hurt, and I could see she was getting off on it, but no contractions. When I discovered what she had planned for me next, I started to resist. Miguel was boiling water on the stove and there were sheets spread out on the kitchen table. I screamed. She tried to force me to lie down. Finally, Miguel intervened. I remember he and his mother arguing violently. But by the time I dressed, she kissed me on both cheeks, touched my shoulders and uttered something. She was smiling, but I knew the old witch was cursing me."

Heather stubbed out her cigarette, went over to the front window and glanced out onto the street.

"Miguel made it clear that he didn't want to have anything more to do with me or the child, but after Garret was born, I started to receive these checks from him. I can't pretend I wasn't grateful. Being a mother alone with a child is an impossible task. The money helped me to finish a business course at Pace, feed and clothe my baby, pay for some day care. Maybe once or twice a year he'd appear, take a look at Garret, ask if there was anything I needed. That's it. The whole story.

You've got what you came for, Mr. Waitz, and now I must ask
you to leave. My fiancé is due here any minute and I don't
want him to meet you."

"Why not?"

"Because he's a very private and jealous man. Because
I've tried to keep him out of that side of my life. Listen, Garret
is a bright, normal child who reads comics and loves *Star Trek*.
Now a man has come into our lives who cares about the two of
us. I'm going to have a husband, and Garret is going to have a
father at a time he desperately needs one. Please, Mr. Waitz, I
beg of you, don't ruin it for us."

I felt her voice in my chest. It poured out like a rich, syr-
upy liquid. All the defensiveness had vanished.

"Miguel wouldn't have wanted us pulled into it. Believe,
me, he wouldn't."

I rose, picked up my coat just as her head snapped back
from the window.

"I have to push you out, Mr. Waitz. He's here. Please,
leave us in peace."

She prodded me to the door, closed it as I was still thank-
ing her for her time.

I met Heather Moore's fiancé between the wall and the
banister on the second floor. He was a stocky man, with short
black hair flecked with gray. His face was square, expression-
less, around gray eyes that looked right through me when I
nodded and smiled.

"Excuse . . ."

It was as if I didn't exist. Nor did he turn sideways to give
me equal berth but came straight ahead, full front, so that I
had to squeeze against the wall to let him pass. He was not a
man used to giving way. If I had met him in Heather Moore's
living room, I might've thought him no more than the "private
and jealous man" she'd described. Now, watching the back of
his dark overcoat disappear, I felt a chill, as though the angel
of death had whispered in my ear.

On the street outside Five Montague Terrace I saw a black Mercedes. It was parked illegally, the only car on that side of the street. It was big, defiant and funereal, like the man who'd pressed me to the wall. An unlikely match for Heather Moore. I scribbled the license number on the back of a receipt for thirty pounds of chopped meat. I'd give it to Bertie to run through Motor Vehicle. Not Christ. He was too close, and I didn't want him sniffing around Ponce's secrets. But I did want to know who he was, this man who'd pressed my back to the wall.

I had to talk to someone. The only person I could think of to whom I could speak freely was brother Zach, but when he answered, it was clear that I didn't have his undivided attention.

"Guess what's going on outside my window?"

"What?"

"These two guys are getting ready to duke it out over a parking space. A Toyota and a Rabbit. I mean, here I am in a respectable neighborhood, and these two upwardly mobile white professionals are nose to nose over a piece of concrete."

"I believe it."

"You might say this confirms the old Darwinian point of view, that 'Nature is writ in tooth and claw,' but that makes it too noble. Actually, we're probably more like bacteria. Every day I watch cultures grow, peak and finally consume their medium."

"You think we've peaked?"

"I do. Sometime around the end of the last century. Wait, Pablo, the Toyota has got the Rabbit in a bear hug. No, the Rabbit breaks his grip and he's, yes, he's going for the Toyota's balls! But the Toyota's putting a choke lock on him. Oh, my God!"

"What is it, Zach?"

"The Toyota has the Rabbit's nose in his mouth. He's like

a pit bull. The Rabbit is screaming bloody murder. He's gonna need a prosthetic schnozzola."

"Why doesn't someone break it up?"

"They've separated. The Rabbit's in shock, he's feeling to see if his nose is still there. Hey, the Toyota has gotten into his car and he's driving away. Now the Rabbit is going after him. Ha! Guess what?"

"What."

"Somebody else is taking the space, a Chrysler Cordoba."

"Zach, today I found out something that blew my mind. Ponce has a kid, a little boy, and he's been supporting him for years."

"The world's nuts, Pablo. Excuse me for a second, I've gotta pop a Valium."

I heard footsteps, tap water, more footsteps, and he was back.

"What did you say? Ponce has a kid?"

"Yeah. That's all. Hey, I'll talk to you tomorrow."

"It's been a hell of a day."

"Keep your eye on those bacteria."

"That's what they pay me for," said Zach.

ROOTWORK

In the month that followed Maria's flight to San Juan with Ponce's coffin, her mood swings were unpredictable and frequent enough for me to edit my activities. I kept the news of her brother's illegitimate son to myself. As far as she was concerned, I had stopped trying to reconstruct the circumstances of Ponce's death. It was easier this way. Her interest in the Tin Angel was also sporadic, but slowly she was learning how to take inventory, do the ordering and avoid creditors. Nor did I see her as much as I wanted to. Without Ponce to spell me on the floor during the early part of the week, I was too tired most nights to meet her for dinner or to walk east after closing. Occasionally she would join me for a meal at the club, but I wasn't the best of company. By early March, business had slipped to a new low; so low, on some nights we barely made payroll.

Forced to acknowledge a souring economy, I began hiring duos, and trios, or, in keeping with our policy of exploring unknown talent, larger groups, like the sextet spearheaded by the Big Licorice Stick.

The Big Licorice Stick had curly black hair and a serious Tyrolean face, which was usually lost in the smoky regions of the upper atmosphere. He would've looked at home in lederhosen playing his instrument to a herd of sheep on an Alpine slope. Instead, he and his vagrant group of musicians wore Army-Navy duds as they played their repertoire of standards, punctuated by a few originals.

One of their originals had become popular at the Tin Angel. Whenever they appeared, Noah or one of the James Boys would call out: "Hey, play 'Circling Uranus'!"

The Big Licorice Stick would look sheepishly back at his fans, then turn to the group.

"OK, here it is. 'Circling Uranus'! Let's hit it, fellas."

What followed was a few bars in three-quarter time which fell apart when the Big Licorice Stick started a crescendoing slur that was picked up by the rest of the group, one by one, until sax, trumpet, bass and cymbals joined the ruckus. This slur was repeated three more times until it sounded as if all the engines in the Great Jones firehouse were responding to a four-alarm; then, after an abrupt rest, the melody was picked up again, only to dissolve once more in a series of slurs. The piece climaxed in a frenzy that produced either nervous collapse or an instant understanding of relativity. After several nights of "Circling Uranus," I usually spent most of the day in bed.

I was doing exactly that, wondering how much longer I could keep the Tin Angel going under the present circumstances, especially considering the thirty-thousand-dollar loan from Chemical Ponce and I had personally guaranteed, when the phone rang. It was my brother Zach, calling to let me know that Carlotta was in Ararat General, being tested for a possible malignancy.

We hadn't spoken since she'd left the Tin Angel in a huff weeks ago, but her voice over the phone was frightened. I dressed, caught a cab and wound up in front of a small white building on a tree-lined street overlooking Grand Central Parkway.

Carlotta was propped up in the middle of a ward wearing a white gown and a gauzy cap they had given her to keep the hair out of her eyes. When she saw me, she forced a smile.

"Don't you think I look like the Poppin' Fresh Doughboy?"

Her stomach, distended by probes, ballooned under the

blankets. A biopsy, said Zach, had confirmed the presence of a lesion on the inner wall of her sigmoid colon. On my way up, I'd talked briefly with Dr. Loftus in the hall. He'd stared at me through bushy eyebrows under a brown toupée and spoke through a waxed mustache. I parroted back what he'd told me.

"They're going to run more tests, Mom. They want to take a look at the outer wall of the intestine."

"Is it malignant, Pablo?"

"They have to check further. There's a suspicion that it is."

Suspicion. That was the doctor's word.

"Yes, of course. I'll just put myself in their hands. Dr. Loftus is an excellent physician."

I nodded.

"Pablo, I've been working too hard. When I get out of here, I'm going to act like a woman of my age. No use pretending I'm a spring chicken. I'll cut down on work and apply for Social Security."

I took her hand. She was pleading. If she promised to be a good girl, maybe God would make her all better.

Cancer is fire season in the body, the structure aflame, alarms going off in the vital organs.

Cancer is the wild flower opening petals of guilt and rage.

Cancer is the music gone mad, notes falling off the staff, a composition that destroys the instrument.

Zach, Bertie and I sat in the glass and stainless-steel lobby of the Ararat listening to Dr. Loftus's barber-shop bass.

"I'm afraid what we suspected has already taken place."

"What does that mean?" asked Bertie.

"It means that the cancer has spread to the peritonium."

Bertie's hand patted the holstered .38 beneath his jacket.

"Can you operate?"

"No, impossible!"

"Are you sure? You're absolutely sure!"

"The peritonium is a thick blanket. The cancer is woven right into it."

Like the rug on your head, I thought.

"The cancer is basted to the pelvis. No operation in the world can separate the healthy from the malignant tissue. I'm sorry."

"What can we do?" I queried.

"We'll put her on chemotherapy. She'll probably get better for a time, but I must tell you that the prognosis isn't good."

"How much time?" Zach wanted to know.

"Two months. Maybe six. Could be as long as a year."

As a bacteriologist with a medical background, Zach was not in awe of doctors. He spoke with controlled anger.

"All I want is for you to keep her comfortable. I don't want to see her in pain. Will you promise me that?"

Loftus's voice descended as he rose to shake our hands.

"You have my personal guarantee she'll be kept comfortable."

"I hope his personal guarantee is better than the one I have with Chemical," I said when he'd walked away.

"I don't trust him." Zach sat back down. "I don't trust him for a minute. He's saying what he must to keep us calm, but none of these guys takes risks. They're experts at steering a tricky course between the law and the patient's relatives."

"Should we take her somewhere else?" There were tears in Bertie's eyes.

Zach thought a minute. He had been the seraphic sibling, the light to my dark, with blond hair and blue eyes. But I could always feel the shadow fall inside of him. When it did, there was a darkness in Zach I couldn't begin to fathom.

"She'd be just another statistic for the computer at a place like Memorial," he said. "No, it's going to be a question of keeping her medicated. There's nothing anybody can do. At least here, maybe she can get some real attention."

"What are we going to tell her," cried Bertie.

"She has a right to know," I blurted out.

"We should tell her what she wants to know. No more, no less," declared Zach.

My head grew warm and I felt an anger I couldn't explain.

"You're both ready to watch her last days on earth turn into a charade? Don't you think, at least at the end, she should have an opportunity to make it real!"

"When she's ready, she'll ask."

"I don't think she can handle it." My mother's lover put his face in his hands.

Carlotta sits up in bed as we enter the ward, adjusts her cap, composes her mask.

Bertie belches. I scratch. Zach stands at the foot of her bed with his hands at his sides, paralyzed.

It's just as we knew it would be. Carlotta knows and doesn't know. Bertie knows one minute and forgets the next. Zach and I know every passing minute, as we will for the remainder of the dance.

"When are they going to let me out?"

"Soon," I tell her. "After they start your therapy. They have to run some tests first. I'd say a week."

"Good."

The thought of leaving makes her smile, then a shadow falls across her face.

"I want to go home where I can listen to my records, take out my cello."

We agree, she should have her music.

Carlotta wants to listen to Delius. More than any other composer she feels closest to him. She tells us what it feels like to be Delius in his last years; the slow blindness, the physical deterioration.

"His sisters carried him around in a sack. Even then, he didn't stop composing. No, right up until the final day he was at work on his music. He ordered his sisters to carry him to the top of a hill where he could see the rolling countryside. You can hear the countryside rolling through his music. For Delius, music was the last thing to go."

Joe Lee Wilson and Monty Waters opened on a rainy weekend with gusting winds that kept people home, except for the hard-core, like The Laughing Budweiser still giggling at himself in the mirror. Maria braved the elements to find me huddled in a corner of the Bowery Café brooding over a Fundador.

"You want to go somewhere else?" I suggested. "I could use a change in scene."

"Sounds good."

Ever since Carlotta had gone into the hospital, Maria had kept her eye on me, and her own moods in check. There was no way in the world I could express my gratitude to her for that, but Robin Kenyatta was playing up at the Five Spot, and Julie Fine, whom I'd been trying in vain to reach, sometimes worked with him. I thought twice about going there with Maria, then decided to do it, if just to see whether or not Julie was in town. By the time Maria and I pushed through the doors on St. Mark's Place, we were soaked beneath our slickers.

Big Baldy towered over the beer cooler behind an empty bar. We pulled up two stools.

"What'll it be?"

"Fundador. Twice. And have one with us."

"For me, a touch of 'Old Underdog,' " said the big man, pouring himself a shot of Hennessey. "Cheers!"

He'd worked the old Five Spot when it was just off Cooper Square. Now he pulled the weekends at the new place on St. Mark's. The owners, Joe and Iggy Termini, took over the rest of the week.

Before us spread an expanse of small cocktail tables of various shapes, colors and sizes, which gave the room a certain warmth when it was full of people. Empty, the chairs and tables were oddments, fragments of other saloons.

"Three weeks ago, Mingus played his heart out to six people." Big Baldy poured us another shot.

"Down the street Joe Lee Wilson is singing to The Laughing Budweiser."

Robin Kenyatta and several others were taking their respective places onstage. One of the septet, in the rear, facing us, was Julie Fine. She sat behind her drums, close-cut honey-colored hair framing dark eyes and pale skin. Suddenly Maria stiffened. I shifted to follow her gaze and saw Rodolfo Colon up front, at a table by himself. He turned as I saw him, waved, motioned us over.

"Let's get out of here." Maria touched my arm.

"Wait here. I've got to talk to him for a second."

"Please, Pablo."

"A second."

"He's nothing but trouble."

She took her hand off my arm, and her face turned hard as plaster set in a mold. For Maria, it was simple. Colon was a gambler and he was street, part of the worlds she held responsible for her brother's death.

As I approached the table, Kenyatta's soprano sax sounded the vamp to "Last Tango."

"Rodolfo."

"You saved me a walk." He showed me his teeth. "I was going to fall by your place later, man."

"Nasty night out there." I sat down.

"Don't want to scare you, Pablo, but you heard about Babar?"

"Heard what?"

He tugged at the collar of his white woolen turtleneck with a hooked finger and regarded me through cocaine eyes, dark periods in his broad forehead.

"He's been putting the touch on everybody for a job, you know? I understand he tried you."

"So?"

"Three of the places that refused to hire him have been hit."

"You think he did it?"

"Same MO every time, a real sledgehammer job, all three turned him down flat; you guess."

"I see your point."

"Just wanted to warn you."

"I appreciate it."

The Cuban gambler filled his glass with the remains of a bottle of Heineken. Julie Fine was moving over her traps as only a woman could, almost riding the drums, her full breasts loose beneath a yellow sweater. She closed her eyes as she beat out the time, her body undulating, as if she were making love. It was clear what had drawn Ponce. When I turned to address Rodolfo, I could see he, too, found her hypnotic.

"What about Black Hattie?"

"I don't know, man."

"I want to talk to her."

"Go to Rio."

"She's been away a long time."

"Yeah. If she were here, maybe Babar wouldn't be acting so crazy."

"How did he survive before he met her?"

"In jail."

"Not a bad place for him."

Rodolfo gave me a twisted Elvis Presley type of smile he'd probably spent months practicing before a mirror.

"You like the Elephant better in a cage? OK, man, don't worry. The minute I see Hattie, I'll let her know you want her."

"Good enough."

When I looked back at the bar, Maria's stool was empty. Big Baldy signaled with his hands that she had left. Women! I'd catch Julie another time. At least, now, I knew she was in town.

"Got to go."

"*Te veo,* man."

"Yeah, Rodolfo. *Te veo.*"

Kenyatta wore an epauletted leisure suit. Holding his sax at his side, peering into the empty vast, he might've been an African statesman trying to avoid a coup. When I stood up, he nodded at me, blew a funky riff. I took one last look at Julie making percussive love to her Slingerland skins, told Big Baldy to give my best to the Terminis, who had been struggling to make their nut for thirty years, and left.

At the Tin Angel, Diamond Jim told me that Maria had returned for her purse, which he had been holding for her, then gone home. I asked him to close up for me and headed for Avenue A. When I crawled into bed beside her, she stirred, pressed her lips against my ear and whispered, "Why can't you leave it alone?"

Carlotta sat upright in a queen-size bed in a room enclosed by blue taffeta curtains hanging between marbleized wall mirrors. A small crystal chandelier with dim red bulbs shaped like candle flames hung over her head. The Sony color tube on the white dresser at the foot of her bed was tuned to "Mod Squad."

Carlotta had spent very little time listening to Delius, and no time playing her cello since returning home. The chemicals that Loftus was pumping into her at his office once a week were taking their toll. Her hair was coming out in clumps. She'd been five days without solid food and the sight of meat nauseated her.

"Most cancer patients lose their taste for meat," whispered Zach.

We served her a one-minute egg, cottage cheese with a Bartlett pear. Bertie brought it to her on a tray, cooing baby talk.

"How's Bertie's sweetums, his tweet, tweet, tweety pie?"

"He's regressing." Zach popped a Mellorill in the bathroom.

Carlotta slumped and shook her head over the tray of food. Later that afternoon, she slumped in Dr. Loftus's office. Sitting in a big leather chair, it was clear her body had shrunk. The black pillbox hat slid down over her forehead when the doctor exhorted her to force foods and liquids. She said she would try.

Bertie helped her to the waiting room as we lingered behind for additional information.

"The pressure she feels around her heart isn't the cancer. It's the beginning of what we call a *bloody asides;* that is, the blood vessels in her stomach are overtaxed and they're superating liquid, which, in turn, is collecting in the tissues. When it grows too big, we'll have to drain it."

In the waiting room, Carlotta's head fell limply on her chest. We helped her into Zach's Datsun. He had taken an emergency leave to be with her twelve hours a day. He had blue rings under his eyes. After putting her to bed, he drove home each night and dreamed she was dying. Before coming back in the morning, he popped a Mellorill.

"Oh, shit!" said Junius Brown. "Do you see what I see?"

My back was to the door. When I turned I saw Babar nose to nose with Noah, who was giving the Elephant Man his Wild Turkey grin. At the prodding of someone behind him, Babar moved past my doorman. As he did, I recognized Black Hattie.

"I don't mind Hattie," sighed Brown. "But whenever I run into her fat friend, he makes me listen to bad Polish jokes."

Hattie's hair was plaited in corn rows that hung around her head like a beaded curtain, accentuating her sharp, sculptural features. A white courtesan in her bloodline peered out of her mocha skin. Her body had the lean grace of an animal capable of moving through dense foliage at high speed. She kissed me softly on the mouth. She tasted like cherries.

"Pablo."

"Am I glad to see you. Let's talk."

"That's why I'm here, fresh off the plane."

Babar squinted at me. I bought him his usual 151-proof rum and coke in a beer mug and left him with Brown, whose head twitched when asked: "Hey, didyuh hear the one about the Polish hockey team? They drowned during spring training."

As we walked towards Watts, Maria rose from the booth where she'd been sitting with Lisa, eating onion rings.

"Hello, Maria."

When Hattie tried to touch her shoulder, she flinched back.

"Hattie."

Hattie continued, as if she hadn't noticed Maria's rebuff. "I'm sorry about Ponce."

"Are you?"

"We were tight for fifteen years, that's a lot of water under the bridge."

"Troubled water."

"Sometimes."

"Nothing stops you, does it, Hattie?"

"I'm really sorry about Ponce."

"Pablo?" Maria turned blazing eyes on me.

"I must talk to Hattie."

"I may not be here."

"That's up to you."

I started towards the kitchen and didn't look back.

"She's not coming unglued, is she?" asked Hattie, slipping through the trap.

"I hope not."

"She never did like me, you know. There was this thing between her and Ponce, and shame on you if you stepped in between."

In my office she removed her quilted blue mandarin jacket and sat facing me on the cot. Her ease was a welcome counterpoint to Maria's stony anger.

"You've been asking about me all over town. Don't you know I like to keep my head down, out of sight?"

"How can a fox like you keep a low profile?"

The three top buttons of her white Mexican *camisa de boda* were unbuttoned. Its collar, pockets and sleeves were embroidered with green and yellow flowers. I could see the swelling of her small breasts almost as far as the nipples. I tried not to look.

"Think I'm a fox?"

"Always have."

Heat rose through my body, pleasurable and, at the same time, disturbing.

"Even foxes get older."

"You're aging like good wine, Hattie."

She lowered her eyes in a way that was almost demure and smiled. It was true. The muscular body I'd first encountered at the Annex years ago had grown less angular, more inviting; something in her face had softened, too. But her voice retained musical traces of her native Jamaican creole.

"Have you developed a taste for fine wine, then?"

This time I was the one to look away, feeling suddenly very shy. Fifteen years ago Black Hattie had waited tables in old sneakers. Now she wore Frye boots and had safety-deposit boxes full of cash in a number of banks. I got up and closed the door, as much out of nervousness as a desire for privacy. Only then did I realize I had an erection. She patted the cot.

"Come. Sit down, Pablo."

I jammed my hand in my pocket, walked back and sat beside her. An audible voice inside warned me I was being reckless.

"You could've waited until I came to you. The cops are pressing everyone."

"I couldn't wait. When things cool down too much, everyone forgets."

"What is it you want?"

"For one thing, I had thirty-five grand tied up in a bad deal."

"You want your money back?"

"Yes. I also want to know why he got killed that way."
Her hand began stroking my head.

"There are things in this life we never know, Pablo. It may
be better so."

She leaned forward, kissed me on the lips. Her tongue was
tentative at first, then swelled in my mouth like a warm animal
with a pulsing life of its own. I slid my hand down her blouse
and my thumb over her hard nipples.

"Hattie, we can't. . . ." I pulled away.

"You sure?" She patted, then squeezed the bulge in my
pants.

"No, I'm not sure. I feel like a pressure cooker about to
explode. But Ponce was a brother to me."

"Ponce and me, we never had handcuffs on each other,"
she explained. "It wasn't that way. Making love would be like
expressing our love for him."

"In my mind you're his, Hattie."

"I don't belong to anyone," she bristled. "I think you still
have him up on some kind of pedestal. Pablo, I loved Ponce;
for years I could hear that man breathing inside of me, but that
doesn't mean I didn't see who he was."

"Who was he?"

"A hustler. The most dangerous kind of hustler there is, a
hustler with a big heart, a love hustler. It made him dangerous
to himself and everyone he dealt with."

I thought about Heather Moore, and Garret, the son
he hardly knew, and wondered how much more of Miguel
Ponce remained hidden. Hattie straightened the collar of her
blouse.

"Pablo, maybe it is better, between you and me. Not that
it wouldn't be nice, but it could ruin a good friendship."

I bent down to embrace her; she returned the hug. We
were still holding each other when the door swung open. Babar
filled the frame.

"Yuh OK, Hattie?"

"Yeah, baby, fine," She let go of me and sat up straight.

"We'll be finished in a minute," I told him.

"Issat so."

He was staring at the hand I'd let rest on Black Hattie's shoulder. I took it off.

"Babar, we'll be up soon, then you can lean on me about a job."

"*Lean on yuh!* Yuh Jew scumbag! I do that for a living. If I decide to lean on yuh, yuh'll know it."

"He didn't mean it the way it sounded," Hattie told him.

Babar walked up so close to me I could smell his elephant breath, an old sausage hero.

"Yuh got some nerve."

"A poor choice of words," I conceded.

"Nobody must've ever leaned on yuh or yu'd know. . . ."

"Babar!"

Hattie's voice hit him like cold water. He blinked. Then her tone turned soft, caressing.

"Baby, we'll be finished soon."

Babar extended his arm towards her and opened his fist. There was a small bamboo peg in his huge palm.

"I wanted to give yuh this, it musta fell offa yer coat, Hattie, an I didn't want yuh t' lose it."

On his way out he gave me a look that plumbed the depth of his pachydermal jealousy. I was certain that the picture of Hattie and me in each other's arms had made an indelible imprint on his elephant memory.

"Pablo, can I make a suggestion?" she said after Babar closed the door. "No, call it a favor."

"Well?"

"I don't know what went down, why it happened that way to Ponce, but I do know the world you're mucking around in."

"I need that money."

"I'll give you a loan, no interest, take a lifetime to pay."

"I appreciate the offer, but I still want what's mine."

"You're swimming in shark-infested waters. It's not your element."

"Will you help me or won't you?"

"What if I learned something, told you, and you went out and got killed because of it? *Yeah, man! Fu' true.* Folks play that way. How'd you think I would feel then?"

"You won't help me?"

"I didn't say that."

"Then you will?"

"Now who's doing the *leaning*?"

She held my face in her hands and kissed me full on the lips.

"I'll do what I can. And Maria, be careful with her. Don't push too hard or she'll fall apart."

Back upstairs Joe Lee was singing the lyrics to a beautiful Gloria Coleman tune, "Good Morning Love."

> Good morning love,
> how do you do?
> Greetings, from
> my warm heart to you ...

But Maria was nowhere to be found. She had decided, once again, to leave. All right. Maybe it was best. I felt scared, angry and lost, but, I told myself, maybe it was for the best.

"What did you say to Babar, man?" Brown interrupted my bitter reverie. "He came back calling you all kinds of mothafucker and little piece of shit, said he was going to wait for you one night when you walk home."

"Let's drop it."

"You musta told him something."

"I called him 'Sweetheart.' "

FIRE SEASON

Maria came out wrapped in a thick red towel, damp curls framing features softened by a hot bath. She smiled wistfully, checking an impulse to speak as I passed her on my way to the bathroom. The mirror was steamy and I could smell her body. When I finished, I found she had gotten back into bed and crawled in beside her. She propped herself on an elbow.

"Oh, Pablo, just when things are good and it feels like everything that's gone before happened to someone else, I see Black Hattie, or Colon, and I'm trapped again in a nightmare."

There was nothing to say. I just held her. There was no answer. She didn't demand one. But the truth was that as long as she held on to me she'd be in the nightmare; I was as much a part of it as Hattie or Rodolfo. Her head cradled in the crook of my arm, she drifted off, safe for the moment. It was only half-past nine. I closed my eyes.

Impossible to say how long I actually dozed, but it seemed no more than seconds before the telephone woke me. Maria and I were tangled vines. I disengaged, careful not to bruise her sleep. It was Noah on the other end.

"Rose and her boys paid you a visit. Good thing I came early to fix the slop sink, you know how it's been backing up? Well, they'd taken out the garbage from the dumper, piled it against the wall and set it on fire. They really had a blaze going."

"My God! How much damage?"

"Not much, scorched wall and door; but another two minutes, the whole place might've gone up. I put it out with the fire extinguisher, then held them at bay with the baseball bat until I saw a patrol car. Actually, I didn't have to hold them at bay; they weren't in a hurry to go anywhere, just sat on the stoop next door shooting craps."

"Did you press charges?"

"I didn't have a chance. The cops let them go."

"What!"

"Told them to walk. They didn't want to do all that paperwork just to give Rose a few days on the city."

"I'll be right over."

"Don't rush."

It had been several weeks since I entered the Ninth Precinct. After Ponce's death, Harris and Toomey had interviewed me every three or four days; then every five or six until, finally, they asked only that I be available if needed. Inspector Borden's door was closed. I wondered if it had been opened since my last visit. Had it been nailed shut? Sealed? Had Borden secured his burrow?

For a fleeting second I considered seeing if Harris and Toomey were in the detectives' office, then dismissed the idea. Instead, I spoke to a beefy desk sergeant, the same one who'd been behind the desk on the night of the shooting.

"I want to see Christ."

"Christ ain't here."

"Somebody responded to a call from the Tin Angel this morning; that's on the Bowery."

"I know where it is."

"Who was it?"

"Patrol car?"

"Right."

"Who are you?"

"The owner."

"Hold on." He thumbed through his log. "Here it is. Martin and Rivera. Come back around four when the shifts change if you wanna see them."

"Thanks."

"Hey, you wanna find Christ? Look in the Last Supper Deli, ha, ha, ha, ha; he may be having breakfast, ha, ha, ha. . . ."

I left him laughing.

On my way past, I peered into the Deli; no Christ. But Armageddon wasn't far away; down here, that meant fire season.

The season began when the tenement boilers were turned off. It lasted right through till fall, when they were turned on again. By the middle of May, I could stand on my roof and watch fires blooming every night between Second Avenue and the East River: hot roses bursting at the heart of the inner city.

A long, black scorch mark on the wall made my blood race. I imagined my hands closing on Wino Rose's throat as I fumbled with the key. Noah opened the door from the inside. He was wearing his plumber's coveralls.

"Am I glad to see you! I've been calling you everywhere."

"I stopped by the Ninth. What's wrong? Did they try again?"

"Worse."

"Whadayuhmean?"

"Boss, I'm sorry . . . but what with the fire and Rose an' all, I didn't notice . . ."

"What!"

"After I spoke to you I went downstairs to get my wrenches and . . ."

"Go on."

"We've been hit. I'll show you."

I had done my best to deal with the scorch mark, but I was totally unprepared for the sight that greeted me at the bottom of the ladder. Maria was on her hands and knees gathering up the loose papers from our payroll and account books strewn over the floor. The door on Ponce's office had been popped. It leaned on a single hinge screw. The file drawers gaped open. Maria looked up.

"Oh, Pablo. Noah called again after you left, and I rushed over."

I started up the alley between Ponce's office and the wall.

"Don't bother," said Noah. "They got the cash box."

"Three days' worth of receipts and a five-hundred-dollar bank. Shit! Almost four grand!"

"Hello, Waitz."

The familiar voice from the far end of the alley belonged to Detective Toomey. He was holding a small pen flashlight.

"I called the Ninth. They sent over these two." Noah shrugged.

"Tough luck, Waitz."

Harris peeped out from Ponce's office, stuffed his mouth with a handful of bean sprouts from the pocket of his charcoal-gray sport coat.

"If winter comes, can spring be far behind?" was the only response I could muster.

The sprouts crunched between Harris' teeth as he spoke.

"I don't know about that, but someone out there doesn't like you."

"We're through. We can't even open the doors."

"Yes, we can." Maria stood to man the barricades.

"How? I don't have money to put in the registers!"

"I've got enough in my savings account."

"I can't . . ."

"Consider it a business loan. After a few decent nights you can pay me back. Pablo, it can't end this way. We can't let it."

"Look over here." Toomey pointed at the liquor room. "They tried to break in and couldn't."

The broken blade of a screwdriver stuck out, wedged between the steel door and the frame we had cemented into a brick wall.

"I thought you two worked Homicide?"

Harris pulled down the knot of his maroon tie, unbuttoned the collar of his blue oxford button-down shirt.

"Normally, we do."

"Let's just say we have a special interest in you, Waitz," explained Toomey.

"There's a pretty fair chance this is connected to our investigation." Harris filled his mouth with another handful of sprouts.

"Whadayathink?" prodded Toomey.

"Couldn't it be a plain old burglary?"

The black detective mumbled something inaudible.

"Harris, I wish you'd stop talking with your mouth full," Toomey interrupted him.

Harris swallowed.

"If it's your ordinary burglary, why go through the files? Maybe they were looking for something in your papers."

"Possibly."

"Or maybe someone wants to scare you, break you. Getting into your files is like getting into your pants; it's personal, a kind of rape."

"He was a psychology major," bragged Toomey.

"You know what Freud said?" asked Noah.

"No, what?" Harris regarded him.

"A cigar is sometimes just a cigar."

"Sheeeeit!"

"Maybe he's right," I said.

"Don't get upset, Mr. Waitz. We know what we're doing. Toomey used to work Vice, but I was in Burglary."

"You gotta understand, if this is connected to your partner's death, you better tell us what you know—I mean *everything*! Next time they might make the message even more personal, if you know what I mean?"

"I've already told you everything." I felt a wave of terror run through me as I spoke.

"OK, then we treat it like a burglary for now. I still have the names and addresses of your employees, but you can update it if there's anything new, if you've fired or hired anyone, had any customer trouble."

"What about prints?" I stared at one, then the other.

"Not a chance," said Harris. "But I'll dust anyway."

Inside Ponce's office, Harris stripped down to his linen shirt-sleeves before opening a small toolbox.

"It's not like you see on *Kojak*. Prints are the toughest things in the world to get. You have to practically stick a glass in someone's hand, then make sure they don't smudge it when you take it away."

"Not very promising."

"Afraid not."

Harris leaned over the top of a metal cabinet and sprinkled some iron filings from a phial. He ran a small magnet over them, waving it, as though it were a magic wand, in tiny circles. Some of the filings jumped to the magnet while others clung to the cabinet, trying to form a pattern.

"You see? Smudges. That's what we got here."

"I see."

"The important thing is the surface. There are very few good surfaces for fingerprints. Anything grainy breaks up a print so bad you can't see the ridges, which makes it a poor surface. So is metal, as you see here. Paper absorbs moisture from the skin, then dries; the prints literally evaporate."

"What are we doing? Wasting time?"

"Not necessarily."

"Sometimes we get a perfect set of prints." Toomey stood in the door. "Only they usually turn out to be your own."

"I don't believe this. . . ."

Toomey continued: "It's true. But we've learned to recognize them right away, because we don't want to waste your time, to say nothing of your precious tax dollars."

Harris spilled iron filings on our battered cash box.

"I dust on burglaries, anyway. Whoever did this, though, was careful not to leave anything. Not a pro, exactly, but not an amateur, either."

"I bet it's an inside job." Toomey cleared his throat.

"Wait a second, I think . . ."

Harris waved his magnet as the filings fulfilled themselves in an unmistakable pattern of ridges and swirls to form a clear print.

"Yes, I believe we've got something here!"

"Looks like your thumb, Harris."

"Sure does look like my thumb."

Toomey beamed.

"Forget prints." I heard myself sigh. "How did they get in?"

"Come with me, Waitz. I'll show you."

I trailed him topside, where Noah sat at the bar with a mug of coffee and a shot of Wild Turkey. He joined us by the door to the Second Street Café, where Toomey pointed to a broken pane of glass. After opening the café door, whoever did it had had no trouble bending back a bar on the metal gate that closed off the café from the interior. It was a cheap gate, one in which the bars were attached to the runner by plastic studs.

"This opening is hardly big enough for a child," I observed.

"Some people can squeeze into real small spaces. Many of the best burglars are under five six. I've also heard about jobs where they used kids, or midgets."

"It wasn't street," said Noah.

"Why not?" challenged Toomey.

" 'Cause if it had been Rose, or any of the hawks at the Kenton, there wouldn't be a full bottle left in the place. What they couldn't take or drink, they'd have broken."

"That's a good point." Toomey rubbed his chin.

It had to have been the Elephant Man. I'd declined to hire him, hurt his pride and inflamed his jealousy. But he was also calling attention to Black Hattie, whose anonymity was her chief asset, a guarantee to the brokers in the drug world that she couldn't easily be caught in a squeeze by cops hungry for information.

"Hey, you guys, down here on the double!" Harris' voice rang out below. "You gotta see this!"

We scrambled through the trap. Maria was on the far side of the basement, in a shadowy corner beyond the walk-in freezer. A few feet away from her, Harris trained his flashlight on the floor. Maria's eyes bugged out while she held a hand over her nose and mouth.

"At first I thought it was an old tire, or maybe a stop at the end of the beer slide." Awe exposed the whites of Harris' eyes. "Incredible!"

Maria brushed past.

"Excuse me. I'm going to be sick."

What I observed in the beam of Harris' flashlight might've been a cobra devouring a mongoose, but it wasn't. It was the biggest turd I ever saw in my life.

"It must weigh at least five pounds," stammered Toomey. "It had to come from a big man."

"There goes your midget theory," chimed Noah.

"Is it cold?"

"Goddammit, Toomey! How in the hell should I know!" Perspiration beaded Harris' forehead. "You don't expect me to touch it and find out!"

"If it's in the line of duty, a piece of evidence, yes, I do. You're a detective, aren't you? You wear a gold shield, don't you?"

Noah stared. Toomey wasn't laughing. Neither was Harris.

"It may be a piece of evidence to you, Toomey, but to me it's a piece of shit."

"You know what Freud said." Noah gave us his sharky grin.

"My job don't call for touching no pieces of shit!"

"Take it easy, Harris."

"I didn't get a master's in psychology to dip around in no shit!"

"A cigar is sometimes . . ."

"If you want to dip around in it, Toomey, go ahead, be my guest. I'll take notes and recommend you for a brown badge instead of a gold one."

"It don't stink," mused Toomey. "It's got to be at least a few hours old."

"Dammit! Stop treating it like a corpse. It's just a piece of shit." Harris snapped around to glare at Noah. "And I don't wanna hear any shit about Freud or cigars."

"It could help us determine the time." Toomey held his ground.

"You really expect to determine that by examining a piece of shit?"

"You're supposed to be a smart guy, Harris, with all those degrees from John Jay, but sometimes I don't get you."

"*You* don't get *me*?"

"Yeah. Sometimes you get . . . prissy."

"*Prissy?*"

"Like a little girl. Wait, listen before you blow your top. OK? Shit's organic, right? It undergoes thermal change, right? Right! As far as I'm concerned, that qualifies it as a piece of evidence."

"Next, you'll want to wrap it up and take it with us to Forensic."

"Excuse me, gentlemen, but I'm going to see about the lady," I told them.

Noah's hands covered his face. I couldn't tell whether it was nausea or hilarity.

"No, I don't want to wrap it and take it with me."

"You want me to call in for a shit specialist to come over and take its temperature?"

"No, Harris, I don't want no shit specialist." Toomey's voice followed me up the ladder. "But it *is* a piece of evidence, goddammit! And every piece of evidence should be treated with *respect!*"

*   *   *

Noah went to the glazier and bought a pane of glass for the café door. Maria went to the bank. Ronald Perry tied a wet towel to his face, shoveled the "piece of evidence" into an empty egg crate and filed it in the dumper. I bent the steel strip until it fit loosely into the runner of the gate and sat down. I was slipping into catatonia when Maria returned. She appeared strangely relaxed, Mother Courage.

"Pablo, go out and see a movie, get drunk, let off steam."

"I thought you didn't like it when I got high."

"I don't like it when you're full of coke. A drink never hurt anyone."

She sat next to me, held my hand.

"I'm broke."

Maria took a twenty from the bills she had just put in the register and gave it to me. She was radiant.

"There, you've got money. Take the rest of the day and do something besides worry."

She meant well.

I left the Tin Angel as a band of Nubian slaves with bare arms and legs danced to keep warm in the parking lot behind the Amato Opera. They had to keep moving as they waited for their cues. So many of these spaghetti benders were set in exotic, tropical climates. Even the spear carriers had to have a certain amount of devotion to work for Tony Amato. *Aida!* It wasn't exactly Nile weather. While spring was around the corner, it was a corner somewhere south of Second Street.

At McSorley's on Seventh and Ale Place, I ordered two mugs of their house brew and remembered that at this very moment Carlotta was sitting at home in her bed watching her *bloody asides* grow as Zach slipped into the bathroom to pop a tranquilizer. Why wasn't I with them? Because my house was burning down and I was trapped inside.

I moved down the bar where Patrick Finnigan reported to a group of regulars that his brother James was "recovering from the jaundice." Next time James touched a drop of alcohol, however, would be his last, according to the doctor. Six ales later, I bid good day to the younger Finnigan, who, at thirty-five, could pass for a soggy Richard Burton, then wove out into a mellow haze.

Passing St. George's Ukrainian School, it occurred to me what an awkward position James Finnigan was in; his greatest pleasure was about to kill him. Fate might have dealt me a better hand, for sure. But considered another way, I might've been a Nubian slave on the Bowery!

"Qué te pica?"

"La cabeza, los guevos."

My response was automatic. It took me a few seconds to realize that the only person who ever asked me this question was dead. Whenever I was under pressure, Ponce would ask where I itched. Depending on my mood, I'd name this or that part of my anatomy.

"What the fuck you doing here! You're dead!"

"What kinda odds you wanna give me on James Finnigan?"

"What?"

"Three to one he falls off the wagon and croaks in six months."

Ponce was sitting on the fender of a station wagon parked in front of St. George's, his slim body as vital as ever.

"Man, did you fuck up!"

"Thought you were rid of me, *cabrón*?" He had a crooked smile.

"Go away. I want to get drunk in peace. I've got plenty of problems, and you're just one of them."

"Stop acting like a baby who can't get at a tit."

"You've got some nerve talking to me that way. Hey, an' what's the idea of never telling me you had a kid? Garret. I found out about it just by accident."

He was dressed in white pants and a loose powder-blue

guyabera. When I mentioned the kid's name, he stared at his highly polished black shoes.

"I want you to promise me something, Pablo."

"Maybe."

"Keep an eye on Garret. You know, just keep in touch, make sure if there's any problem . . ."

His voice trailed off into a morose silence.

"I can't pay the bills, my mother's a martyr to chemotherapy, and you want me to check up on a kid you never even acknowledged was your son."

"Correct."

"Ponce, I've gotta admit you've got balls to sit and tell me that after losing thirty-five grand out of the business. . . ."

"With your permission. It was an investment opportunity."

"You make it sound like I was dealing with Merrill Lynch."

"There's always an element of risk."

"With that money I could pay the butcher, the produce man, our restaurant supplier. Shit! I could have paid the March liquor bill with the money it cost me to send your carcass to San Juan!"

"That's another bone I want to pick with you."

"Shove it." ·

"Don't get nasty. You know how I hate it down there, man! Why you let them do that to me? It makes you laugh to think that the ducks and chickens are shitting all over Ponce's grave?"

"It wasn't my idea."

"And another thing, Maria . . ."

"Fuck off! You were always overprotective."

"My ass!"

"Even back when we were seeing each other, you got between us. I was afraid to call you on it, God knows why."

"I know why. You needed me."

"Well, I need her now, and I'm not afraid of you."

He took a toothpick from his shirt pocket and started to pick his teeth.

"So I notice. I get killed and suddenly you're *macho-chamaco,* grabbing all my women."

"I couldn't help it. Besides, Hattie's not really 'your woman' ... and she didn't think you'd mind. She thought you'd like it."

"You gotta head full of *garbanzos.*"

"And stop treating Maria like one of your private stock. She's not your lover, she's your sister."

He wiped the toothpick on his pants before speaking.

"She's delicate, Pablo. She may talk tough, but she was always delicate. Listen, here you are, fuckin' knee-deep in shit, no money, cops all over your ass, and you're bringing her nothin' but grief. . . ."

"You created the situation, mothafucker. . . ."

"Don't call me that."

"Well, you did. You brought her grief all your life. You've got no business on my case, especially because I'm trying to clean up after you."

"Lay off her. I know what I'm talking about. I swear on my chicken-shit grave, if you don't, you'll never get another good night's sleep."

"What makes you think I sleep so good now? You blew it, man, *you blew it!*"

Gradually, I realized the kids playing punchball on Ale Place were staring at me. What they saw was some drunk yelling at the fender of a green Ford Torino station wagon. They were pointing at me and laughing. I gave them the finger and headed for the Last Supper Deli. What I needed was available there: a cup of sump water and a radioactive bagel. When I glanced back, Ponce was gone.

Benson Supper, in a white apron full of mustard stains, sat alone at a table in the rear. When he saw me, he waved me over, scratched his gray muttonchops and regarded me with bloodshot eyes. He was a puddle of sympathy.

"What's wrong?"

"Where do I start?"

"How about a bagel and coffee?"

He served the coffee with two little containers of dairy substitute; by the time the bagel was finished having its atoms scrambled in the radar range, the prospect of eating it had nearly sobered me. Butter substitute bubbled through the dough.

"That should do the trick," he said.

I began a litany that ran from my partner's death to this morning's burglary and the water and sewage bill I'd recently received from the city that covered the past two years.

"First thing tomorrow, I'm sending over Hunkey, my plumbing specialist, to put a fifty percent bypass on your water meter. He'll be there at nine. The other stuff I can't help you with."

"Thanks, Benson."

"Hey, maybe there's something you can do for me?"

"Shoot."

"I've got a ticklish electrical problem. Know anyone?"

"So happens I do, a guy named Manny Wu. He put a bypass on our electric."

Benson's face turned a bright red.

"Manny Wu? A Jewish Chink?"

"Short for Manchu. He comes from illustrious ancestors. They call him the Electric Chinaman."

"Terrific! Hey, you want a radar range like the one I got? Brand-new, wholesale! I mean, it fell off a truck. It's worth about four hundred, but you can get it for less. Anything off the street, they'll ask for half and settle for a third."

"Those radar things scare me."

"How about some wholesale meat, or a cash deal on liquor, no tax, pure profit?"

"What I need right now is a miracle. You know someone who makes miracles?"

"As a matter of fact, I've got just the guy for you, calls himself Smokey the Bear. A real artist. He can burn anything. Even stone."

"I don't . . ."

"He builds shopping centers; says that before you can burn a place down, you gotta know how to build it. If you wanna burn it right! Only thing he has a little trouble with is brick."

"My place has lots of brick."

"But he can make brick smolder. Remember all the building I had to do when I took over this place from Ali? Looked like an Arabian whorehouse, with all those hanging lights."

"Delis aren't Ali's thing."

"Smokey came by while I was puttin' down the floor, and he says, 'Benson, I don't know about those tiles, they're a mixture of brick and linoleum. We might have a slight burn problem with them, but I guess we can start from the ceiling.' "

"What about the people upstairs?"

"Smokey's never lost a tenant. He works mostly by day, checks to see that people are at work."

"I'll keep him in mind."

"He made me drive him to Brooklyn to see his last job. We pull up to this vacant lot near Sheepshead Bay where there used to be a four-story building? Nothing. Flat as a plate. Before I know it, Smokey's out of the car, bending down, running his fingers through the ashes, an' he's whispering, 'Ain't it beoooootiful!' Just like that, 'Beoooootiful!' The man's an artist."

Manny Wu, the Electric Chinaman, claimed to have his high-decibel ear pressed to half the bugged phones and bedrooms in Manhattan and several boroughs. I'd been meaning to talk to him about Ponce's death, and now Benson's request gave me the push I needed to contact him. I left word at Moe's, a mod barber shop in St. Mark's, that I was looking for Manny.

Moe, a Roman who sported a mustache that covered the bottom half of his face, told me Manny would be in touch.

On my way down Second Avenue, I bumped into Frankie Palermo, whose family owned a funeral parlor around the corner from the Tin Angel. Small, dark, in a suit and blue overcoat, he looked like an understudy for Al Pacino. He was organizing a demonstration to try and get the men's shelter moved from Third Street. It wasn't fair to the people who lived in the neighborhood, dumping all the derelicts and crazies there. It made our streets sewers, and Third Street was the drain. Frankie's idea was to rent wheelbarrows, put a wino in each, wheel them down to City Hall and dump them on the steps.

"A hundred winos with their flys open, stinking like sour milk!"

He practically jumped up and down, he was so excited.

"Sorry, Frankie, but right now I've got other problems. Say, you know anybody interested in buying a classy bar and restaurant?"

"Your place?"

"Yeah."

He scratched his chin.

"Maybe I do. I'll ask around."

I wished him luck with his wheelbarrow assault on City Hall and continued to a hole in the wall below the Palace Hotel called CBGB's, the mecca of punk rock, wondering if I were really serious about selling the Tin Angel. It had come out unexpectedly. Certainly, a part of me wanted to unload some of this terrible weight. At the very least, it was an alternative to Smokey the Bear.

The down-and-out residents of the Palace Hotel mingled freely with the children of the white middle class who spilled in and out of the small club. You could always tell the grifters from the punks because the latter dyed their hair green, yellow, blue or red; wore neck chokers, chains around their shoulders, spiked belts and wristbands, rings through their ears and noses, shoes with six-inch heels.

A man with a gray Vandyke waved me past the admission. Patti Smith's "Piss Factory" played on a machine our jukebox man had once told me he hated to service because there was usually rat shit in the coin box.

They stood three rows deep at the long bar, packed the tables around the stage in the rear of this electronic zoo. I was shouldering my way towards the bartender when a hand reached out and touched my shoulder.

"Can I buy you a beer?"

It was Christ. A young couple wearing (him) leopard skin and (her) a zebra bodystocking parted to let me in.

"Better make it ginger ale. I'm trying to sober up."

"You were looking for me this morning?"

"Wino Rose and her quiffs. They almost burned me out. Noah flagged down a patrol car, but the cops let them walk. Maybe it would've been better if they'd torched the place."

"You don't mean that."

"No? When I need help I don't get it. I carve a little piece of civilization out of this wilderness of monkeys and no one gives a fuck."

"I do, Pablo. I'm sorry. Most of the time I feel like a man in the middle of a stampede trying to stop it by blowing a whistle."

"I don't know anyone else to bitch to."

"I hear you got hit."

"Word travels fast."

"Have any ideas?"

"Nothing I'd swear to."

"Why don't you give me what you have and let me work on it?"

"Hey, man, you've had forty men out there on the street squeezing everybody they could touch."

"We don't have forty men anymore."

"How many?"

"Five, six."

"All right. So, what've you found out?"

Christ shook his head.

"It doesn't make sense, no sense at all. Is there any coke in town at the moment?"

"Not really," I lied. "But I'm turning in my coke spoon. No more white lady."

"Maria?"

"She gets upset when she sees my pupils boil."

"Love is a better high. Not that I care about the drug, mind you. I'm just trying to make the pieces fit. You say there's nothing around, but a couple of days after the shooting up until now everyone is walking around with their eyes popping."

"Something has come into town, recently," I volunteered. "But the people who have it don't do business this far east, and definitely not on the street."

"I'll tell you this much." Christ returned the favor. "It's a *house* connection we're looking for, not a street one."

"Anything else?"

"The old Russian lady picked a guy out of a lineup, a black dude wanted for armed robbery in New Jersey. I don't think he's the right man. Sound like anyone Ponce knew?"

"Nope."

"Pablo ..."

"Listen, man, I've a lot of feelers out; if something comes back, I'll let you know."

"I don't like the way this thing is moving. Be careful."

"I'll keep you posted."

"Please."

"I better get back."

He held up two fingers in a V.

UNDERSTANDING RELATIVITY

The *bloody asides* had grown to the size of a medicine ball. Carlotta lay in bed and stroked it. She petted, cuddled and held it as if all her grief were suddenly gathered there and a display of tenderness might make it go away.

"I can't tell her." Zach's voice clotted in his throat.

We stood in her kitchen. There was bird song and the first delicate buds of spring on the tree outside. I noticed that Zach's blond hair had begun to thin at the crown, that there was dandruff on the shoulders of his wrinkled gray crewneck.

"We can't wait any longer," I said.

"How can I tell her she's not getting well, that she has to go back to the hospital?"

"I'll tell her," I replied.

"There's no choice. We can't take care of her anymore."

"You're right."

You can't take care of her anymore, old Zach, waiting by her bedside day and night while I try to hold my life together in another part of town. Of course you can't.

Dr. Loftus assured me over the phone that there would be a bed waiting for her in the morning. We returned to find her hugging the burgeoning bulge in her abdomen. She tried to smile, but when I told her she had to go back into the hospital, she turned away.

"They've got to drain you, get some nourishment into your system."

As I said this, it was clear that while they might be able to drain the liquid, there was no way they could nourish the will that had begun to seep from her spirit, her *spiritual asides.*

When Carlotta buried her face in her hands, the vertebrae in her back stood up through her nightshirt, a range of flannel mountains, a Delius landscape. It trembled when she spoke.

"I wish they'd put me out. They shouldn't be doing this to a woman my age, dragging me around, humiliating me."

Although her chest heaved, she was too weak to cry. After a minute she stopped trying, patted my hand. I sat at the edge of the bed, searching for something to say.

"Mom . . ."

"It's all right," said Carlotta. "It's all right."

It was a few minutes before two on a balmy Saturday afternoon, the second one in April, when I called Julie Fine from the Market Diner and woke her. She agreed to see me if I'd give her twenty minutes to wash and dress. I hung up, chose a booth and gave a middle-aged waitress with strawberry-blond hair my order of eggs over easy, rye toast and coffee.

The Market was one of the few all-night diners left in Manhattan. I often found myself in the same booth, savoring the smell of bacon, gazing at the Hudson through the decaying girders of the West Side Highway. Often, in the wee hours, you could see stragglers from the gay leather bars like the Ramrod walking back and forth by the docks.

Over coffee, I flashed on what Christ had told me. If it were true that Ponce's last deal had been connected to a *house,* that is, from a major source directly to a large supplier, then Black Hattie would know about it. She was covering up. I had to get back to her again, and quickly, before she dropped out of sight. But now it was time for Julie Fine.

During the last few months of Ponce's life, Julie had been an obsession. Not that he'd ever talked about it, but there had been this special tone in his voice, a quaver, when he spoke her name, or a concentrated, glazed expression on his face when he whispered to her over the telephone. And they had told me at the Hip Bartenders' Consciousness-Raising Group that he'd actually admitted to being frightened, uninterested in other pussy! Most of the women in the endless procession I'd observed marching through Ponce's life had been more beautiful than Julie—he had preferred showstoppers. Nothing pleased him more than walking into a room with a woman who made the conversation dissolve. The lady drummer did not have that effect on a roomful of men except when sitting behind her drums. As I paid my check, I concluded that for the first time since I'd known him, Ponce had been in love.

Julie lived on Greenwich Street, in one of those loft buildings south of Canal that had gone cooperative. Tribeca, as the area was called, was the new frontier of factory and warehouse space slowly being populated by urban pioneers: writers, painters and musicians. It was deserted on weekends, with no trucks pulling in and out of loading platforms. I yelled her name twice before a head popped out of a window on the third floor. She dropped a white sock with a key in it. I opened the door and climbed the wooden stairs. She was waiting for me on the landing.

"Excuse the mess. I was working last night."

She scratched her head of thick honey-colored hair as I followed her inside.

"Who you working with?"

"Buddy Rich's big band at the Vanguard."

"Sounds like a nice gig."

"Yeah, I love Buddy. Come in."

She was small, no bigger than five three. Astride her drums, she appeared to be larger than life, but here, in the middle of a huge white room, wearing a black V-neck sweater, she was timid, childlike, as tousled as her loft.

"How about some coffee?"

I pulled up a seat at a round Formica table, across from a large unmade bed with sheets and a comforter piled on it. The floor was strewn with clothes and magazines. At the opposite end of the loft her Slingerland drums, still packed in black cases, sat on an area rug. There were also an electronic keyboard, a shelf of hi-fi stuff, records, sheet music, percussion equipment: a gourd, a bell-tree, claves, a birimbau and cungas.

Julie put down two cups of coffee, then started to roll a joint from a grass-filled cigarette case in the middle of the table.

"I suppose you want to talk about Ponce."

"That's right."

"I've already told the cops everything I know, which is nothing. I've talked to more fuzz in the last two months than in all my life."

She drawled the words. Her movements were slow as she took another long pull on the joint. My cup was dirty. The room was chaotic. Making love to her skins Julie was a goddess, but at home she was simply depressed. Had that attracted Ponce? Had he been her white knight?

"Tell me what you told them."

"Sure. The night he got it I was playing a gig in Jersey, a place called Richard's Lounge. He called me that morning to say he'd try and pick me up after the set, but if he wasn't there, to go home with the cats. They wanted to know if he'd talked about a robbery, or a dope deal. I told them he hadn't."

"That's it?"

"Just about. They asked me who he associated with."

"And?"

"I didn't know. The time we spent together, we spent together, you know? I mean, we'd see a movie, have dinner, come back here. Occasionally, we'd go out and listen to some music."

"You never had a hint of anything about to pop?"

"The only thing Ponce ever did when we were together was try and get close to me."

"Did he?"

"That really interested the cops. They wanted to know all about it."

"What did you tell them?"

"I said, yes, we had a little scene, OK?"

She pulled her hair back over her ears and held it for a minute. Her light blue eyes were moist, either from sorrow or dope, I couldn't tell which, but the set of her jaw was familiar. Heather Moore. They had the same jaw.

"Was that all it came to, a little scene?"

"What difference does it make?"

"It makes a difference."

I refused the joint she handed me; instead, had visions of myself going wild, throwing furniture, jumping up and down, anything to scare her out of her stoned lethargy.

"You really want to know? All right. Ponce clung to me closer than dirt. I couldn't play a gig that he wasn't at the front table. If I went to the bathroom, he was there to pull the chain. At first I was flattered. He sent cards, flowers, the whole corny routine. No one ever paid that kind of attention to me before. I ate it up."

"Did he love you?"

"That's what he kept saying. He said that was why he was a washout in bed."

"Ponce?"

"You sure you want to hear this?"

"Go on."

Julie lit a straight cigarette, a Pall Mall. There were nicotine stains on her fingers.

"Go on," I prompted.

"At first it was OK, you know? No fireworks, but very sweet. Then he ... you know, couldn't do it, couldn't get it up. It didn't particularly bother me. I had a good time with him. But it bothered him. He kept saying that he could go all night with most women, but because he loved me, it was different. Strange. Do you understand that?"

I avoided her eyes.

"I think so."

"The real problem was that I didn't love him. I was, uh, fond of Ponce, but I didn't love him. Once I realized that, I tried to let him down easy, to back off, but he just came at me harder, started talking crazy. . . ."

"Crazy, how?"

"Well, he had his cards read somewhere, and they told him that we'd been lovers in another life, like in Atlantis— what do you do with that, man! I didn't know. Then he started making plans, asking me if I'd move into a house with him, somewhere outside the city; visions of a little ivy-covered cottage, that kind of thing. I told him, man, I'm a musician, I gotta play. Then he wanted to know if I liked kids."

She exhaled the last of her cigarette, stubbed it out and started to roll another joint. Her mind left the present, drifted elsewhere, perhaps to a cottage in the suburbs, the sounds of tiny feet on the stairs. It shattered when she shook her head violently, stared at me.

"I really tried to be nice. I told him, man, it wasn't me he loved. I wasn't a character in that story. He wanted someone else."

"What did he say?"

"Ponce didn't like not getting his way. He didn't even hear me."

This time I accepted the joint.

"Hold on, I have to go to the bathroom," she said.

After she closed the bathroom door, I strolled over to the drums and Fender Rhodes. On my left, two large windows opened slightly on Greenwich Street. The air smelled of incipient spring, of thawing earth and watershed rains washing away dead leaves. The faint sound of an alto rose from the loft below. On a table to my right were charts and arrangements, mostly big-band scores. An old Fake Book lay open. A bookmark stuck up between two Quincy Jones tunes, "Blues Bittersweet" and "Bone Dance." There were some penciled notations in the margin of the latter in a microscopic, illegible hand. The writing on the note Julie had used to mark her place was different. It sprawled across the scrap of paper, the letters falling over each other as they raced towards the end. Before I'd even made sense of the message, I'd read the note.

> Julie *mariposa,* meet me at Bradley's after the last set. I love your white-petal eyes.
>
>> Rodolfo

Jesus, but Colon was a flowery turd! And what was he doing talking shit to Julie Fine, anyway? I recalled the fixed, dilated eyes of the card player as they had stared at Julie riding her drum at the Five Spot. I slipped the note into my shirt pocket and returned to the table where my coffee sat, un- touched. Soon the toilet flushed and Julie appeared.

"Well, I guess that's it," I told her.

"I don't know what else I can tell you," drying her hands on her jeans.

I stifled the urge to confront her with the note then and there; the voice of a greater wisdom told me to exit quietly, let the information settle. I rose and removed my jacket from the back of the chair.

"Listen." She stopped me at the door. "That stuff about Ponce not being able to make it?"

"What about it?"

"I understand it. It's not what he thought. There was nothing wrong with him."

"What are you getting at, Julie?"

"Ponce thought that because he loved me, he should be Superman in bed. He kept blaming himself that he wasn't. It never occurred to him that maybe he couldn't perform because I didn't love him! You see?"

She looked up at me with sky-blue eyes set in skin so pale it was almost translucent.

"Shhhhhh." Carlotta puts her fingers to her lips. "I don't want to be embalmed. Bury me in a closed coffin."

She lies in her private room at Ararat General, the vein in her neck throbbing with panic blood; not pulsing but racing, a river trying to jump its meandering bed. The liquid from her *asides* flows into a plastic bag pinned to the bed rails, as does the fluid collecting from her chest, which runs down through tubes inserted in her nostrils. She closes her eyes.

"Look at that. It's just passing through her."

Zach points out that the yellow glucose entering her as nourishment through the IV on the far side of the bed is coming out the draining tube beside us. He shakes his head, seraphic blond curls around his forehead, his eyes dark pits in his face.

Sinking into a delirium, Carlotta tears at the tubes, throws off her blankets, begins to pull at her dressing gown. She rips it off her body and we see how thin she's become, except for the edema around her ankles. Flesh hangs from her arms. She tears at curtains of air, trying to part them, to see what's on the other side. Then she falls back into a medicated limbo, patting her monstrous pregnancy, gently mothering the child of her demise.

"What am I suppose to do with this?"

Maria put the note I'd taken from Julie's loft down on the table.

It was a handle on something, I told her. It was a hard piece of information that took me under the surface of Ponce's life. Had he talked about his relationship to Julie? About Colon? Had he seemed troubled, angry, desperate?

I watched her face change, her eyes dart. She looked at the note, color washed from her cheeks. So Miguel's girl friend was two-timing him, wasn't that the implication? So what! Did I expect her to pin a medal on me for bringing back that piece of indigestible material?

"Don't you care?"

"No! Dammit! No, I don't. How many times do I have to

tell you, Pablo? Look, already, that one, Colon, he's calling here and leaving messages."

"When? Why didn't you tell me!"

"I forgot. No, I didn't forget. I don't want him calling. I'm trying to clean my house and you're bringing *trash* into it!"

There were long white candles in brass sconces on the table. The settings were china, the napkins linen, the utensils silver. There was a roast in the oven; wild rice on the stove; fresh string beans simmering in ginger, butter and lemon. An unopened bottle of French claret bent the light of a candle into a ruby star.

"Ponce's dead and somebody's got my money. How do you expect me to walk away from that?"

"You put one foot after the other."

"It's that simple for you?"

"We're different, Pablo. I can close the door on all of that; for me it's only pain, nothing more. But being in the middle of it gives you pleasure."

"I couldn't live with myself if I didn't try...."

"You're like a dog with a bone. It'll never be over for you."

"That's not true."

There were flinty sparks in her eyes. Her voice rose and broke, but there were no tears.

"It is. You're always in the street, halfway out the door."

"And you draw a curtain on the world."

She didn't answer. The argument had grown old; we both knew the terrain. There was nothing more to add. But I fumbled with the buttons of my denim jacket, hoping she'd make an effort to detain me. She didn't. I picked up the note from the table, still waiting for a signal, an excuse to kneel beside her, touch her cheek, but Maria just stared straight ahead, into a flickering flame. It was deathly quiet. The thought of her, with dinner on the stove, in all this elegance while the wind blew and thieves raged outside her window filled me with sorrow.

I walked out on tiptoe, closed her door so that the sound of the tongue clicking into its groove was imperceptible.

I found Bertie stretched out on a piece of black naugahide in the waiting room of the Ararat. He was gazing out the picture window, watching the red-and-white necklaces of traffic headed to and from Kennedy in the darkness. His belly had begun to bother him. No longer did he have the sprightly appearance of Hans Christian Andersen. He looked more like Red Nichols about to give birth to all Five Pennies. A brown paper bag with a bottle of Georgi vodka peeped out. He belched and passed it to me.

"Carlotta's got company?"

"Mrs. Sawyer. This morning she asked me to phone her, and that guy who calls himself a swami, what's his name?"

"Sri Mudra."

"That asshole," belched Bertie. "He sat with her for an hour, holding her hand and humming."

"What?"

"That's right. I peeked in, and she was just lying there while he held her hand and went *hmmmmmmm*. Just like that. *Hmmmmmmmm*. Now you tell me, what the fuck is that supposed to do? She's dying, and that greasy little fartbag is sitting there going *hmmmmmmmm.*"

I handed him back his bottle.

"Take a hit, Bertie. You're getting upset."

"Goddamn right. She kicks me out so that phony can hold her hand and whisper in her ear!"

"He wasn't whispering, he was humming. Who is that in there with her now?"

"Her Christian Science practitioner. Well, maybe the old cows can work a miracle. She can't do any worse than these doctors."

"Hey, Bertie, would you do me a favor?" I found the folded piece of paper in my wallet, between my license and my

Blue Cross card. On it I had scribbled the plate of the Mercedes parked in front of Heather Moore's the day I had visited her.

"What's this?"

"Would you run it through MVB for me?"

He scanned the note, folded it and put it into his shirt pocket.

"Something important?"

"I don't know. Maybe . . ."

"Consider it done."

I sat quietly as Bertie talked about the new gambling unit he'd been assigned to. During recessions gambling increased, but this detail, he said, was almost a bonus for organized crime. They make a few cosmetic busts on the small numbers joints and everything settles; the big boys never get touched, don't even have to pay off. Only lately there were also a lot of numbers joints being robbed and the guys who ran them were packing guns, so the cops had to be careful when they moved in. He told me this story about an incident that happened the other day when three guys pulled guns on a numbers man who stood, safely, behind bullet-proof glass. They asked him to give up his money and, when he refused, held a gun to the head of a woman waiting in line, they thought, to place her bet. What they didn't know was that she was the numbers man's wife. When they told him to give up the money or they'd blow her head off, the man behind the glass yelled: "Fuck you!" hit the deck and pushed the alarm.

"Did they shoot?"

"No, but her husband sure wishes they had."

I turned just as a beefy woman in her seventies dressed in black with salt-and-pepper hair approached. At one time she must've been a beauty, but now the delicate lips, the small nose were lost in the hills and valleys of her buckling flesh.

"I left Carlotta sleeping peacefully," she tried to smiled. "I reminded her that she was God's perfect child. You must not think of her as sick and infirm. That is Error. Think of her as whole and well, the Carlotta whose vitality knows no bounds. Do not admit this Error to your consciousness. It's an illusion."

A tear rolled down her cheek. We stared back at her. Bertie belched.

GLOBAL BACTERIA

I'd been in and out of the Ninth Precinct often enough over the last few months to have established a nodding acquaintance with most of the cops on the front steps, two desk sergeants and the beautiful café-au-lait paraprofessional in the midiskirt who worked the files and computer. The black wreath with its long streamers still hung over the doorway. Now there were also two bronze plaques on the wall to the right of the front desk with photoengraved portraits of Eddie Marovitch, a man with broad cheeks and close-cropped hair, and Bill Greene, who had flaring nostrils and large, close-set eyes. There were half a dozen other plaques on the same wall, but only these two were as shiny as new pennies.

Toomey lifted his head from the *Daily News* when I entered. He was alone in the office. Even the bullpen was empty.

"What happened? The criminals on strike?"

He glanced at his watch, then back at the paper.

"Come in, Waitz. You're right on time. Goddamn stock market has me by the balls. A friend—ha! some friend—he gave me a tip on a gypsum mine in Vancouver. Right from the source. Said there was a gold play, too. Toomey, he says, we're sitting in a jewelry store. Naturally, I buy ten thousand shares. Six months later I find out the stock has been printed by the mayor of a small town in New Jersey. And where is the stock at this moment, you may ask? You wanna know? Well, so do I! But nobody can tell me. Not even my fucking broker. It seems to have slipped right off the Exchange."

"Where's Harris? Taking a crap?"

"Jeezus, poor shit! Wait till I tell you what happened to Harris."

"Is he all right?"

I was suddenly aware that I liked the guy. More to my surprise, I was forced to admit to myself I liked Toomey.

"He's gonna live. You know how he gave up smoking, never ate a hot dog, jogged, chewed on those bean sprouts all the time? He had bowels like Big Ben, hands that never shook; even his farts smelled like a health-food store."

"So? What's wrong with him?"

"He's got a bleeding ulcer. Poor shit! He got these pains yesterday sitting at his desk, doubled over and we rushed him to Bellevue. They gave him a GI series. A fucking bleeding ulcer!"

"Will he be coming back?"

"I hope so. But he's got to lay low for a while. If he stays out too long, they're gonna team me up with somebody else, and God knows it took me a long time to get used to Harris!"

"Tell him I hope he feels better. OK?"

"Sure, Waitz, sure."

For weeks after the shooting, the place had been buzzing with detectives, and I'd been hustled in every few days for questioning along with anyone else who was close to Ponce. Slowly, I'd watched the ranks of investigating officers thin until now, with Harris gone, Toomey was the only one left on the case.

"What's new?"

"I'm supposed to be asking you. You tell me."

He leaned forward in his sharkskin suit, biting the dry end of a cheap ballpoint.

"Nothing. No big discoveries."

"Figure out who might've knocked over your place?"

"No. How about you?"

"Are you in a hurry?"

"Me?"

"Yeah, you. You appear to be in a hurry to finish this interview, Mr. Waitz."

"On the contrary, I always enjoy visiting you, Detective Toomey."

"Good. Then hang around a few minutes and tell me about a guy called Ali."

"Who?"

"You heard me. He's an old guy, been around since the year one."

"Ali who has the *bodega* on Avenue B?"

"Right. That's the guy."

"Like you say, he's been there since the year one."

"What's his racket?"

"He sells food."

"What else?"

"Aw, shit, Toomey! A little bit of numbers, that kind of stuff. Nothing heavy. Maybe a bet on a football game."

"That's it? He never fences anything?"

"Once in a while, maybe."

"Was he a friend of Miguel Ponce's?"

"More like a father. Miguel hung around his store when he was a kid, ran errands."

"Were they ever . . . in business together?"

"I don't know what you're getting at. Ali is a good man. Ponce's death shook him up. What kind of a case are you trying to build?"

"Why get upset? All I asked you was if they did business together. Are you hiding something, Waitz?"

"Why don't you ask Ali yourself?"

"That's an idea."

"Take my word for it, he doesn't have a thing to do with what happened to Ponce."

"Can you prove it?"

"Do I have to?"

"You can go now, Waitz. Remember, keep in touch. You know the number."

By the time I hit the street, I felt like a toy that Toomey had wound so tight its legs could hardly move fast enough to make the spring unwind. They carried me to Avenue B. I wanted to see Ali, find out how his name got into the picture.

The sight of Ali's *bodega,* or what had been Ali's *bodega,* stopped me in my tracks. It was now a black hole full of ashes. Some plywood boards had been hastily nailed over the broken windows, and there was a rope tied across the entrance. What had been a wooden door lay splintered on the other side of the threshhold. I slipped under the rope, walked into the sodden, chalky smell of water and cinders. The place was in ruins, but the fire had stopped at the ceiling, leaving the rest of the building untouched; a torch job worthy of Smokey the Bear.

There was movement in the rear. I kicked through a pile of scorched tins and waded into the acrid darkness until I saw China, in her pea-pod dress, squatting in the rubble. She held a flashlight, busily selecting tins which she put in a canvas bag.

"*Donde está Ali?*"

"Ali no here."

"*No me recuerdes, China?*"

She let the beam of her flashlight play on my face.

"*Ah, sí, señor. Ali se fue.*"

"*Díme, China. A donde?*"

"*No se, señor.*"

She had to know something. Was he at home? With a lady friend? A relative?

"*No se, señor.*"

Was there a number I could leave a message at?

"*No, señor.*"

"*Que pasa aquí?*"

"*No se, señor.*"

China wasn't at her conversational best. I couldn't even

find out if the fire had been a genuine accident, an insurance scam or an act of retaliation. What had it to do with Ponce's death? Toomey, that bloodhound, had set me in motion for a reason, had wanted me to come here and find what I had. Drop Waitz over the side and see what goes after him. I felt like a worm on a hook.

"China, if you see Ali, tell him Pablo was looking for him. Tell him to be careful. Remember, Pablo said to be careful."

She aimed the beam at me again.

"*Sí, sí, Pablo. Comprendo.* Okey-dokey."

China winked. At least I thought she winked at me. When my eyes had adjusted to the semidark again, I told her, "*Adiós,*" left her sifting through the spoils.

On the sunny side of Avenue B, the door of Pop Farkas' Fishing Club stood open to a mild spring afternoon. Inside, four gray-haired men were playing pinochle. Further up the block, in front of my old tenement, several Latinos banged their dominoes on a piece of cardboard resting on garbage cans.

I climbed six flights and knocked at the door of apartment sixty-two. Papo answered, all knees and elbows in a T-shirt and cutoffs. He spoke in an urgent whisper, jerking his head towards the roof.

"I've got something for you. Upstairs."

"*Quién es, Papo?*"

His mother's voice floated from the interior.

"*Un amigo mío, Mama.*"

He closed the door and followed me to the roof in his bare feet. We leaned on the parapet, watched the domino players, some kids at stickball. I pointed to Ali's *bodega.*

"What happened?"

"I don' know, Pablo. Maybe a week ago, I jus' had somethin' to eat an' I sit down to watch TV an' I hear sirens. So I look out an' it's on fire. She went up like a match box.

An' where is Ali, I jus' don' know. Ain't nobody seen him."

"Anyone hurt?"

"No, man. It's lucky, too."

"What have you got for me?"

"I know who sold the car to Ponce."

"Good, Papo!"

"It was hot, you know. If the cops had run a check on it when they stopped them, they'd have grabbed Ponce for sure."

"I think they were sitting on a lot of coke, Papo."

"Then it woulda meant jail, for years, man! Or getting turned back out on the street as a fink. The way I see it, the dude who shot had no choice."

"Where would a check on the car lead?"

"No place. Newark, Union City, wherever it was lifted. But plates, engine number, everything was changed. All they know is it was hot."

"Who sold it to him?"

"A brother."

"Dynamite Brother?"

"Yeah. Cat lives on Fourth Street, around the corner from you."

"One of the guys at the Social Club?"

"You got it."

The guys who hung out at the Social Club did all their work right out on the street. They ran electricity out of the club, put cars up on blocks, stripped them, changed whole chassis. Sunday mornings on Fourth Street were like visits to an open-air garage.

"His name, Papo?"

"José."

"José what?"

"Jus' José."

"If I stand there and yell *José!* the whole Social Club and half the people on the street will answer. Every guy on that block is named José."

"They call him Chocoláte."

"That's better."

"He's a little guy with big muscles and a tattoo of an eagle on his arm."

"And this Chocoláte, he sold Ponce the car personally?"

"Yeah. He was the mechanic."

"Ponce was alone?"

"I don' know, man. I told you what I found. You gotta do the rest."

"Solid."

I slapped his palm, then Papo stopped me as I started to reach for my wallet.

"Hey, man, no way!"

"Why not?"

"What you think I am, a snitch? You pay a snitch. I did this for friendship, an' because I owe you."

"No more, Papo. We're even."

"Do you remember when I used to play with you in the bath, Pablo?"

We sit Carlotta up in bed for the supreme pleasure of her gargle. Bertie has become the high priest, the Master of Mouthwash. He empties the contents of a small packet into a glass of warm water, a pink powder he stirs while whispering baby-talk incantation.

Zach is Altar Boy. He holds the silver rinse pan at her chin. The pan is crescent-shaped, the moon of Islam.

I am Choirmaster, holding the napkin in case she dribbles, singing out hosannas of, "Isn't that good!"

We hold her carefully. The glass trembles at her lips. *Sip. Gargle. Spit. Sip. Gargle. Spit.* A drop runs down the side of her cheek, her hands wave, a silent alarm goes off and I jump into the breach between Bertie and Zach, the Napkin Bearer, Nabob of Tissue, whose function it is to make certain the smallest drop of spittle does not touch the counterpane. Should this come to pass, it would resound like a tidal wave through Carlotta's condition.

Her world is a network of delicate balances. If anyone draws too close to the tubes plugged into her on either side of the bed, she flails in mortal terror. When the nurses come in to put her on the bedpan, she insists we speak sweetly to them.

"You boys have power over the nurses."

Henny Penny, under a slowly descending sky, can no longer eliminate the fullness in her gut, the pressure around her heart.

"Can't you do something for me!"

Carlotta has caught the oncologist, Dr. Dick, by pretending to be asleep as he tiptoes in to peek at her chart.

"Just keep up the drainage."

His face is a cluster of marshmallows as he backs towards the door.

"We can try cobalt," says Dr. Loftus.

"Can't you give her stronger medication?" pleads Zach.

"I'll double her present dosage."

Carlotta is sleeping now, dreaming about her life, past, passing and to come. She has begun to speak of this state as *"going to the tropics."*

Before heading over to the Tin Angel, I went home and soaked in a hot bath. I felt like Jonah in the belly of the whale. And like Jonah, awash in the gastric flood. I considered those my life had touched, whose lives had foundered and sunk, then tried to free myself from this position; there was nothing one could do locked in the belly of the beast.

Tomorrow I'd go over to the Social Club and talk to Chocoláte. Rodolfo had been trying to reach me. All right, I'd confront him with the note and see what happened. Then there was Hattie. I'd start putting pressure on her, too. If Babar had knocked over my place, she owed me. She was the Gamekeeper.

I was getting somewhere. I could feel it. Bits and pieces of the puzzle were falling on me. Suddenly I felt tears in my eyes which took me by surprise, and I could do little more than sit in the hot tub and let them come. When there were no more tears, I washed my face, dressed and left for the club. I couldn't wait to catch a glimpse of Dinah in her beaded bra. I wanted to watch her gyrate and clank her finger cymbals to the strains of "Summertime."

Dinah was Jeremy Stieg's old lady. While I hadn't exactly hired him because of her, after their first weekend I was grateful for her presence. When he had handed me his audition tape, I'd been intrigued by the haunting, breathy quality of his flute. After making a few inquiries, I learned that Stieg had paralyzed one side of his face years ago in an automobile accident and in order to continue playing had developed this way of stuffing his mouth with cotton to control the airstream. Even after he had regained some movement, it left him with a sound like no one else's. I booked him and his statuesque girl friend but found the music flat, unconvincing. His breath wove in and out of the notes, yet the haunting quality I had heard was missing. Jeremy Cottonmouth, with his droopy mustache, had even suggested it was because of the Miguel Ponce memorial sound system, that it kept shocking him. No matter. As far as I was concerned, all was forgiven for Dinah's sake.

At the end of every set, Dinah emerged from the cordoned-off Second Street Café to the opening bars of "Summertime." It began delicately, chirping finger cymbals, tiny bells ringing on her toes, then broke loose when, rooted to the floor, she began vibrating and swaying. As she swayed up and down the aisles, her beaded bra shimmered and men held their breath to hear the sound it made. Dinah was a jewel to set off any sultan's harem.

Word had spread quickly. Last night, before the end of the second set, people poured into the Tin Angel from every other bar within a five-block radius to stand rubbernecking for the duration of "Summertime."

Noah greeted me at the door.

"They're about to start another set. I tell you, Pablo, she really adds a new dimension to jazz."

The crowd was young, made up of people who liked the crossover fusion stuff Robin Kenyatta once told me was the "wave of the future." I scanned the room for Dinah, but she was still secreted in the Second Street Café, which had become her private dressing room. I had just settled into the Bowery Café with a cup of black coffee when Noah appeared.

"There's a guy to see you, says his name is Clarence Bowman, from WRVR."

A tall man in his forties with a lantern jaw waited behind my doorman. He might've just blown in from East Egg, with his dapper mustache, hair neatly parted in the middle. He wore a Harris tweed jacket over a tan sweater and an old school tie. Choate or Exeter.

"Show him in."

I'd been mailing copies of our music schedule to him and a number of other jazz critics and DJs for over a year in the hope of getting some exposure. It had been like whispering into the Grand Canyon. This was the first time one of them had walked through my door.

Bowman extended his hand.

"Good to meet you after all this time."

"Please, sit down."

He joined me in a Fundador, then relaxed enough to tell me what had brought him. It hadn't been my impassioned pleas, those cries from a man on the brink of bankruptcy. When he spoke, his words ran through me like an electric current.

"Joe and Iggy Termini have decided to close the Five Spot."

"So they're throwing in the towel."

"Apparently."

"I'm sorry to hear it."

The loss of a place like the Five Spot was like the loss of a great musician, of a Monk or a Mingus or an Eddie Jefferson. Good rooms, like extraordinary people, were spectacular accidents.

"Ted Curson was scheduled to open there next week, his first appearance since he left the US ten years ago. We wanted him to open in the same room he and Dolphy played with Mingus in the sixties. Now I don't know what to do."

The DJ leaned forward. His original impression of faded elegance was confirmed on closer scrutiny. The cuffs of his Brooks Brothers blue oxford shirt were frayed and his cordovans badly worn at the heels. Such were the fortunes of jazz.

"I can either cancel Ted's opening or find another place."

"Like the Tin Angel?"

"We'd post a sign on the Five Spot door. I'd get it into the listings of a number of papers."

I'd been trying to get listings, critics' choices, for so long with no luck that I wanted to make him sweat just a little. Here was a man with the power to keep my room alive, who had come to me only because he was in a corner. Here he was, throwing his musical weight behind a returning musician of formidable gifts, with no room to place him in. I cleared my throat.

"Of course, Ted will play for free. I'm going to try and pull every critic in town who writes about jazz, make it the event of the year."

"My only hesitation is that I've booked a group for that weekend. . . ."

"How about if we schedule Ted between whatever you've got coming?"

A double bill, with Ted Curson as the main event! Not bad. Would Bowman have made that offer, I wondered, if he had known that in the interest of our budget I had booked none other than the Big Licorice Stick?

As I considered the proposition, the opening bars of "Summertime" sent a shiver through the room. Men began salivating at the sound of Dinah's tiny bells. My own lips moistened at the thought of her in diaphanous veils rolling her hips, bending back to touch the floor with the top of her head, bumping and grinding between tables as the fish started jumping, the cotton got high and the Tin Angel became a forest of hard-ons.

"Is it agreed?"

Bowman was waiting for an answer. Chairs began to creak as customers mounted them for a better view. The population had doubled as drinkers from CBGB's, Phebe's, Sobosseck's, Lady Astor's, the Colonnades and McSorley's jammed in.

"Agreed."

"Good."

Bowman raised his snifter.

"Here's to Ted Curson at the Tin Angel."

We clinked glasses as "Summertime" burst into its full exotic flowering, punctuated by ohhhhs, ahhhhs, grunts and catcalls.

The DJ craned his neck.

"Hey, what's going on out there?"

III

NERVE ENDINGS

THE HANGED MAN

I tried shutting him out of my mind, locking an imaginary door, drawing a curtain embroidered with the Zodiac, but he kept seeping through every obstacle to call me names in Spanish, a language that has produced the world's greatest name-callers. In Spanish my mother was a *putana* and I a *hijo de puta, cabeza de culo,* a *pendejo* and a *cabrón;* in English I was simply no fucking good with women and never would be—which might indeed be the fact. But I wasn't about to take it lying down from a skinny, tight-ass ghost. Shaking my fist, I insisted that the same held true for him, to which he replied that it no longer mattered since he was dead and not in a position to hurt women anymore; besides, it took a heel to know one. I asked him how it felt to be ravaged by jealousy even after he could no longer lay claim to flesh and blood. You were jealous in life, I told him; at least in death you could be more graceful.

"I ask a simple favor of you—keep an eye on my kid, make sure he's all right."

"Give me a chance, man!"

"Instead, you run around trampling on everyone's toes."

"Ha! You've got some nerve. What happened to Ali? Why was Colon meeting Julie. . . ."

"Leave her out of this!"

"Where is our money and . . . why couldn't you get it up!"

"Those questions, the last one especially, are beneath my dignity."

"What dignity?"

"Listen, fuckface, you jumped into a muddy bottom and stirred it up; when you do that, everything rises to the surface and you find things you didn't want to find, things you can't do anything with, that are also *none of your business!*"

I apologized for bringing up his impotence. He just stared at me, said I could think whatever I wanted about his manhood, try and pretend, with him off the scene, that I had a new pair of balls, but the fact remained that while I might be OK with women on the short stroke, I had no staying power.

"Bullshit!"

"You walked out on Maria over a week ago and haven't talked to her since. Right?"

"She doesn't want to speak to me."

"Balls!"

"Shithead!"

"*Pato! Maricón!*"

"Corpse! Fruitcake!"

"Fart breath! *Boca de mierda!*'

"Blow it out your ass!"

I felt a ring of pressure closing around my Adam's apple and fought back, determined not to let any spook in a hospital gown strangle me.

My eyes popped open. My pillow was drenched with sweat and I had managed to wrap my neck in the top sheet. After freeing myself, I lay back, listened to the telephone ring five or six times before picking it up.

"It's Joe Termini, from the Five Spot."

"Hi, Joe."

"I know it's early for a night owl, hope I didn't wake you."

I looked at the clock-radio. It was a few minutes after one.

"No. I was just getting up."

"Iggy and I would like to talk to you. Do you think you could come by later? Maybe this afternoon? We'll be here all day. Whenever you get ready, OK? Just knock."

A red chemical sun had cleared the trio of Con Ed stacks

which were belching clouds of poison waste over Manhattan. It seemed like the ultimate in public relations that they were painted with bands of red, white and blue.

Closing my eyes again was useless. Ponce was waiting behind my lids. It was time to get into the world, feel concrete under my feet. I rubbed cold water on my face, slipped into gray corduroy pants, a white pullover sweater and greeted the May afternoon on my way to St. Mark's Place.

For a quarter of a century the Termini brothers had championed jazz. Iggy, small and round. Joe, tall, bespectacled, with hair like foam on the Bay of Naples. They'd come back from the last noble war and brought music to their club at Number Five Cooper Square. When the old Five Spot was torn down, they moved to Number Two St. Mark's Place and for a while tried to make a go of it under the name of the Two Saints. And for most of the people in the jazz world, they were indeed two saints. There were nights, said Big Baldy, when they'd had to borrow money from him for cab fare home. In a last desperate attempt to make ends meet, they had changed the name back to the Five Spot.

The Terminis had championed Mingus, among others. Mingus, in return, had poured his time and talent into their latest effort, trying to give it the transfusion it needed. In the end, in spite of the old name, the urgency and devotion of the jazz community, there had been no alternative. It was over for them. Even so, it was Joe and Iggy who had petitioned the court to let Billie Holiday sing at the Five Spot after her drug bust, offering their personal guarantees, insisting that every day Lady Day remained silent, the world was poorer for it. Naturally, the court had refused.

When I reached the Five Spot, I saw there was already a poster on the yellow doors announcing Ted Curson's appearance at the Tin Angel. I knocked gently. Iggy opened, ushered me in with a soft, "Hello."

Joe sat on a stool in the middle of an empty bar. I

might've been entering the hold of an old Liberty ship in the boneyard. Captain Joe gave a sweep of his hand.

"All she needs is a coat of paint."

"Everything in the kitchen is fully operational," echoed Iggy. "All you have to do is put a little grease in the friolator."

Ponce's ghost floated in front of me as I made a tour of the place. This time he hadn't come to harangue me; he, too, was considering the pitted linoleum, odd-lot tables and chairs, listening to the way they spoke in broken phrases of a long struggle to survive.

There was no natural light in the room. What were supporting arches that had let in light had been bricked up to form a solid wall against the street. A collage of posters circled the room on the back wall; it was the only clue to what had gone on in this space: Coltrane, Mingus, Dolphy, Monk, Coleman, Cherry, Taylor. The very corners were spiderwebbed with unheard music.

"A fresh coat of paint," called Captain Iggy.

"Two days with a roller," agreed Captain Joe.

"It would take more than a coat of paint to whip this place into shape," whispered Ponce.

I noted the two mirrored pillars that divided the room disastrously, cutting off a view of the stage from much of the bar. Those would have to go.

"No way." Ponce read my mind. "They're supporting the place. You'd have to move in steel. Then you'd have to tear out the front and build a new one, something light, airy, lots of Plexiglas. Know what a number like that would cost? And you haven't got the price of a haircut."

Iggy walked over and stood beside me.

"I don't know what you've got in mind, but if you'd take it over we'd give you a release on the name. The Five Spot is a pretty good name, you know?"

Joe remained seated on his stool.

"It's just that we're tired. We've been at it a long time and we're ready to hang it up."

"We don't have the endurance," said Iggy. "A young guy like you could keep it going. That's what it needs, young blood."

The Five Spot had been their baby and they were pleading for its life. I knew how they felt. I felt the same about the Tin Angel.

Iggy held out both hands, palms up.

"Listen, you don't have to pay us anything right away. We'll work with you until you've got it going, then you can start to pay us back, little by little."

Could it be done? Ponce shook his head. It would be easier to resurrect Lazarus. The Five Spot was just another one of many jazz clubs perishing this year. Good-bye, Boomer's. Good-bye, Rust Brown's. Good-bye, St. James Infirmary. Good-bye, Buddy Rich's. Good-bye, Willy's.

What I heard was the Five Spot's death rattle. Zach might've said the situation was bacterial, that the medium had been consumed.

"Let me think about it," I told them.

"How long will you need?" asked Joe.

"Give me a week."

Leonard Dandy, in his chef's whites, was busy turning out orders of eggs Benedict for a roomful of Sunday brunchers. When I told him about the Five Spot, his only comment was: "So it finally happened."

Waitress Maggie called over the warming shelf: "Hey, Leonard, can you lighten up that hollandaise? The eggs are sticking to the plates like they were dipped in glue."

He gave the double boiler a stir and frowned.

"All right, honey, I'll see what I can do. They're really sweet guys." Leonard shook his head. "Too sweet, if you ask me. Musicians were always walking over them roughshod, particularly that Mingus!"

"No kidding."

"When I was working at the Five Spot, Joe gave me permission to keep my motorcycle in the kitchen; you know how big that kitchen is. Well, Mingus, he was always hanging around the pots and pans."

Dandy added hot water to the sauce.

"They say that Mingus helped them out when they were in trouble, agreed to play for what he could eat."

"I don't doubt it."

"You still don't like him."

"One night he was hanging around my steam table, picking his teeth with a chicken bone, when he gets a bug up his ass, walks over to my machine and kicks it. The motorcycle goes crashing to the floor. When I ask him for money to replace the broken mirror, he refuses: 'This motorcycle has no business in the kitchen,' he tells me, as if he had any business there himself."

"What happened?"

"I had to let him know that if he can fuck with my machine, I can fuck with his bass."

"Shit, Leonard, you didn't . . ."

"Let me tell you what this faggot did. After everyone goes home, I go over to where he keeps it, open the case and cut the strings. Next day, when he goes to open it, those strings popped out at him. He screamed, cursed, told the Terminis that it was him or me. He was their bread and butter, so of course I was the one who went, but don't think for a minute they didn't stop to consider the alternatives. I still remember Joe whispering to Iggy, 'Hey, maybe this is our chance to get rid of him.' "

"Pablo," called waitress Maggie. "There's a guy outside says to tell you that your electrician is here."

"I'll be right out."

I left Leonard Dandy thinning his hollandaise and found Manny Wu in the Bowery Café.

"Jeeezus!"

Manny leaped from his chair with such force he nearly struck his head on a hanging pot of Swedish ivy.

"There's my electrician."

"Man, don't you ever send me on a Micky Mouse job like that again!"

"How about a drink?"

Maggie brought him a Heineken. I waited until his lean body stopped twitching before asking him what he was talking about. As he spoke, he twisted in his chair to look behind him.

"That Benson guy, at the deli, the number you gave me? He played Sam Spade with me for three hours, asked me all kinds of questions, who I knew, where I spent the last ten years, man! That clown wanted to creep right up my asshole!"

"Don't get upset."

"Easy for you to say."

"I thought it might be a quick buck."

"A buck, that's exactly right."

Manny Wu had a bony face and straight black hair graying at the temples, a cross between Sun Yat-sen and Paul Henreid. He wore a space-age utility belt full of tools and meters around a khaki bush jacket. It was rumored that while in the slam, the Electrician Chinaman had developed a number of surveillance devices that worked both telescopically and by remote control which were so small you needed tweezers to plant them. He had gained his reputation by wiring most of the gambling houses in Chinatown with early-warning systems, but he made his bread-and-butter money with a key that allowed him to open terminal boxes inaccessible to lesser mortals.

Maggie put another bottle of beer in front of him.

"Thank you, doll. Hey, talk about standing out like a bouquet of roses on a shit wagon," he yelled.

"Shhhh."

Several issues of the Sunday *Times* rattled in protest. It boggled the mind to imagine Wu's mandarin ancestors farming silkworms with their long fingernails. All that was left of them was Manny's yellow skin and folded eyes; beyond that, he was pure New York.

"Sorry." The Electric Chinaman cast a quick smile around the room. "After they questioned me at the store, they drove around Harlem in a white Seville. I mean, dig it—Harlem, in a white car, two honkies and a Chink!"

"What were they doing?"

"Questioning me, creeping right up my asshole!"

A chorus of Sunday *Times* rattling.

"Sorry."

"How about another beer?"

"Jeeez, I could use it."

Wu had managed to talk, twitch, scream and finish the bottle in front of him. I signaled Maggie.

"Where did you find these guys? After all that, I do a job in the deli, a hundred-dollar job he chisels down to eighty, then he tells me there's more work for me and he'll be in touch. Pablo, man, I ain't used to doin' business that way."

"Manny, I wanna ask you about something else, about the Avenue B shooting. . . ."

"Thanks, doll." He patted Maggie's hand. "Your partner got iced in that one, didn't he?"

"Right. I'm trying to find out what happened."

"Promise you won't tell that Benson guy how to get in touch with me?"

"Deal."

"OK. I didn't know your partner, so I don't know how he got mixed up with these people. I can only tell you what I heard, and it's for your ears only, you dig?"

"I dig."

"*Marone!* What a stupid bloodbath."

He stopped, waiting for me to say something. So I did.

"Sounds like you've been spending a lot of time in Little Italy."

"Don't be a wise guy." He waved a long bony finger. "The

cops, all they wanted to do was tell the dude he had failed to signal for a left turn."

"That was in the papers, Manny."

"And there was a chick in the car."

"Same paper."

"Remember Mickey Jelke, the playboy pimp who made a big splash in the fifties with a high-class call girl, Pat Ward?"

"Sure. Every kid on the street corners of Flatbush Avenue wanted to be a high roller like him."

"The chick in the car was—dig this now—she was the old lady of Micky Jelke's partner, and the driver was her boyfriend!"

"What!"

"You heard it first right here."

"Get off it. Wu . . . Ponce didn't know anyone like that."

"I don't interpret information, *gumbah,* that's for the guys with college degrees. My degree's from Attica, I just pass it on. The cat they're holding now is a fall guy."

"Thanks, Manny."

I should've added, *for nothing.*

"Anytime."

"Something else I want to run through your hot line. Heard anything about a guy named Ali? Runs some numbers, fences sometimes out of a *bodega* on Avenue B."

"Don't know the cat myself." Manny rubbed his chin. "But what I heard is pretty heavy."

"Don't tell me he's got cancer because I already know that."

"Nope. Nothin' like that. Your friend Ali is a gunrunner."

I could hardly suppress my laughter.

"Come on, Manny. First you tell me Ponce was hooked up with Mickey Jelke, and now Ali is a gunrunner. Those are the kind of stories my mother makes up."

"Take my word for it, he's running guns for the Palestinians. When it comes out in the wash, remember who gave you top value for a few beers. *Basta!* You need me for anything righteous, Pablo, tell Moe. But remember your promise."

He drained his bottle and stood up.

"I'll keep Benson in the dark."

"Where he belongs. Later."

Manny twitched as he walked out the door.

Pat Ward, Mickey Jelke, Ali a gunrunner; for a man who was suppposed to be plugged into most of the important conversations in greater New York, all the Electric Chinaman had succeeded in giving me was a headache. And through the incipient throbbing Ponce's voice repeated that when you jump into a muddy pool, you stir up the bottom. Now there were all these fragments floating around me, things I didn't want to know.

I didn't want to know that Ponce couldn't get it up, or that Ali bought guns for the Palestinians, or that Maria's only defense against the nightmare of her life was the fragile elegance of bone china; I didn't want to know that while Danny Mac sailed over the bounding main getting his cock sucked, Joe and Iggy Termini could no longer keep the Five Spot's doors open, or Harris had a bleeding ulcer and Toomey worthless stock in gold and gypsum; I didn't want to know that Julie Fine drank her coffee from dirty cups, or that my brother Zach had stopped seeing the future of the race through his microscope to watch Carlotta starve to death. But how could you move in this world without stirring up bits and pieces of it? I did want to know why my partner died as he did and who had my money. So I set out to find a man they called Chocoláte.

The Social Club was a large room three steps down from the street. A sign over the door read: FOR MEMBERS ONLY. The door was ajar.

The room was lit by pink fluorescent bulbs, what was left to the racial memory of sunsets over Santurce. A half-dozen members clustered around a regulation-size pool table in the middle of the floor. There was a bar to the left. An old juke, flashing cheap rainbows behind the players, blasted out *salsa*, probably Ray Baretto.

Chocoláte was one of the men watching the game. I recognized him immediately. There was a big eagle with bloody talons descending the bicep of his right arm. He lifted his eyes along with the others to stare at the intruder. I nodded at him, assuming he knew me from the street we had shared for years, motioned to him. Me? He pointed to himself. Nobody seemed disturbed. I was a local. It was cool. His friends resumed their game as Chocoláte came bounding out on small sneakered feet.

"Hey, man, wazhapnin'?"

From the sound of his voice, I guessed he hadn't been born in Puerto Rico.

"I got a problem."

"What? You need wheels?"

"No. But if I ever do, I'll know where to come."

At first he beamed, then grew suspicious.

"I'm the best. Was you name, man?"

"Pablo."

"Entiende español?"

"A little."

"But you no Latin?"

"No."

He had a wispy mustache on an otherwise hairless face, the complexion of which had earned him the name Chocoláte. I judged him to be in his early twenties.

"You have a Latin name."

"My mother liked Pablo Picasso."

"Ha, ha, ha ... Pablo Picasso, Pablo Neruda, the Latin is the best. I'm Dominican, but my father was French. You Americans got to learn to like the Latin people. You know why?"

"Sure. Because Latin is the best."

"No. Because there are too many of us an' you got to learn to like us, even if we a little crazy, like the Japanese."

"My partner was a Latin."

"I know him?"

"Miguel Ponce. He bought a car from you a few months back."

"A few months, that's a long time." His eyes narrowed. "No, I don' know nobody by that name."

"About three months ago. He was shot getting out of the car you sold him . . . on Avenue B. You must have heard about it."

He stared at his adidas.

"Yeah, I heard about it. I got frens over there. But I don' know this guy. Who toll you I did?"

"A little birdie."

"A pigeon."

"OK, Chocoláte, listen to me a minute."

"I lissen, but only 'cause you name is Pablo."

"Miguel Ponce was my partner, my friend, my brother, *comprende*? I want to know what happened to him. I think you can help me."

"Why?"

"He bought the car from you."

He shifted his weight from foot to sneakered foot.

"So if you know this, you know everything I know."

"What did he say to you when he bought it? Who was he with?"

"Hey, man, maybe I jus' sell the car to him an' he don' say nothin'."

"And maybe there are some cops over at the Ninth who would like to find out for sure. As a matter of fact, they're dying to find out. You understand what cops are like when other cops get iced, don't you?"

"Man, I am a mechanic. I sell cars to dudes who don'

wan' em traced. I don' ask what for they wan' a car, it's no my business. Guys in the club, they got *niños, familias,* they feel bad if you fuck'em up, *comprende?*"

"You're a tough guy, Chocoláte, but I'm a tough guy, too."

"I ain't no tough guy."

"Tell me about Rodolfo Colon."

"Who?"

The sound of La Lupe drifted out the door. Chocoláte did a little dance around the parking meter. When the tune ended, he stopped precisely on the upbeat, spit into the gutter.

"You wanna do it the hard way?"

"OK, because you name is Pablo, I tell you what. I speak to my frens, you come back *lunes, martes,* we talk again."

"Fair enough."

He started inside.

"Chocoláte."

"*Si.*"

"Here is a card with my business address and number on it. Call anytime."

"OK."

"One more thing."

"*Que pasa, hombre!* I gotta game inside."

"Next time you sell a car, make sure both turn signals are working."

"Pablo, this is Bertie."

"Bertie. How's Carlotta?"

"She's *in the tropics.* But that's not why I called. You remember that license number you gave me?"

"Yeah. You got something?"

"Came back yesterday from MVB. Pablo, what kind of business have you got with Matt Rosen?"

I grabbed a pencil and a scratch pad on the table beside my phone and started jotting.

"Who's he?"

"Big league. He's a Brooklyn boy, a tough Jew in the rackets, mostly gambling, though I wouldn't be surprised if he had fingers in dope and prostitution as well. We can't touch him, though, never gets his hands dirty. One of the new breed, well mannered, college educated [belch]; excuse me, Pablo, my fucking stomach. Be careful, the man plays hardball. Can you tell me what's up?"

I explained to Bertie that this guy, Matt Rosen, was marrying the mother of my ex-partner's illegitimate son. He belched again and asked me why I was interested. Did it matter, now that Ponce was dead? Perhaps not. I couldn't figure out why a lady like Heather Moore was interested in a gangster, or vice versa; but then, neither could I understand why Ponce had been obsessed with Julie Fine. And now Garret, whose picture I had seen, was going to have Matt Rosen for a father.

"Some of these guys are great family men." Bertie read my mind. "The bloodiest scumbags, guys who are responsible for hundreds of hits, to see them at home in these quiet little communities [belch], sorry, with their rosy-cheeked kids and blowsy wives, man, you'd think it was all American-flag-and-apple-pie."

"That makes me feel a lot better."

His voice became a whisper.

"Pablo, my stomach is so big I can't button my pants. I can't hold anything down. See? All I do is fart and belch. You think I've got cancer, too?"

"Just nerves, Bertie."

"Are you coming over?"

"Sure. I'm on my way."

TIME IN THE TROPICS

On impulse, I called Heather Moore. The child's voice that answered was high but self-assured. He said that Mama had run to Montague Street to pick up some milk and dessert, chocolate-swirl ice cream, he hoped. Who was I? My name was Pablo, a friend. Did I know that there was going to be a Trekkie Convention at the Americana Hotel? Mr. Spock wouldn't be there, nor would Captain Kirk, but Bones and Scotty would. Was I going? No? Well, lest I think that it was all kid stuff, did I know the age of the average Trekkie was somewhere close to thirty? He suddenly got shy when the door slammed, told his mother the call was for her and said a quick good-bye. I told him if I went, I'd go as a Vulcan.

"Mr. Waitz, I must ask you not to keep calling. I gave you whatever information I had, and now you must respect my privacy."

"Would you mind terribly if I got to know Garret a bit? Like take him to the Star Trek Con ..."

"Out of the question."

"I feel ... Ponce was ..."

"Absolutely not ... Garret, if you want to eat ice cream, do it in the kitchen!" She lowered her voice to a whisper. "I gave birth to him alone. I live with this child day in and day out."

She paused. Her resentment filled the silence.

"If you keep bothering me, Mr. Waitz, I'll have to file

a complaint against you for harassment. Is that clear?"
  I told her it was.

  Zach picked me up in his Toyota.
  "How's my breath?"
  "Everything smells like Lavoris."
  His recent attention to good grooming was the result of a
tirade Carlotta had delivered a few days ago in her new role.
She had discovered the incredible strength in abject weakness
and, between periods in the tropics, had begun to rule from her
bed like Queen Victoria. Her three pages farted, belched,
bowed and awaited her every word. This discovery had in-
vigorated Carlotta's will to live.
  One afternoon, propped up in bed, the fluid running
smoothly in all directions from her tubing, she had riveted
Zach with her gaze and recited "Little Jack Horner"—after
which she'd told him: "You can stop being a *good boy*."
  Zach had winced through the nursery rhyme, especially
the part about putting in his thumb and pulling out a plum.
  "It's important to be groomed," Carlotta had lectured
him. "There's too much dirt in the world. It's a dirty world."
  The combined effects of her disease and its treatment had
been peeling layers off her personality like the leaves of an
onion. We all stood speechless before the terror of finding out
what lay at the center.
  "Zach identifies with his cat. His clothes are always full of
cat hair. You should take better care of yourself, Zach, not
slink around eating tunafish. He even smells like his cat. Zach
should grow up, keep himself clean and eat in cafeterias."
  There was some truth in her observation. The beautiful
golden child had grown into manhood neglecting his appearance.
  Bertie, as was his wont, had jumped into the breach with a
jar of Nivea in an effort to stave her off. He was always there
with the cream, or her gargle, or perfume which he dabbed on

her forehead. But she stopped him before his fingers full of Nivea had touched her lips.

"Out! All of you, get out. I want to sleep."

I was lifting my jacket from the back of a chair before following the other two into the hall when she turned to me.

"I'll be leaving soon."

"I know. Be peaceful."

Softly, "I am."

"I spoke to Dr. Loftus this morning. He told me she was comatose again, didn't think it would be much longer."

Zach breathed one more medicinal breath at the mirror of his Toyota. His shirt was clean, pants pressed, but his eyes were shot through with blood.

"I'm not sure how much more I can take, either," I confessed. "My hemorrhoid is so big I can hardly sit."

"Me, too. Mine is doing the Hustle in my asshole."

Instead of finding the dying woman we had braced ourselves for, we entered the room to encounter Mary, Queen of Scots. She dismissed us as soon as we entered.

"Why don't you boys go into the waiting room? It's easier for me if you just look in from time to time. Bertie is in there already. Keep him company. He gets lonely."

She was sitting bolt upright; the oxygen mask that Dr. Loftus had strapped to her face hung over the guard rails of her bed. We kissed her on the cheek and left.

Bertie was half reclining on the black naugahide couch, his stomach distended, a brown paper bag clenched in his hand.

"These damn doctors and nurses. There's no water in her pitcher, they've let her milk go sour [belch] and nobody [fart] has cleaned her bedsore."

Carlotta had developed an angry red hole at the base of her spine that was growing brighter every day. Ten days ago we had asked for anesthetic spray, a rubber doughnut to take the weight off that part of her body. Nobody had heard us.

"I'd like to put one into the head nurse on the night shift." Bertie patted his gun. "Make her look like a piece of Swiss cheese. If we weren't here, they'd never even give her the bedpan!"

"Can I have some of that vodka?" asked Zach.

Bertie handed him the bag.

"I'd like to fill them all full of lead." He squeezed off a fart, then whined, "And she wants to be alone. She says our company [belch] tires her out."

I left them bending their elbows and went to peek in on Carlotta. The lights were off and I tiptoed in so as not to disturb her. I was on my way back out when I heard a lisping whisper. It was the voice of a child, age seven or eight, and it floated on the air behind me. The words were indistinguishable. I followed the sound until I was leaning over the guard rails with my ear practically to Carlotta's lips.

"I don't underthand you," she lisped.

"What don't you understand?"

"I haven't had any tholid food for dayth. I haven't had a bowel movement for longer than that. What are you going to do?"

"I can only try to make you comfortable."

"You can't do anything else?"

"No."

"You mean you're jutht going to leave me here to die?"

I couldn't answer. Finally, she had asked me for the truth I had been so impatient to give her, and all I could do was bury my face in her neck and cry.

"What about a *colostomy*? No. Of course not. I couldn't live with that."

It's all right to cry, I kept thinking as my tears ran onto her pillow and I inhaled the odor of her decaying body. Go ahead, Pablo Waitz, you mixed bag of tricks, you hemorrhoidal optimist, sly child, dumb child, numb child, street child, mothafucker, cry!

"Then there's nothing you can do for me? Nothing!"
I raised my head.

"No, Mom. Nothing more than we've already done."

"I see."

In the course of our exchange she had grown from childhood into the full flower of her adult powers. Her hand reached out, touched my cheek, touched me without guilt or seduction.

"I love you," I told her.

"I love you, too. Now get the others."

With Zach, Bertie and me around her bed, Carlotta took charge for the first time since the onset of her illness. Her voice rang out clearly with the request for stronger medication.

"It isn't fair to rob people of dignity. I want to be kept in the tropics. If it drags on too much longer, I want you all to promise me you'll find a way to put me out."

Bertie gulped, grabbed his gut. I sat there, frozen. Zach nodded dutifully.

Later, on our way back to Manhattan, he pulled over at the entrance to the Fifty-ninth Street Bridge and handed me something from his jacket pocket. It was an ampule of insulin. He'd gotten it from a doctor friend at Einstein; had been carrying it around for days.

By the time Maria answered the door in a gray smock full of paint stains, I felt like a supplicant. Standing there, dark curls framing her face, she seemed smaller than I remembered her.

"Hello." Curtly.

She walked inside. All I could do was follow. There were two small suitcases in the middle of the room.

"Going someplace?"

"Yes."

"Where?"

"You're interested?"

"You know I am."

A wave of panic filled my chest; the child riding it looked like me in an early photo.

"Would you have known the difference if I had spent the last ten days in Barbados?"

"Please . . ."

"Well, I didn't. I spent it here, working. Coffee? Some wine?"

"Coffee will be fine."

"I've got some made."

She took a mug from the kitchen, filled it from a pot on the table; it was a ceramic mug, with brown and red glazes, in beautiful taste and spotlessly clean, like her floors, her rug—even the stains on her smock had an order to them.

"How's your mother?"

"Not so good."

"I'm sorry."

After a pause: "The Five Spot is closing. I feel bad for the Terminis, but maybe it will give us a fighting chance."

"Us?"

"You're my partner."

"Am I?"

"Yes, Maria. Regardless of anything else."

"Oh, Pablo, it's just so *hard*!"

"I can't help it."

"I know. When things are good with us, I forget everything that's happened, then, just as I'm beginning to get comfortable, something comes along and knocks it apart."

"Maria, I can't cut myself off from what has happened to me."

"Remember, after we came back from the morgue, I told you that I'd wanted to kill myself?"

"I remember."

"You were sitting right where you are now. When I said it, the tenderness in your eyes made me want to live."

She lowered her head.

"I'm glad."

"My dentist, you know what my dentist told me? He said I've been grinding my teeth in my sleep, that if I didn't stop, I'd wear them down to the gums."

For the second time tonight the words stuck in my throat; that I had, perhaps, caused such a thing was intolerable. All I had ever wanted to do for Maria was to ease her.

"I've got to protect myself, Pablo."

"I understand."

Suddenly she took both my hands in hers and sat beside me.

"What do you want? Tell me. If you want me, you can have me! If you *really want me, all you have to do is reach out, but you can't keep dragging me back into the nightmare. I ... I'm simply not strong enough. There'll be nothing left of me.*"

We looked at each other for a long moment. She was waiting for me to embrace her, to reassure her. I couldn't. There was no way I could promise her what she was asking for. She stood.

"Where are you going?"

"Boston. I won't be away long."

"Why Boston?"

"I've been asked to represent Puerto Rican womanhood at the Second Minority Survival Conference. I was at the first one in South Dakota. Everyone present agreed that the pregnant Puerto Rican mother with no male in the house had a survival problem, but it wasn't as pressing as that of the poor white farmer in South Dakota."

"What about the vanishing New York jazz club?"

"I'll ask."

She took a pencil and a note pad from the table by her telephone, wrote down a number at which she could be reached.

"There's got to be a way to work this out, Maria."

I could feel her trembling when we embraced by the door.

"Let's give it some thought. Think about what I said, seriously. Weigh it, inside."

"I will."

My arms didn't want to release her. For a moment she lay her head on my shoulder, then gently but firmly pushed me away.

"We'll talk when I get back."

I arrived at Ararat General as the sun was rising over Jamaica Bay in an attempt to catch Dr. Loftus making his rounds. I was informed at the nurses' station that Dr. Loftus had gone on vacation; the man I had to see was Dick, the oncologist, who moved about the wards like a shadow. I took this opportunity to remind the head nurse that we still hadn't gotten anything to relieve the pain of Carlotta's bedsore, that open mouth screaming at the bottom of her spine.

I teamed up with an irate schoolteacher from Flushing, whose mother was dying at the other end of the hall. She was a big woman, and her classroom experience had rendered her immune to intimidation. We both wanted the same thing from Dr. Dick.

"I don't know what they're giving her, but it ain't worth a shit," she told me. "My mother's in pain all the time. How can those bastards do it!"

We lurked in the shadows all morning. Finally, when she had gone downstairs for coffee, I caught a glimpse of the oncologist peeking out of a room. He was looking both ways, to see if it was safe. As soon as our eyes met, he raised his surgical mask. It had been hanging beneath his chin. Too late! I had him. He ducked back into the room, but I waited outside the door thinking, "The game's up, you prick!"

I waited several minutes before he poked his head out. His eyes flared above the mask. He tried to outpace me on his way to the nurses' station, but I kept right beside him.

"Dr. Dick, can I have a word with you?"

"What is it?"

His voice was clipped, if muffled by his sanitary disguise.

"My mother's in pain. It's her bedsore. Can you give her a little stronger sedation?"

"I saw her already. She's not in pain."

"She is. I spend every day with her. Believe me, she is in pain."

"Absolutely not!"

"I just want her to be comfortable. Dr. Loftus promised us he'd keep her out of pain."

He lowered the surgical mask with a hooked finger. A bad case of prickly heat was blossoming along his upper lip.

"If you want to come with me, I'll show you a case, a woman with advanced cancer of the colon who is doing fine on an aspirin a day."

"I'm not interested. I want my mother's discomfort stopped. Half a grain of morphine would do it."

"We're already giving her a quarter-grain."

"It's not enough."

"I will not treat your anxiety by giving her enough drugs to kill her."

"Only a quarter-grain more."

"I know what you want me to do, and I won't do it. I will not kill your mother!"

Before I could respond, he disappeared through a door marked EXIT.

Just wait until the high-school teacher from Flushing finds out you're only giving her mother an aspirin a day, I thought. She'll strangle you with your surgical mask.

Carlotta spent the day safely tucked away in the tropics. By early evening, the high-school teacher from Flushing decided to give up her vigil at the elevators until tomorrow. But she did swear an oath: "When I do catch him, I will complete his circumcision."

Zach arrived with Bertie in tow, farting and belching. Carlotta woke briefly. We sat her on the bedpan, which was merely a ritual gesture; her passage was blocked. We turned her, to take the weight off the bedsore, to promote circulation. Surprisingly, a nurse brought us the anesthetic spray and, after she'd given Carlotta her shot, told us, in the hall, that Dr. Dick had prescribed some Thorazine.

Drifting off to sleep, Carlotta whispers: "Where is my limousine? Isn't somebody going to send the limousine to pick me up?"

"Yes, my darling," Bertie answers. "We'll send it as soon as we can."

Going up in my tiny elevator, painted whatever color is on sale once a year, this year's color being "Songbird Yellow," I felt dizzy. Rather than acquiesce, I scratched a new piece of graffiti into the yellow wall. Someone had asked: *Are you a turtle?* I answered: *I was until I converted.*

Exiting on nine, I started up the flight of stairs that led to my apartment. Mine was the only one on the roof. As usual, the bulb on my landing had burned out. The hall was dark, but I knew my way. I took a step, then tripped headlong into my door over something heavy and soft, like a sack of flour. Jabbing at my lock with my key, I finally found the niche. Inside, I reached for the light. What I saw when it burst on made my head explode with a scream to wake the dead. Only it didn't wake Rodolfo Colon, whose head lolled on his chest, a red hole in his temple the size of a dime, and from it a trickle of blood down the side of his face like a big red tear.

CIRCLING URANUS

Nothing can be anticipated with certainty, least of all one's reactions in a crisis situation. I only screamed a couple of times before my breath caught on a hook in my throat. I ran to the bathroom, dry-heaved, then came to my senses on a closed toilet seat. Fear rose and overflowed through my pores. Evaporating on my cheeks and forehead, the end of my sweat left me cold and trembling. I reached Christ at home.

"Don't touch anything."

"Shall I lock my door? Turn out the lights? No, I don't think I could stand being here with the lights out."

"Whoever wanted you to find that body has seen your lights go on. If they meant to hurt you, you wouldn't be making this call. Someone is sending you a message, Pablo. Hang on, I'll call it in and come right over."

"Hurry."

His voice had given me a quick shot of courage that began to flag as soon as I put the receiver back on its cradle. I stood in the center of the room, my short hairs prickling with the sensation of being watched. Were there eyes on me at this very moment?

I checked on Rodolfo. No, I wasn't hallucinating. He was right where I'd left him, one hand cupped over his groin, the other arm, the right one, twisted behind his back. His body had achieved an odd torque, against the natural tendency of living muscle. He hadn't been propped gently, rather, he'd been dropped, a huge stuffed doll in a refuse pile. Already there was the same exotic pallor Ponce had displayed when I'd seen him last, like that of a man too long in a freezing pool; only, Rodolfo was less green, more yellow, the last phase of a violent sea change. With his single bloody teardrop, he was a dead harlequin whose lower lip hung slack, as if about to drool.

Unlike Danny Mac, I'd never beheld anyone's head blown off his shoulders. Though once, in Saigon, I had witnessed a man's stomach ripped open by plastic explosives set in a radio. He'd been thrown in the air and dropped like a stuffed doll, too. Only the stuffing had come out of him. Rodolfo's seams were still intact.

No more than two weeks ago I had dared to hope things were starting to make sense, that the wall of silence surrounding Ponce's death was yielding stone by stone. One stone was Chocoláte. The other, Colon's note to Julie Fine. I had dared to believe I could pull them out, a little at a time, until the wall collapsed.

What does a wall of silence sound like when it falls?

As if the powers that be had decided to answer my question, the phone rang. I lifted the receiver slowly, waiting for a voice that belonged, perhaps, to a mysterious set of eyes watching my apartment. Silence.

Then: "Hello? Hello? Pablo, is that you?"

"Zach?"

"Did I call too late?"

"Depends on what you mean."

"Sorry to wake you. It's only a little after one, but I had to let you know that the mackerel are coming. They're tooling around Chesapeake at this very moment. I can hear their migration song clear as your voice over the phone."

"Zach, there's . . ."

"They sound a little like the Mormon Tabernacle Choir singing the 'Hallelujah Chorus' in a hot tub. Kinda like this: 'Hallelu . . .' "

"It's not that I don't care, but at the moment I'm in a little hot water myself."

"What's wrong?"

"There's a corpse in my hall."

"Pablo, get your ass out of there!"

"The cops are on their way."

"My God!"

Footsteps on the stairs.

"Gotta go."

"Why is this happening to you?"

"I wish I knew."

Christ appeared at the door, followed by a flock of uniformed and plainclothes cops.

"The law has arrived. Talk to you later."

Christ was diffident, almost embarrassed when I turned to face him.

"Bad times, Pablo."

"Worse for him."

We left a crew of specialists going over the scene and walked to Fifth Street. Up in the detectives' office, I automatically sat in the chair beside Toomey's desk. The door of the interrogation room, the one with the one-way mirror, opposite the bull pen, opened and short, square-shouldered McGrath came out. He was chewing an unlit cigar. He took it out of his mouth to whisper something in Christ's ear. Both men laughed, then McGrath left.

"See the guy in the bull pen, the one in the panama hat?"

Christ was talking about a thin white man in his forties, disheveled but well appareled in beige slacks and a tan vented jacket. He was wedged between two blacks and an Hispanic with tobacco juice on his T-shirt. Clearly, he wasn't the least uncomfortable; the mustachioed corners of his mouth turned up in a tight-lipped smile reminiscent of The Laughing Budweiser.

"He'd stand out in a crowd. What did he do?"

"He was caught trying to ... fuck a duck."

"Come on."

"They heard this loud quacking coming from a car on A

and Seventh, checked and found this guy with his fly open trying to fuck a duck."

"Where's the duck?"

"They're feeding it a little lettuce downstairs, trying to cheer it up. It can't testify, so we're holding it as evidence."

"It?"

"We think it's a male duck, but we're not sure."

"What a guy!"

"Red suggested it was no longer a matter of simple assault, but rape and sodomy."

The door of the interrogation room opened again; a group of men came out, led by the familiar figure of Harris.

"Hello, Waitz. Back so soon?"

"Can't stay away. How's your ulcer?"

He saw me staring at the cigarette in his hand.

"The doctor thinks an occasional cigarette is better for me than unrelieved stress."

I wondered what had broken him. Could it possibly have been the large turd in my basement?

"Next thing you know, you'll be eating hot dogs."

"Be right back, Waitz."

"He used to call me 'Mr. Waitz,'" I told Christ as the black detective stepped out, probably to look in on the duck.

A few minutes later Harris returned with Toomey and a group of men wearing gold shields and baggy suits. Smoking his cigarette down to the filter, Harris conducted the questioning, supported by brief interruptions from Toomey.

What was my connection with Colon? His connection with Ponce? When had I last seen him alive, and what had we talked about? Why would anybody want to kill him? Why dump his body on my doorstep? Who wanted to scare me to death? Where was I between the hours of eight and ten? At the hospital? Why? Your mother has cancer!

Harris stubbed out his cigarette.

I told them what I could: Colon was a street cat from Alphabet City who made his money playing and dealing cards; Ponce was a gambler; the last time I had seen Rodolfo alive was about three weeks ago at the Five Spot, where we talked about jazz; I had no idea why anyone would want to kill him, or scare me. Then I took the note Colon had written Julie out of my pocket and handed it to Harris, who read it over several times before passing it to the impatient Toomey.

"What do you make of it, Waitz?"

"I went to visit her because she and Ponce were seeing each other, pretty hot and heavy. She wasn't very helpful, but when she went to the bathroom I found this on her table."

"Why did you take it?" snapped Toomey.

"I wanted to show it to Colon, to surprise him with it."

"What conclusions did you come to?" Harris lit a Winston.

"I never got a chance to confront him with it. Next thing I know, he's dead. Judging by appearances, I'd say he was making it with Ponce's girl."

"Did Ponce know?"

"If he did, he never said anything. And he didn't come back from the dead to put a bullet in Colon's head."

"Very sharp, Waitz. I'm going to hold on to this," Harris put the note in his desk drawer.

Toomey stood up and paced around the desk. He looked like a big seabird with his wavy silver hair and sharkskin suit.

"What about Ali?"

"What about him?"

"Was Colon connected to him?"

"Toomey, we all knew each other. What do you mean by *connected*? That we lived in the same neighborhood? Said hello when we passed on the street?"

"You know what I mean."

"I told you last time, Ali made some policy, fenced a few things, but that's it."

"Sure. A little numbers, a little this, a little that," Toomey mocked me. "What else?"

"An occasional torch job, very discreet, just enough for insurance purposes."

"Isn't there more?"

It was McGrath. His curly red head bobbed behind a cluster of baggy suits.

"Well, once, when he had the deli on Second Avenue, he ran a marriage service for Arabs who wanted to immigrate. He arranged marriages for them with local girls, mostly Puerto Ricans."

"Sounds like a good business."

"I don't know why you guys are laying all over him; he's a sick man."

"Did you know he was buying guns for the Palestinians?" asked McGrath.

I took a deep breath. Not that; not that Manny Wu shit. Did my electrician trade information with the cops? How else would they have gotten a bee like this in their collective bonnet?

"All right, I see what you're building. Now you think that Ponce and Colon were killed because they were hooked up with Ali, running guns. Right?"

I couldn't help it, I started laughing. As I did, the faces around me became fixed, hard; it was obvious I was laughing my way into a tight spot.

"What's so goddamn funny about it, Waitz!" demanded Toomey.

"First, you build a case for armed robbery. Next, you bring this basically decent man into it because of a bullshit rumor, somebody's misinformation. After all this time, you guys are still fishing, sitting with your lines over the side jumping at every nibble."

"What makes you so sure our information is wrong?" McGrath spat out a piece of his cigar on the shoe of the detective standing beside him. "Sorry."

"Because I've known Ali for fifteen years."

There was a general silence, during which the men in baggy suits looked at one another. Finally, Toomey turned to me.

"Do you want police protection, Waitz?"

I considered the offer as Harris crushed an empty pack of Winstons. It would certainly be reassuring to know that someone who played rough was watching out for me. On the other hand, it would make me an untouchable. Who would talk to me about Ponce's death with a cop on my shoulder? I could also say good-bye to my thirty-five grand.

"Not right now, thanks."

"Think about it a minute," said Toomey. "That wasn't only a body on your doorstep, it was a message, Western Union. Somebody's got you in their sights."

I swallowed involuntarily.

"I'll let you know, OK?"

"Have it your way," said Harris. "You can go. But stay close. We're going to want to speak to you again, say, Monday morning at ten?"

"Fine."

"OK, OK, good-bye, Waitz," said Toomey.

"Uhhh, listen . . ."

"It's all cleaned up, no messy bodies, no embarrassing stains," smiled Harris.

"We're all domestics at heart." Toomey thought for a second, then added: "Nothing personal, Harris."

Zach was waiting for me at the Tin Angel, in the Second Street Café, dipping pita bread into an order of Mel's *babaganoush.*

"Are you all right, Pablo?"

"No. How's Mom?"

He shook his head. I noticed his teeth were yellow, unbrushed for days, probably, and his sweater was once more full of cat hair.

"None of her vital organs are affected. She's starving to death, but they're giving her just enough to keep her going. She could go on for months in pain."

He handed me a piece of pita. I scooped up a dollop of *babaganoush*.

"Or she could get pneumonia and go tonight." A wedge of garlic exploded on my tongue.

"That's possible, but I doubt it."

"Why do you say that?"

"Because she's stubborn, doesn't want to die, and she's used to doing things her own way."

"I don't know how much more I can take, Zach."

"Bertie is about to shoot every nurse and doctor on the ward. When this is over, Pab, I'm going to reserve a room with kitty litter at some New England inn and stay there until mackerel season."

"Is she conscious?"

"Enough to make it bad. Let's put her out," he said.

We both stopped eating.

"How sure is that stuff?"

"Pretty sure. There are certain risks with insulin, but it should work."

"What risks?"

"If I don't inject the right amount, she could survive as a complete vegetable."

"A big risk."

"No, a small one. I know what I'm doing."

He dipped into his Middle Eastern eggplant, then pushed the dish away. I tore another piece of warm pita in half.

"Say we put her out," I asked him. "What happens next? Will they be able to find out we did it?"

"Not unless there's a postmortem. They won't do that, though, unless somebody is suspicious and raises the question."

"What about needle marks?"

"She's already a pincushion."

"I don't know, Zach. I've had enough killing."

He chewed, considering.

"I understand." He finally spoke. "If she's in pain, I'll do it myself. She asked us. You heard her. In a more civilized world, there wouldn't be any question about it."

"Who ever told you the world was civilized?"

I recalled a piece of graffiti painted on a building on the corner of Third Street and Second Avenue. It read:

Q: Mr. Gandhi, what do you think of Western civilization?

A: I think it would be a very good idea.

"I'm going to do it, Pablo."

"Please, Zach, give it another week. If she hasn't died by then, I'll help you."

"Will you stand chickey?"

"Sure."

"OK."

My stomach went queasy. Zach wiped his mouth.

"See you tomorrow, Pablo. Put it on my bill."

Before he left, I brushed the cat hair off his collar.

The more elegant members of the music world had come to hear Ted Curson, and the Big Licorice Stick, with his vagrant group, seemed out of place. Curson and Bowman seldom left each other's sight. The musician held on to the DJ's raveled sleeve as if it were the only stable entity in a shifting world. As a prodigy, Ted had played Birdland in his early twenties. Later, he had held the chair beside Dolphy in that magical Mingus group that filled the Five Spot. Now, a decade later, shy but no longer precocious, he had come home from Europe. The only callous on Ted Curson was the one his mouthpiece had made around his lips.

A round, mocha-colored man wearing heavy gold bracelets and a leather vest, Ted was talking about making another album.

"They all want to control your music; Arista, for example,

would let me make a new version of my last record, but that's not what I want."

"You'll get just what you want, hold tight," Bowman reassured him, then regarded me. "I believe Ted is already playing on a par with Trane and Miles. It's time he got out, and I'm going to see that he does. Excuse me, looks like it's time for me to go to work."

The DJ rose to greet a party of tuxedoed VIPs at the door. When I excused myself, I sensed a moment of panic in Ted, who was about to be alone.

"That Bowman is a strange bird," the Big Licorice Stick told me at the bar. "I introduced myself as the leader of the other group, and he hardly noticed me."

Disc jockeys and critics, I cautioned him, shouldn't be taken too seriously.

The Big Licorice Stick responded with a coughing fit that lasted thirty seconds by the bar clock. Diamond Jim handed him a glass of water and whispered, "Play 'Circling Uranus.' "

They were the first act of the evening. As the sextet mounted the stage, I was reminded of an old engraving of Peter the Hermit leading the Children's Crusade.

" 'Circling Uranus'!" shouted Noah from the door.

In deference to the occasion, the Big Licorice Stick called a set of standards. I was thinking about how well executed they were when Bowman sidled up to me at the jukebox.

"You know the Terminis would love to see their room stay with jazz. That's why they want you to take it over. Are you talking with them?"

"Yes, I'm talking."

"Anything about the negotiations I can mention on the air?"

"No, not right now," I said, realizing that I'd never take it on.

"Can I say that you're talking?"

"Sure."

"Why do you think they decided to close?" The DJ knit his brow.

"They're tired."

"You think that's the reason?"

"I do."

He pursed his lips. It was difficult for him to believe that people, institutions, whole civilizations could shut down for such a simple reason.

Julie Fine was standing at the door. I signaled Noah to let her pass. Her honey-colored curls broke over the worn collar of a denim jacket, and her shoulders slumped. Her expression, when she stood in front of me, was the most articulate statement of abandonment I had ever seen. Hundreds of broken capillaries crisscrossed the white of her eyes to make a crazy red pattern; her voice was nearly inaudible.

"What happened?"

"I don't know, Julie."

She tried to say something else, but no sooner had she opened her mouth than the tears flowed and her small body started shaking. I put an arm around her, and we shuffled out of the crowded room into a private corner of the kitchen, a nook by the coffee burners.

"Two cops come to my loft . . . ask me about Rodolfo, tell me he's dead, shot. . . ."

The spasms started. For all of my recent experience, I had not become resourceful under these conditions.

"Take it easy, Julie. How about a cup of coffee?"

To my surprise, she nodded her head. I took a cup from the shelf, filled it. I recalled the dirty one she had given me, the unkempt apartment, the vacant look on her face when she had greeted me on the landing. At least in sorrow her face came alive. I steadied the cup while she took a couple of sips. Then she started talking.

"Right after you were up that morning, I talked to Ro-

dolfo. He wanted to know what we'd talked about. I told him
we'd discussed Ponce, that was all. Nothing about him. Suddenly he explodes, calls me names, said I was a dumb
bitch...."

"You loved him?"

She nodded.

"Did Ponce know?"

"No ... yes, towards the end. At least I think he did.
Ponce was a good guy; I didn't want to string him along, but
... Rodolfo said to wait, that he'd tell me when to let him
know...."

"Julie, think for a minute; did either one of them talk
about the other?"

"Rodolfo, in the beginning, he was very jealous, even
when I told him that it wasn't any good between Ponce and me
in bed. Then, you know, he just stopped questioning me about
it, got real cool ... just told me not to rock the boat."

Julie stood motionless, cup poised at her chest. I tried to
give my head time to clear, to find the right question, the one
that would tie it all together, but I couldn't frame it.

"Rodolfo," she gulped, "he was difficult, didn't have
a lot of friends. I know what people thought of him. They
told me."

"I didn't say a word."

"But I know what you're thinking!"

She let her shoulders slump still further. Yes, she was
right. I'd been thinking, What did a creep like Rodolfo do to
earn such fierce loyalty?

"He was sharp and quick, but he was also soft, and hurt. I
knew a side of him nobody else did."

I believed her, even though I resented the fact she had de-
ceived Ponce to be with a low life like Colon. The more I discovered, the less I thought of Rodolfo. Hidden in the recesses
of his heart had been a small muddy slug.

She started to blubber.

"He was tender. When he touched me anywhere, my cheek, my thigh, anywhere, my whole body opened up, you understand?"

I told her I did. Perhaps she'd never come before except hovering over her cymbals.

"I didn't mean to hurt Ponce. I didn't love him. I just couldn't. . . ."

"I'd like to help you, Julie, but . . ."

"Tell me why Rodolfo had to die!"

"I don't know."

She lifted her head, took a deep breath, then put the cup down on the warm-up shelf.

"Yeah. OK."

I led her to the kitchen door. When I took her hand briefly, to say good-bye, I saw that her eyes had again gone vacant.

The Big Licorice Stick caught me as I came back into the room. He bent low enough for me to see his face, which I found pleasant in a Germanic way.

"Gee, that Ted Curson is good. I want to thank you for the opportunity of playing beside him."

"My pleasure. Now go up there and knock their socks off with a little music of the spheres."

He got my drift, and I was grateful. I needed something to erase the apparition of Julie Fine from my immediate, if not long-range, memory. If anyone could do it, it was the Big Licorice Stick.

He opened with a rendition of "Circling Uranus." As the first throbbing slurr annihilated the melodic refrain, Ted Curson's head snapped up from his plate of chicken Kiev and Bowman's eyes glazed over. The slurr built into a hemorrhoidal crescendo which moved many of the black-tie audience to wriggle in their seats. But unabashed delight was fixed on the faces of both James Boys, and my mind was on the verge of becoming a tabula rasa, when I noticed Noah motioning me to the door.

"I've got something for you."

He handed me a sealed envelope. There was a dirty thumbprint right below my name written in shaky block lettering. Harris could get a clear set of prints from this envelope.

"Who left it?"

"A kid. Ran in, gave it to me, then took off."

"Recognize him?"

"Puerto Rican, fourteen, fifteen, plaid shirt, faded jeans, old sneakers; could be any one of a hundred out there."

Chocoláte, I thought. He's ready to talk.

Downstairs in my office, I opened the envelope and found a message written in ballpoint with the same block lettering:

IF YOU WANT TO KNOW WHAT YOU WANT TO
KNOW BE AT THE BROOKLYN ZOO TOMORROW
AT THREE WHERE THEY KEEP THE SEALS
                                        A FRIEND

"Careful, Pablo."

It was Ponce, lying on my cot.

"You could save me the trouble. Who has the money?"

"I can't."

"All right. Who was with you in the car?"

"I can't tell you that, either."

"Why not?"

"It's against the rules."

"Since when did that stop you?"

"Always. Even at cards, I played by the rules. *Chamaco,* you want to know what a rule is?"

"I'm all ears."

"A rule is something you run into, a brick wall. If I tried to tell you about the past or the future, well, I'd disappear."

"Not a bad idea."

"I can tell you two things."

"Speak."

"Watch your ass."

"That's one."

"There's a . . ."

He must have been about to tell me something contrary to the rules because his face suddenly turned red; he grabbed his throat with his right hand and disappeared.

Friday: High-Stepping to an Elephant Dance

I paused on the corner of Flatbush and Empire Boulevard, where Zach and I had hawked Dodger buttons when the "Boys of Summer" were still in their prime. After a few silent seconds of respect to the departed Ebbets Field, I started up the hill that ended more than a mile away at Grand Army Plaza.

Trees lined both sides of the grade. On my right, across the street, were the Botanical Gardens; on my left, the Prospect Park Zoo. There were kids with red and yellow balloons everywhere (but they would never savor names like Pee Wee Reese, Duke Snider and Branch Rickey; never swipe hot loaves from the conveyor belt of the Bond Bread factory that divided Flatbush and Washington avenues).

Stopping at a Sabrett wagon, I ordered a hot dog and took the opportunity to check the street behind me. A gaggle of young mothers clustered on benches along the cobblestone sidewalk while their kids played monkey-in-the-middle or raced back and forth in front of them. A leathery woman who looked like a man put mustard and onions on my hot dog before I continued to the entrance, then turned left on my way to the Seal House.

The ivy was brilliant green against the red brick colonnade. I dedicated the first big bite of my hot dog to Detective Harris and listened as the seals applauded inside their concrete bunker. After scanning the faces seated on an outdoor patio, I

failed to see the brown skin of Chocoláte, or anyone else familiar. An empty chair on the north side of the patio provided me
with a clear view. My watch read ten after three. Suddenly a
220-volt current shot through my body. There would be no
Chocoláte here. Only Babar, who came strolling around the
Seal House, hands thrust into the pockets of his dark trench-
coat.

He appeared in the blink of an eye, stopped fifty feet from
where I sat, raised his jowly head; it was as stony as a cement
gargoyle's. He was sniffing the air. I turned away, hoping the
fact I wasn't looking at him would make it more difficult for
him to see me—a child's game. It didn't work. His eyes burned
the back of my neck. I didn't have to see him to know he was
approaching. My nerve endings sat up, opened their mouths
and screamed like chicks in a nest waiting for a worm. In an
attempt to appear nonplussed, I shoved the remainder of the
hot dog into my mouth.

"Pablo Waitz."

He stood in front of me, his greasy hair shining in the sun.

"Hey, Babar. What you doing here?"

"I live in Brooklyn. Remember what I toll yuh, about
things happenin' in Brooklyn? Mind if I sit down?"

He sat, without waiting for a reply.

"I bet you like the seals. I like the seals. Always have, ever
since I was a little nipper. Were you ever a little nipper,
Babar?"

Why was I always saying the wrong thing to the Elephant
Man? His piggy eyes narrowed. There was definitely something self-destructive at work here. I vowed to examine it later,
if I survived.

"Yeah, I was a little nipper, but I ain't no more and you
still are."

"That's ... probably ... very ... true."

"What happened to Colon?"

"I found him in my hallway one night."

"Yuh don't know who did it?"

"No. Thought maybe you might."

"Colon was a good guy, didn' try bein' a smartass with me, yuh know? Not like people who go stickin' their nose in people's business. I thought since yuh know so much, maybe yuh knew what happened to him."

"Man, I was sure you'd be able to tell me. I guess I was wrong. Come to think of it, I'm sure I was wrong. Rodolfo was shot. You never use . . . I mean, you don't like guns any more than I do, do you?"

I'd done it again. But instead of the evil eye, he smiled as he removed a small penis-dowel from his coat pocket. He pointed it at me.

"Bang! Yer dead."

"What did you say?"

"I said, 'Bang! Yer dead.' "

He was staring straight at me. My mouth started to work like a junkie's in a jam. Confront a junkie and he will jabber at you as if his life depended on it. As long as I kept on talking, I was still alive. Junkie-mouth.

"It's been nice seeing you, Babar, I mean, how often do we get together like this, here at the Seal House, chew over old times, but I think I left my tub running . . . it happens when I step out to get a paper, you know, run into someone, or leave water boiling on the stove. . . ."

Before he could put his dowel back in his pocket, I bolted. My strategy was to stay beyond arm's reach in a public place. If he tried to close in on me in a crowd, I'd scream his name out and point at him. He was a few feet behind me. It had started as a lark, a scare; or maybe he thought I really knew something about Rodolfo's unfortunate death. He wouldn't have chosen a place as public as the Seal House if he'd wanted to ice me, but just now as he moved something flashed in his sleeve, silver, the small blade he carried. A voice in my head whispered that it had turned serious; it was Babar's voice, clear as day, saying, "I might as well ice the fuck."

I'd also scream his address and telephone number. But I

didn't know his telephone number, just that he lived some-where close to Atlantic Avenue, around Deane Street. It was humiliating to scream like a hysterical woman, but it was bet-ter than a blade in the kidney.

The seals applauded in their bunker. They cried, *"Earth! Earth! Earth!"* The orangutans in the Monkey House picked their noses. Several young representatives of the world beyond their bars picked noses in reply. I kept to the domiciles; every animal watcher was a potential witness.

For a man his size, Babar moved with great stealth. I headed south, through the park. A large white grizzly invited spectators into an arctic embrace. I passed up the invitation. But a solid wall of children lined up for the pony ride delayed me long enough to make my neck hairs quiver. He'd already gotten closer than I had resolved to let him before screaming, but not a sound, not so much as an "Excuse me," passed my lips.

I broke through the startled line of boys and girls, knock-ing a couple over as I ran, the harbinger of things to come rip-ping through their world of ponies and balloons. Outside the entrance, I noticed a phone booth in front of the Botanical Gardens across the street. I made for it. Even if he tried to get in, I could hold him off by wedging my body between the walls and the door. Why hadn't I accepted Toomey's offer of protec-tion? Clearly, I hadn't been constructed for heroism. The Creator had fashioned me for grace and speed; hadn't I been around long enough to realize that in a confrontation between brute force and grace, brute force wins! Shit, even Papo knew that. And here I was, small-boned, subject to every virus in the air, trying to hold off the Elephant Man from a phone booth!

He lingered on the corner, outside Prospect Park, as if he were biding time, arrived early for a date. Behind him, the wooden horses on the carousel bobbed up and down. I dialed.

"Tin Angel. Diamond Jim speaking."

"It's Pablo."

"What's up, boss?"

"I'm trapped in a phone booth in Brooklyn."

"Is the door stuck?"

"No."

"Is this a riddle?"

"No. Babar is after me."

"Babar? Why?"

"Because he's lonely."

"Anything I can do?"

"Listen, if you don't hear from me in an hour, call Christ—his number is in the address book in the drawer beneath the register—tell him . . . at four-twenty I was in a phone booth in front of the Botanical Gardens . . . I'm going to try to make it back home."

"Gotcha."

"Now's my chance. . . ."

I left the receiver dangling by its cord. Babar had bent down to examine the condiments in the Sabrett wagon. Before you could say, "Mustard and onions," I was in the Botanical Gardens, jogging north through the cherry blossoms, toward the Seventh Avenue stop on the BMT.

It was dark by the time I made it to Maria's. I had no idea how long a survival conference lasted, and was therefore greatly surprised and relieved when she buzzed me in. She met me in the foyer, where I watched her features transform themselves into an expression of raw dread in anticipation of the nightmare I continually brought to her doorstep.

"Pablo, you're shaking."

She tried to keep her voice steady.

"I just finished a survival conference of my own."

"Are you hurt?"

"Just terrified."

Even in my condition, I could feel her stop, fight to control her own panic. I more or less fell on the couch.

"I almost got . . ."

"Not now, *cariño*. Shhh."

She held my head to her breast, stroked my cheek, cradled me. I inhaled her through a cotton T-shirt. Finally, she propped my head on a throw pillow.

"Relax, I'm going to run a hot bath."

While she filled the tub, I called Diamond Jim. He'd been about to phone Christ, tell him I was a prisoner in a booth near the Botanical Gardens. I asked him not to mention a word of this to anyone.

When I stood on the bathmat peeling off my clothes, I could smell the fear on them. There is no more pungent odor than that of nervous perspiration. It's different from the sweat that comes from making love, or laboring under a tropical sun; it has a mustiness like something surfacing from a grotto.

Sinking into a hot tub full of bubble bath, I watched light play on the soap as my muscles unlocked. Tiny bubbles, each a world, a prism about to burst. But this was a safe place, full of aquamarine heat against green tiles.

"Camomile tea, *cariño*. Sip it. It will help you to relax."

She had taken me in without a word of protest. I was grateful. The steaming mug touched my lips. I sipped. She sat on the edge of the tub, drinking from a mug of her own.

"Close, baby. It was . . ."

"Not now, Pablo."

"OK." Stretching out, "I love the heat."

"Good. *Calmas.*"

Putting down my mug, I kissed her. When her mouth opened, I touched her camomile tongue with my own. Her chest heaved, her hand traced a line down my neck, across my shoulder. She was braless under her shirt. I lifted it over her head, kissed her under her raised arms, needing her, listening to her breath, feeling her chest rise and fall. I fumbled with the button on her jeans, raised her so I could slip them over her thighs; see that curved, scalloped roundness of her hips. Trying to gather up a woman's body is like attempting to embrace a wave. I stood, pressed my wet flesh to her dry skin, then kneeled to touch her belly with my mouth, brushing the sea-blue vein that ran from the top of her thigh to the mossy black hair; arching her back, I felt her blood rushing, swelling her vulva's lips as I parted them to drink her, an ocean in a goblet.

After love, in bed, the animal inside me curled up, as if the danger had never been. No urgency now, just the steady ebb and flow of our breathing, and her voice saying, "Shhh, sleep, Pablo, sleep." Then my lids shut and I was standing at the door of Carlotta's apartment, as I had at various points in my childhood, on the run from my father, school, the law. She opened it, shaking her head, irritated at this invasion of her privacy. Hadn't she done enough for me already? When they apprehended me jimmying open parking meters near the Albemarle Theater, hadn't she used her connections to reach a judge? Yes, I agreed, but this was different. I was in *real* danger now. No, she insisted, it was the same; I was in danger now for the same reason I had always been. I'd been a difficult birth, kicking and screaming, fighting to get out of the womb, then crying to crawl back in. What did I expect, after all, associating with criminals, running a bar on the Bowery? Besides, couldn't I see she wasn't getting any younger? Was I like my father, a secret woman-hater, with, yes, possibly even fairies at the bottom of my garden? Couldn't I see that she wasn't getting any younger!

"Yes, I can see you're not getting any younger."

Her body spilled out of a shorty nightgown. She had the full breasts of a young woman, but the wigless head was spiderwebbed with time. She had a face that no longer bore the clear markings of either gender, and her hands, I saw, reached down to support a *bloody asides,* which ballooned from the right side of her stomach.

What did I expect from her? She stamped her foot. A purple heart!

No. My heart was already purple. Without her help, I told

her, it might soon become defunct. Not only that, but she would continue to grow older whether she helped me or not.

My logic moved her to surrender the keys to her office. I could hide there for one night only, she said. I thanked her, took the subway to Broadway and Forty-second, walked to the Theater Arts Building, where a nightwatchman led me to a register. I signed in as *Perdido.*

The elevator stopped on the fifteenth floor, where I let myself into a dark room after opening a glass door on which was stenciled: SUMMIT THEATRICAL AGENCY. I felt my way to Carlotta's desk and reclining chair, where I sat surrounded by the silhouettes of file cabinets containing résumés and glossy eight-by-ten's of hopefuls waiting to dance and sing their way out of those metal drawers into the hearts of America. A small silver key on the same ring fit the lock in a bottom drawer of the desk. Inside, I found a small Beretta, took it out, checked the magazine, then put it down in front of me. I waited. I had spent most of my life waiting for my life to begin, and all the while it had been rushing past. . . .

Footsteps in the hall . . .

I reach for my piece
and . . .

it's plastic!

PLASTIC!

Mama, you hear?

You left your son.

You left me with a plastic gun!

"It's all right, *cariño.*"
"No."
"A bad dream."
"No good at all."
"Pablo, it's Maria. Everything is going to be OK."

The smell of bacon, toast and coffee makes everything OK. Over breakfast I told Maria about my dream. She sat quietly, taking tiny sips from her cup.

"You ran from the dangerous world out there to me, then dreamed about running to your mother."

Sitting there in a yellow terrycloth bathrobe, I felt as naked as the day I was born. I had always considered myself the anchor for Maria, something she could hang onto in the terrible drift of our common world. But as she had presented it, the very opposite was true.

"Are you angry?" Maria poured herself a fresh cup of coffee.

"I don't know."

"Lovers are supposed to know one another, aren't they?"

"I suppose."

"Friends, too. Did you know Miguel?"

"He wasn't easy to know. I used to think so, but lately I'm not sure. He lived different lives, kept them all separate. I feel like the left hand that never knew what the right hand was doing."

"You know where we grew up?"

"Sure, Twelfth and Boo."

"Have you ever thought about how it was for us, in a rat hole with no father and a poor, twisted Puerto Rican mama? Do you believe for one minute that Miguel ran from women to cards to coke because he was having a great time?"

"I never said I did."

"He was scared. It was dangerous out there on the street, and there was nobody to run to. Just like you, Pablo, with your plastic gun."

"It wasn't the same for him."

"It was. He handled it differently, made it appear a certain way from outside, but I knew him from the inside out. Consider this: If you two men, born into a man's world, were scared, what do you think it was like for this little girl?"

"You make me feel like a fool, Maria."

She fixed me with her eyes. They were dark and sad.

"I'm going to tell you something about Miguel and me that no one else knows."

"Why?"

"Because it's time you knew the friend you lost, and the woman you're sleeping with."

"Go ahead."

"Our father ran off when Miguel was nine. I was seven. Mama never married again, she was too angry, didn't even have boyfriends. The only man in her life was her *niño,* her Miguelito. Do you know that if I got up early I was forbidden to make a sound until he was finished sleeping! He was everything to her . . . *everything!*"

"At least he had that."

"He had *nothing.* When you're everything to someone, you're nothing . . . the person gets lost."

"I wouldn't know."

"Miguel didn't like school, stayed home from it most of the time. Mama didn't care. By the time you knew him he could read and write, figure percentages and odds better than most, but as a kid, the only time he went to school was to score."

Tears began rolling down her cheeks.

"One day I came home early. I'd gotten food poisoning from the free lunch—it was tuna fish and carrot cake. I was eleven and had this white woolen bonnet that pulled down over my ears and tied under my chin. It was my magical hat. As long as I had it on, nothing could harm me; only it didn't protect me from food poisoning, so I came home, let myself in, put my books down in the living room. Then I heard these strange sounds coming from the bedroom where Miguel and I slept. They terrified me. I thought someone was hurt. I rushed back, found them together in bed. . . ."

"What?"

"She was on top of him, Pablo. Fucking him."

"Maria!"

"Incest isn't as rare as people think. I know that now. But then, to a little girl in her magical bonnet . . ."

"Shit! What happened?"

"I may have screamed, I don't remember, but when Mama turned, I saw such rage in her face that I knew I was in danger if I stayed. If she had gotten her hands on me at that moment, she would've killed me. I still believe that. I ran back into the street."

"My God, Maria."

"It was the dead of winter. I couldn't spend the night on Avenue B. I went up to the roof, nearly froze. When I returned the following day, it was as if nothing had happened. We never spoke about it."

"Not even with Miguel?'

"Once or twice I tried, when we were both older and I was in therapy. It was the only time he ever raised his hand to me."

"You were in therapy?"

"A friend in a women's group turned me on to it. It saved my life."

"I didn't know that."

"After a few years I could talk about it pretty freely with my shrink. I learned how common incest is, especially in Hispanic families, only usually it's father-daughter. I dealt with my pain, but I couldn't deal with his, and that was inside me, too! Miguel knew it. That was why he hovered."

"I begin to see."

"After that, do you think there was a woman out there Miguel Ponce could trust?"

"Besides you."

"How could I refuse him, knowing what I did about him, feeling his pain, living with what drove him?"

She put her head in her arms and started to cry. I held her shoulders until her breathing grew regular.

"It's going to be OK, baby."

"How do you think I know what's going on in you? You're so familiar, Pablo. Always were."

"So? What do I do?"

"Open your eyes."

"They're open."

"No. You believe that because you're always out there in that hip ... devastation, in the thick of it, that your eyes are open, and because I close the door on it that I don't see. Pablo, if you really want to see what it's about, look at the person sitting in front of you."

"I see her."

"Does she frighten you?"

"Maybe."

Maria took a deep breath.

"Well, she should."

Saturday: Tiny Bubbles

"Get up, Mom is dead!"

Zach's voice over the phone was full of accusation, as if she'd died because I'd been sleeping. Maria sat there, watching me, somehow knowing what this phone call meant, though she couldn't hear a word.

Carlotta had died strangling on her own mucous, too weak to spit.

In the cab to Queens, my conversation with Maria wove in and out of thoughts about my mother; images and impressions of Carlotta blew like solar debris through the vast empty spaces of my head. I pinched my arm but felt nothing.

Mom is dead!

I tried to figure out what that meant.

There had been two Carlottas. The first one was a vague memory from my childhood, with her hair pulled back in a bun as she bowed the Bach cello *Suites*. I lay on the living-room floor trying to understand the expression of ineffable sorrow on her face, hoping to follow the music into the mahogany dark of her heart.

And then there was the second Carlotta, the diva with blond wigs, the seductress who talked like a seaman.

My God, did we all become tombs for earlier versions of ourselves?

But for a moment by her bed in the hospital I had told her the truth, and she had stroked my head.

Zach and Bertie were waiting when I arrived at the Funeral Parlor on Queens Boulevard. We gave the dark-suited young man a death certificate, signed the deed to Carlotta's family plot and picked a coffin. It was only slightly more ornate than the one we had buried Ponce in. It was lined with red satin. It reminded me of an open mouth.

A shirtless youngster was sitting on the stairs leading down to the Social Club. I asked him if Chocoláte was inside.

"Chocoláte? Who he, man? I don' know no Chocoláte."

"Funny, he used to shoot pool here. A short guy with an eagle tattooed on his arm, right here."

"Oh, yeah. I think I know the dude you wan'. He move, man. I think he go back to Santa Domingo."

The kid took several quick puffs on a roach, snuffed it out between his thumb and forefinger, swallowed it, then vanished inside. I wasn't going to get any help from the guys in the Social Club.

Papo was sitting on his stoop, turning the pages of a Spanish romance comic book. The pictures were drawn in black and white, and the heroine promised to pop out of her dress in the following frame but never did. Papo was annoyed by the interruption.

"You musta said something to him, man."

"Of course! How am I supposed to find anything out if I don't talk to the cat?"

"Well, you didn't do it right, man. Chocoláte *se fue.*"

"No forwarding address?"

"You scared him, man. Fo'get it."

If I had had the energy, I might've found Chocoláte on Amsterdam Avenue, in the Nineties, shooting pool in another basement social club, but I didn't. Papo merely grunted in response to my *"Te Veo,"* undressing the comic-book heroine in his mind.

I had to find Black Hattie before she took off for Rio. It wasn't nearly as hot for her down there as it was here in Manhattan. She might even decide to stay down longer than her usual couple of months, lounging on the beach at Copacabana, partying with friends. By the time she met her Argentine connection in the bush, returned to the troubled waters of New York, the entire episode might be as cold as Colon's corpse. When I found her, I wasn't going to let her be coy with me.

After dinner at the Tin Angel, Maria insisted upon accompanying me to the Gaming Club. I was going to leave a message that would move her. If she didn't respond, I'd lead the whole Ninth Precinct to her doorstep, as her late, unlamented colleague had wound up on mine.

"I won't get in your way," promised Maria. "I'd like to see where Miguel spent so much of his time, not to mention his money."

The taxi dropped us at the corner of Bleecker and Jones; from there we walked a short distance until we reached a blue door sandwiched between a candy store and a fish market. I knocked. An eye moved behind a peephole.

"Who is it? Oh, it's you."

A man I knew only as Sal greeted us. He was a vision in a black silk shirt open to his potted navel, a gold crucifix recumbent on a bed of black chest hair.

"Sal, this is Maria."

"Ponce's sister?"

"The same." She managed a smile.

"We all liked your brother, miss. Please be my guests for the first round."

"Thanks, Sal. When you have a minute?"

"Yeah. Soon as I can get somebody on the door."

Maria gave my hand a squeeze.

"Charming."

We proceeded down a carpeted ramp to a circular bar in the middle of the room. With one exception, the stools were empty. A brunette in a white sleeveless blouse paced the inside track; nothing provocative about her, the money here was made on cards. She nodded when Sal gave her a high sign from the door.

"I'll bet they liked my brother here. He probably paid their rent."

She shifted until she was comfortable on the stool.

"What are you drinking? Sal's buying."

"Fundador . . . no? OK. Make it two Remys, soda back."

By midnight the empty room before us would be jammed with folks who thought nothing of extending their night into the following day, many of them restaurant people getting off work. Maria wasn't listening as I tried to describe the early-morning scene; she was more involved with what was going on in the back room, visible through a broad archway, where six players sat at a green felt table. It was a semicircular table, at the center of which a dealer, sporting a green eyeshade, presided. Once upon a time that position had been occupied by Rodolfo Colon.

I couldn't see the face of the man handling the cards, but his hands were quick, in full control of the probabilities. Blackjack was, I explained, a game of skill.

"Can we go in?"

"Come on."

We settled behind a black man in a white Stetson seated between two blondes. They were all drinking tequila gold from tulip glasses. There must've been a thousand dollars worth of chips in front of them.

"White cost five, yellow ten and red are twenty-five," I told her. "The minimum bet on this table is five."

A bearded man I recognized as a bartender from the Upper West Side threw a twenty and a five on the green felt.

"Give me five white."

"Here you go, Lou."

The dealer pushed five chips his way, then shoved the two bills through a slot in the table that fed into a metal strongbox bolted to the underside.

"I'll take five of the same," I called.

The dealer took my money, gave me my chips and the obligatory rap to new players.

"We play Vegas rules. House wins on a draw."

Maria's eyes showed some of her brother's fascination with the game.

"Bad for us, no?"

"Bad for us, yes."

"People play anyway?"

"As you see."

"Why does he use all those decks?"

She indicated the dealer's shoe, a tray which held three decks of cards.

"To foil card counters. Some people can remember what cards have been dealt. When there's only one deck, that puts the odds against the house."

On the first round we went bust along with everyone else, except Lou, the bearded bartender, who stuck with seventeen showing. Then I felt a hand on my back. It was Sal.

"Finish these chips," I told Maria. "Stick at sixteen."

Sal led me into a back room furnished with a couch, Formica table, chairs and a refrigerator.

"I've got Beck's and Bud."

"Bud is fine."

After twisting off the cap, he handed me a bottle, took one for himself, swallowed.

"*Salud!* Maria enjoying herself?"

"I think so."

"Careful. Gambling can run in the family."

"Too bad about Colon."

Sal sat cowboy style, legs astride a chair, his gold crucifix gleaming in the light of a naked bulb overhead.

"Yeah, too bad. He was a good dealer. I never seen hands like that before, don't think I will again. He was born to the cards like some people are born to play the piano or paint pictures. And you know what else? I kinda liked the kid."

"You're one of a very select few. Have any idea why he was hit?"

"Are you serious? Man, it coulda been anything. How the hell should I know? As long as nothing goes down in my club, I don't care what kind of deals people make, and most of the people in this joint are wheeling and dealing some kind of way. Now I got the fuckin' cops putting the squeeze on me, saying they're gonna make my life miserable unless I tell them who Colon was tight with. They want me to solve their fuckin' murder for 'em."

"And?"

"Nuttin', man. The fuzz will probably close my ass down for a while because I can't tell them what they wanna hear."

"Can't, or won't?"

"No difference. I'll tell you someone I'd like to hand them gift-wrapped, though: that tub of shit, Babar."

"Why is he on your mind?"

"You hear what he did, man? Cocksucker! A cousin of mine gave him a job in a place downtown, the Twenty-two Club, you know it? I thought, well, the cat sometimes works for Hattie, he needs a hand, so I tell my cousin he's OK. I figure, how much damage can you do as a salad man working lunches, right? *Wrong!* You're not going to believe this, Pablo, but I swear on my mother's grave it's true. The cocksucker starts an argument with my cousin, and you know what he does?"

"Is this twenty questions?"

"You couldn't guess with forty. He starts swinging with a

paring knife, ends up cutting off one of my cousin's balls!"

"Jesus!"

"My cousin, mind you, ain't nobody to mess with. I mean, if you start, you better finish, because he's gonna kill you, right? So my cousin runs back to his office, holding his ball in his hand, gets his gun, but by the time he returns, the suma-bitch is gone."

"How did it start?"

"Who the fuck knows? I think my cousin told him not to use so much oregano in the house dressing."

"Go figure it."

"He's lucky if he makes it past Hoboken. My cousin, he put the word out. That man is a walking tombstone."

"When did it happen?"

"Thursday, after lunch. Why? You seen him?"

"Friday, in Brooklyn."

"Wherever he is, I swear by Jesus, Mary and Joseph the cocksucker is a walking tombstone."

I'd been most fortunate. Babar had flipped his lid. I only hoped that Sal and his cousin were men of their word.

"The shit's hitting the fan all at once, Pablo. What's your guess about Colon?"

He took a folded bill from his shirt pocket, handed it to me. I was speeding already. A little more wouldn't matter.

"That's one of the things I came here to find out. I have a hunch Hattie can shed some light on it."

"I haven't seen much of her. I guess I'd be pretty scarce, too, if a couple of my associates had been blown away and a third was blowing his top."

"Sal, do me a favor. Hattie comes by, tell her that if she doesn't call me in the next couple of days, I'm taking my trou-bles to Christ. OK?"

"You're religious?"

"She'll know what I mean."

"You got it. If she don't call you, you're taking your trou-bles to Christ. Those words, right?"

I handed him back his coke.

"Thanks, man."

"You think you got troubles. They tried to reattach my cousin's testicle up there at Bellevue, had him on the table for five hours."

"Did they do it?"

He stood, opened the door.

"They got it sewed back on, but whether it works or not is anybody's guess. He's fucking fifty-three years old, anyway. You don't need two balls after fifty, right?"

"Right."

Maria was where I had left her, only there were no longer any chips in front of her. As I took her arm, I could feel the coke filling me with those illusions of power that rise when fear has been numbed.

"How could anyone possibly walk away from this a winner?"

"Not many do, but that's not what it's about."

"Tell me, what is it about?"

"Action."

"Just like that, win or lose?"

"Just like that."

Sunday: The Bubble Bursts

"It's Hattie, Pablo."

I could hardly hear her over the din of Monty Waters' Big Band, which Pepe Nero once called "the horniest band in town."

"When can I see you?"

"Tonight. Soon enough?"

"Where?"

"Corner of Bleecker and LaGuardia Place, about one."

"I'll be there."

"Alone, Pablo. Don't tell anyone where you're going

—that includes Maria. I've got your word on it?"

"You have my word."

"Make sure no one's behind you when you leave. They may be staking you out. If they are and you can't shake the tail, go back to the club and I'll call you."

"I'll be careful."

"Later."

"Later, Hattie."

The bar clock read eleven-thirty, bar time, which is always fifteen minutes fast. A little more than an hour and a half to kill. I occupied the empty stool next to Junius Brown, in the middle of the bar. Monty was doing a tune of his own called "Ghosts," in which the musicians jump up and down making eerier sounds every few bars as their leader gestures frantically to make sure they pick up the melody at the same time.

"You know, Pablo, everything is sixty–forty," Brown squinted at me over a glass of wine. "I mean, at times you may think it's eighty–twenty or seventy–thirty; it ain't never really fifty–fifty, even when it looks that way! When you get up close, eyeball to eyeball, things is usually sixty–forty."

Rodeo Jim gave me the keys to his Duster. It was parked on Bowery, in front of the Kenton Hotel. A breeze blew from the east, salted with currents of warm air. I observed that there was no one in the doorways, not even a wino. The Duster turned right over. Pulling out, I made certain there was no one behind me. For a second I considered the possibility that Harris and Toomey might be watching me, but the streets were empty. I was alone.

It was a few minutes after one when I parked on the corner of Bleecker and LaGuardia. Handsome Willy Hoover, the singing bartender, was doing his thing inside the Village Inn; his voice drifted out the open door, sustained itself above the street noises. He did a decent imitation of Jimmy Rushing, especially considering he was pulling beers as he sang.

Black Hattie turned the corner of LaGuardia wearing a white silk mandarin jacket with red-and-yellow dragons embroidered over both breasts. She was slightly out of breath.

"No company?"

"I was careful."

"Good. How is Handsome Willy tonight?"

"Better than Rodolfo Colon."

She didn't miss a beat, just locked her door from inside and fastened her seat belt.

"Make a left at the corner, Pablo."

"Where to?"

"Off Lafayette, not far from the Tombs."

"What's down there?"

I beat the light across Houston to West Broadway.

"Ever hear of the Nose?"

"No."

"The name Caviar Henry mean anything to you?"

"Sounds familiar."

"Half the places in SoHo garnish their dishes with salmon eggs because he imports his dope from the West Coast packed in government-inspected cases."

"Never met him."

"Salmon eggs from Vancouver, what a cover! He's big, Pablo, probably one of the oldest wholesale outlets around."

The Café Roma was dark, as was the rest of Little Italy along Mulberry Street. We turned uptown on Lafayette, not far from the municipal jail, a huge stone building with passageways connecting to the courts, known affectionately as the Tombs. Hattie instructed me to make a sharp right down a narrow street and pull over where a man stood waving me into the only parking space on the block. He was an Oriental, in jeans and a sweat shirt.

"Don't be nervous." Hattie buttoned the top of her mandarin collar.

"I figure I'm safe with you."

The statement was only half true. It hung in the air between us. It would be even easier for Hattie to set me up than it had been for Babar, if that was what she had in mind. Our Oriental guide opened the door on Hattie's side. When she had gotten out, he pushed down the button to lock it.

We followed him to what appeared to be an old loft building that housed a couple of sweatshops. He pressed a button on an intercom, listened to some unintelligible words, answered back in a foreign tongue, either Japanese or Korean, and waited. A clicking sound released the lock. The door was not an old wooden one, as it had seemed from the outside, but was made of reinforced steel with hinges welded to a steel frame.

"Henry's a nut about security," smiled Hattie.

Our guide didn't give us any indication he understood or was interested in what we had to say. He unlocked a padlock on the elevator gate, then yodeled up the shaft, whereupon a wrought-iron behemoth started a lumbering descent.

The elevator operator, another Oriental, was shorter and squarer than his colleague, who remained at the door. He gave us a sharp, abbreviated bow. I noticed that his knuckles had been broken so many times, they formed a single bar of bone across his hands. When we stopped, he opened the heavy iron gate as if it were rice paper.

The room was the size of a banquet hall, with ceilings nearly sixteen feet high, a medley of woods: knotty-pine floors, rough wood wainscoting, oak beams overhead.

"I'll be damned if this isn't the Shogun's castle."

"Wait till you meet the Shogun."

There were track lights with pin spots, one of which beamed down on the cast-bronze statue of a nose! This monument to the great Sniffer must've been at least five feet high on a base of a foot and a half thick.

"Hooray for Hollywood."

"As a matter of fact, Henry does a lot of business with

Hollywood. They've got him half convinced he'd do better to let them make a movie of his life and retire from the drug trade like a gentleman."

"Must be tempting."

The tables and chairs were horizontal slabs cut from giant redwoods; couches and huge throw pillows lined the walls. Black opaque shades that prevented light from showing through covered the windows. A few people watched a color TV at the far end; others sat casually, alone or in small groups.

They were a mixed bunch, white, black, a smattering of Latino, but they shared the look of easy affluence that marks successful young drug dealers who compose an ever-growing percentage of America's middle class. They wore expensive jewelry, leathers, tailored sport clothes, imported sweaters, custom shirts, designer jeans; among them were future Danny Macs, charmers who would find their way into the upper echelons because they fit an image, were nerveless and sentimental.

"So this is where you hang out?"

"Sometimes, and only during business hours. I prefer a little more funk in my social life. Not that it's so different anywhere else these days. Even the brothers in those uptown supermarkets have surburban souls."

Superknuckles, the elevator operator, bowed to us.

"You come, pease."

"Thanks, Toshi."

He used one of many keys on a ring to unlock a door that opened onto a long corridor. At his request, we emptied our pockets on a table. He used a magic-wand metal detector to check us for concealed weapons, after which he led us to a door halfway down the hall.

Toshi knocked three times lightly, then escorted us inside.

"Hattie! Hattie! Hattie!"

An adenoidal voice rang through a pea-soup fog as hot and damp as a Turkish bath.

"Henry?"

"Over here. How do you like my new hot tub, Hattie?"

"I can't see a thing."

"Come closer. Come, come. . . ."

Holding my arm, Hattie inched towards the voice until we found ourselves confronting a huge wooden barrel about twelve feet high and perhaps eight in diameter. Wooden steps led up to a semicircular platform around its lip.

"Aren't you supposed to put these things outside, Henry; you know, with a view of the sun setting behind mountains?"

"I could put it on the roof and watch the sun go down behind Ferrara's, but the air gets too sooty. You understand the concessions we're forced to make in our line of work. At least indoors, I have steam, too."

It was an oversized kiddie pool for a jaded kiddie, except instead of rubber ducks, a naked geisha-type frolicked in front of him. She tittered at us over the rim. When she moved aside, I saw a small carroty head and a droopy mustache.

"You haven't told me if you like it, Hattie. Of course, you and your friend are welcome to join me. In civilized parts of the world, where they know how to live, the most informative conversations take place under these conditions."

"Another time, Henry."

"It's redwood and ponderosa pine; had it shipped from the Coast with a truckload of Blackfoot mushrooms."

"Groovy, Henry, but my schedule is kinda tight."

"Oh, Hattie, why are you always rushing off to catch the next plane? Don't tell me. I don't want to know. All right, I'll be with you as soon as Hidieko walks on my back."

Toshi conducted us back to the main hall. We arrived in time to hear Bacall talking to Bogart over Henry's Sony Trinitron.

In about twenty minutes Toshi came to fetch me. Hattie remained behind. We walked down the same corridor to a room opposite the one with the hot tub. He let me in and closed the door. I listened for footsteps walking away. I didn't hear any. Either Toshi moved like a cat, or he was posted outside.

A thick-pile white carpet covered the floor wall to wall. At the far end was a mahogany desk on which a green Tiffany Nautilus lamp cast a glow that drew everything into a snug circle. The filing cabinets behind the desk would probably be worth a small fortune to the Feds. I settled into a deep upholstered chair.

"Greetings. No, don't get up. Contrary to appearances, we're informal."

Caviar Henry was no more than two or three inches over five feet. He padded to the desk in flip-flops, wrapped in a yellow-and-black kimono that clashed with his freckled face and flaming hair. Removing two humidors from a cubbyhole, he placed them on the desk, then slid one toward me.

"Smell."

It contained swatches of shriveled black material that gave off a dank, musty odor.

"What is it?"

"Dried Blackfoot mushrooms. They came with my hot tub. They're grown in the traditional manner by Blackfoot Indians."

"Some of my best friends have black feet."

He pushed the other humidor. It was full of *nieve pura*. I nodded, put it back on the desk.

"Try some. It's very delicate, the beating of butterfly wings in the nose."

"Another time."

"Would you prefer cannabis? I have an Indonesian selection they call 'heart of the buds.'"

"I don't think so."

"You're not impressed by my tub, you're not impressed by my wares," he sighed. "I guess I'll have to stop trying to impress you."

"It would make things easier."

"I only do it, you understand, because I'm very shy."

"I understand."

"There's something else you should know."

"What's that?"

He gestured around the room with one hand.

"We're private here. No cameras, mikes; it's the only room in the complex that's completely cut off from the monitor."

"Why live so dangerously?"

"Exactly! What fun would it be if I had absolutely all my bets covered? A bit of a risk spices things, don't you think? Of course, I do have a button under my desk that signals a red alert, but if you were very fast, now that you know it's here, you could wring my neck in complete privacy."

"That's not what I came for."

"Naturally, if you succeeded, you'd never make it out alive."

"Beware of kamikazes."

Henry seemed to be sneezing into his hand when he laughed.

"Kamikazes . . . ha, ha, ha, very good. You know, when I started selling drugs in the early sixties, I considered it an act of civil disobedience. But everything at that time had a political implication. Radicals took showers, reactionaries took baths. And I was part of the effort to undermine the bad guys and give the good guys a chance. Turning people on was like freeing the slaves. You remember?"

He released a wheezing laugh into cupped hands.

"There was a lot of bad rhetoric around in those days."

"I believed it. I really thought that the more people I turned on, the harder it would be to keep the war going. Vietnam . . ."

"What do you believe in now?"

"Hard to say." He scratched his chin. "One thing I learned

is that men are slaves with or without drugs, if that's what they were born to be. Maybe I don't believe anything across the board. Yes, I think that's true. I merely find the appropriate position in relation to things as they arise."

"Very diplomatic."

"Practical."

"Henry, if you don't mind, Hattie has led me to believe that you can help me answer a few questions."

"*Who? Why?*"

"Exactly. . . ."

"Do you realize, Mr. . . ."

"Pablo will do."

"Mr. Pablo, did it ever occur to you that no other animal behaves in the form of a question? I mean, intelligent animals can express a wish or a need; sea mammals, like the whale, can even beach themselves in gestures of suicidal despair, but only the human animal can frame a question."

"Very interesting."

"The final irony, Mr. Pablo, is that while the questioning posture is commonly considered to be a humble one, it's probably the one that elevates us above all other life forms."

"What's your point?"

"Do you find your questions elevating, Mr. Pablo?"

"It's more like a tickle in my throat that won't quit, Henry."

"Perhaps if you took something for it?"

"That's why I'm here. Some answers would help."

"Hattie tells me you own a restaurant."

"The Tin Angel. It's a jazz club."

"I've heard of it."

"Ever hear of Miguel Ponce? Rodolfo Colon?"

Henry pulled on his earlobe.

"Most unfortunate, particularly the first name."

"He was my partner."

Henry turned in his swivel chair.

"Terrible! Terrible! What would you say if I offered you a good deal on salmon eggs?"

"What?"

"I can deliver them at cost, less than the price of gherkins."

"I'm not interested."

"It would probably be more germane than what you've come for."

"I'd hate to think so."

"Here, I give you an unbeatable price on salmon eggs and you accept. Your customers are pleased with a touch of added elegance, you make a bigger profit, your waitresses get bigger tips and I get to ship more goods. Everyone benefits. I'd call that a fruitful discussion. Now, consider the order of business you've come to pursue."

"Let's do that."

"Ask yourself, 'Will it result in making people happy? Will it alter the complexion of things in a way that's advantageous to all?' "

"You're being evasive."

"Bear with me. Most people think as you do: if they ask the right questions, they will get the right answers; if they get the right answers, they'll be able to alter the unpleasant conditions of their lives. But I put it to you, Mr. Pablo, consider it further. This man wants to know why he can't get an erection; another, why his doctor has just told him he has a fatal malignancy in his lung; a mother wants to know why she sometimes hates her child, dreams of throwing it into the garbage disposal: all of them believe they have a right to answers that will change their condition."

"What about you, Henry? You play in your hot tub, naked women walk on your back, and here you sit talking with supreme detachment to a fool who has come to you for help."

"Isn't mine a reasonable position?"

"About as reasonable as selling drugs to stop a war. Bro,

you may think you're some kind of sage, but you're just a little redheaded guy with freckles sitting across from a nervous guy with a big nose."

As soon as the words were out, I was sure I had blown it, until I saw Henry was laughing himself into a coughing fit. When it subsided, he took a deep breath before continuing.

"Each of us lives out a fantasy, Mr. Pablo. Ever see the Japanese film *Sword of Doom*?"

"Sure. At the Bleecker Street Cinema."

"It's my favorite. If I ever made a movie of my life, I'd love to have Tatsuya Nakadai play the lead."

"Anything is possible if you have the money."

"I'm afraid not. As you so accurately observed, I'm a little redheaded guy with freckles."

Henry blew his nose in the handkerchief he pulled from his kimono in time to catch a sneeze. Then he leaned towards me.

"Recall the scene at the end, when Tatsuya is killing all those samurai around the house? He's been mortally wounded himself, but he goes right on killing—it must go on for ten minutes!"

"Yes."

"A beautiful dance. We watch him, this infernal machine, moving with such grace; we become fascinated, fall in love with his dance of death. It's magnetic, it pulls us, until, to paraphrase Yeats, we can no longer tell the dancer from the dance. We can't make that distinction anymore because our perception is clouded with the bloody truth of our own desire . . . do you know what for?"

"I haven't the foggiest."

"The desire to comprehend death, to do battle with it until we understand that it isn't something other, but a reflection of ourselves. A kind of negative mysticism, Mr. Pablo. By the time Tatsuya sees this, he has become Death, littered the groves with corpses."

"Is this some kind of elaborate threat?"

"Consider your questions as a kind of sword. You wave them around like an avenging angel, people all around you are falling; you dance around like Nakadai, slicing everywhere."

"There *are* dead bodies around me, Henry. Not long ago I found one propped in front of my door. The other one belonged to a friend I keep seeing in my dreams."

"Do you really think it's a matter of a couple of names? One or two individuals? Don't you know that when you start rocking the boat you discover it is full of passengers; and when you sound the alarm, they all head for the lifeboats at the same time, perhaps trample each other trying to save their own lives?"

"That won't do. I want names and reasons."

"For every name, there are four or five more dead bodies."

"What am I supposed to do?"

"Listen to me!"

"What the hell you think I've been doing!"

"We take care of our own dirty laundry, Mr. Pablo."

"Meaning?"

"Your answers no longer exist."

"The thirty-five grand from my business, that doesn't exist, either?"

"First things first. You mentioned a body on your doorstep, Mr. Pablo?"

"Damn right! Doesn't exactly give me a feeling of security!"

"Exactly. But instead of considering it a threat, why don't you think of it as a piece of dirty laundry delivered for your inspection? A reassurance, one of your vital answers."

"I don't understand."

"I just told you, we take care of our own. The answers to your questions no longer exist. As for your money, you made a blind investment, Mr. Pablo: you took a risk and lost."

"I accept the risk. But nothing was recovered, Henry! My money is still out there."

He opened a drawer, withdrew a large manila envelope and held it out. I took it.

"I'm going to give you an opportunity they'd never give you on Wall Street, Mr. Pablo. Count the money."

It was all there, wrapped and faced, thirty-five stacks with ten hundred-dollar bills in each.

"Thirty-five grand."

"It's yours, under certain conditions."

"Why?"

"You're incorrigible, Mr. Pablo. The condition I'm giving this to you is, *no more questions.* You drop the matter as soon as you walk out the door."

"Jesus!"

"Let's say it's worth it to me to keep you from rocking the boat. Call it an investment in futures."

"I don't know."

"Think carefully. You have my assurance the matter has been dealt with. Take the money. Accept my conditions. Next time we get together, we can discuss a shipment of salmon eggs for a comparable order of gherkins."

He folded his hands on the desk, content to let the ball rest in my court. Caviar Henry had taken his best shot. A great deal of what he said made sense. If Ponce were here, he'd be the first to take the money and get out. And perhaps, as Henry pointed out, there were people on the sidelines, people like Black Hattie, who could only be hurt by my stubbornness. I stifled the revulsion that rose in my throat when I picked up the envelope and stood before my host.

"Wise move. I applaud you."

Henry patted his palms together a couple of times before sticking his right hand out. I took it. The hand was hot, clammy, the bones delicate, like a woman's.

"I'll show you out."

But my feet wouldn't move.

"I can't do it."

"Don't be obtuse."

"I know. I know, but . . ."

He was right. Guys who think they're too good for this world don't stay in it long. They wreck the hard-won negotiations others have hammered out in order to survive. I put the envelope back down on the desk.

"If this is my money, I want it without conditions."

"Then it's not your money."

"Fine. I don't accept charity."

"That's that then."

"Another threat, Henry?"

"More questions? But you're not looking for answers, my friend; you're looking for yourself, and I can't help you with that. Good-bye, Mr. Waitz."

Black Hattie crossed her arms as we descended in the elevator.

"Well?"

"Well?" I shrugged.

"There's nothing more I can do."

She gazed down at the metal floor plates.

Caviar Henry had shaken me up. I'd stood before him with money in my hand and given it back. No, it wasn't only the money. Nor was it revenge. Maria had allowed me to understand that Ponce's death hadn't been a matter of a cop's bullet, but the flowering of a seed planted long before. Nor could I ascribe my persistence to a passion for justice. I could accept the idea that people lived and died in a drama in which the answers made no difference. Yes, I could live with that. What I could not live with any longer was the feeling that I was being pushed around.

* * *

We were approaching Rodeo Jim's Duster when I heard something move in the shadows of the building behind it. An alley cat foraging, I thought, until I perceived the outline of a massive shape.

"Hold it right there!"

The voice came from a warehouse with a graded driveway and loading platform. The outline disengaged itself from the shadow of the platform and walked slowly down the ramp into the sodium pink of a street lamp.

Black Hattie took a step back.

"Babar!"

His voice was soft, caressing.

"Hello, Hattie. I been keeping my eye on yuh, like always."

"What are you doing here, baby?"

"Watchin' out for yuh, Hattie. And I've got some unfinished business with this scumbag."

"Easy, honey. Easy does it."

"Better for yuh if I take care of him now. He's been on your case."

"Easy, baby."

"I'll do it slow and easy, so he don't miss nut'in. Don't yuh worry, Hattie."

The trembling in her voice made my blood freeze. For the second time tonight my feet were rooted. I waited for my adrenaline to kick in so I could run, the old "fight or flight" response that's supposed to be built into the species. Where was it?

"Babar, baby, you shouldn't be within a hundred miles of this town."

"Maybe I can help," I managed.

"Yuh can shit in your pants, that's what yuh can do. Yer the one who needs help, yuh Jew scumbag! I'm gonna bone yuh like a chicken."

"Hold on, Babar," cautioned Hattie.

My eyes scanned the street for something I could use as a weapon: a pipe, a stick, a garbage-can cover. But even if I held a pipe, where would I hit him? He was armor-plated, just head and thorax. I'd have to drive a wedge under his chin to find his Adam's apple; as for his knees, they had more flesh over them than foam in a football pad. His groin? His balls were probably as small and hard as cherry pits. The thought struck me funny. I snickered.

"Big joke, huh?"

"Not for a second, Babar. I didn't mean it like that. You know how I am."

"Listen to Mama," pleaded Black Hattie. "It's already past time for us to be outa here. We can't make any more waves, you dig?"

"It's not my fault, Hattie. It's him, with his big mouth and scumbag hands he can't keep to himself. I seen him touchin' yuh."

He stood before her, arms hanging at his sides. When she reached out to caress his cheek with her fingertips, he leaned towards her with this dreamy expression.

"Listen to Mama, baby."

"Yuh shudda listened to me, Hattie. Yuh wouldn't be in trouble now if yuh did. I ain't so stupid. People think, 'That Babar, he ain't good for nut'in but muscle, he's even got muscles in his head.' But that ain't true, Hattie. I got brains."

"I know, sweetheart."

"Jus' cause I ain't got a big mouth, like him!"

"Shhh."

Gently she turned his face away from me, back towards her in an effort to distract him long enough for me to run, but I couldn't move!

"Trust me, Hattie."

"I always trusted you."

"No, yuh didn't. Yuh used to trust me, then yuh stopped. Yuh got involved with those other hot dogs. . . ."

"No, baby."

"I ain't stupid, Hattie."

"Whatever I didn't tell you was for your own protection, baby. That's the truth!"

Babar turned to me. There were tears in his eyes, and as he walked slowly in my direction I could see something had snapped in his brain.

"Babar, listen, honey, Pablo's all right, he's my friend."

"He's a piece of shit! I'm yer friend and he's nut'in!"

"There are already folks out there looking for you, Babar. Remember the guy you cut?"

"I ain't worried."

"But I am. If you hurt Pablo, it's going to be impossible to get out from under."

"It'll be all right. We'll go away, you and me, and that's the way it shudda been all the time."

"Right now, before anyone else gets hurt."

"I gotta hurt him."

"There won't be anyplace in the world for me to hide if you do."

"He's been burying yuh, Hattie, with his questions, his talks with cops. I gotta hurt him."

"No, Babar!"

"Get outta my way, Hattie."

"Babar, you're the one who's put me in danger, not him!"

"Don't say that!"

"It's true. Look at what you've done, robbing those bars, cutting Sal's cousin, threatening people close to me ... and now you want to kill one of my oldest friends! *Babar, you're blowing me away!*"

Run, I implored my feet.

"He's gotta be taken out, Hattie. He knows. He can put you away for life."

The tendons in her neck stood out.

"He doesn't know anything. You! You're putting me away."

"I'm the only friend yuh got in the world, Hattie."

He spoke so gently, I barely noticed his palm until it covered my face, pushed back my head.

"Babar!"

"I'd do anything for yuh. Those other hot dogs, they want to use yuh, to touch yuh."

He kept bending my head back with one hand while pulling my spine forward with the other. Applying a steady pressure, he palmed my face like Goose Tatum palmed basketballs, and his words came through a ringing in my ears. Then it got dark. I was in a movie watching the action on a screen at the back of my mind—a woman was racing down the sidewalk, Avenue B, carrying two suitcases full of pure cocaine. Why had I always assumed the woman had been as white as the contents of her luggage!

Because you is a prejudice mothafucker! whispered Junius Brown.

It had been there all along, ticking. Suddenly the alarm had gone off. Hattie! It was you in the car!

"Babar, stop it!"

Her voice washed over me. I heard her scream, *No, no, noo,* then I felt something probing my nostril. He was trying to jam his dowel up my nose, make good his promise to leave me noseless, to pry it off my face. *Carlotta, what happens next? Forgive me, Maria. Good-bye, Zach.*

There was water rushing, a bell tolling a buoy, like Ambrose Light; there it was on the movie screen, a steel horse in the middle of a bay ringing as the tinker mackerel, numerous as stars in a southern sky, shot across the blue surface, dappling it with their silver bodies while they sang like the Mormon Tabernacle Choir belting out the *Hallelujah Chorus* in a hot tub—until everything dissolved into a candle flame that flickered against the walls of my cortical chamber, lower, dimmer as the dowel moved up my right nostril, then a rush, a sigh of air . . . then a deep gurgling as my knees went weak, buckled because there was no longer anything holding me; the sluggish engine that was my heart started turning over, my lungs like a monstrous bellows attempted to rekindle the blood with oxygen so it could rush its message to the brain: I was still alive!

Something warm, sticky blossomed on my chest. Babar's hand slipped through it. I focused on his face. It was close to mine. There was a bouquet of red bubbles forming along his lips; a jet of blood was spurting to the rhythms of his pulse, fading from a severed carotid. The Elephant Man managed to twist back towards Black Hattie, who held a straight razor in her hand, then fell to his knees, face gazing upward. His expression changed from one of confusion to one of relief before his eyes glazed with the icy surface of shock and he lurched forward to touch her ankle with the finger of one hand.

I removed the dowel from my nose. He may have created a second ridge in it, but, except for a little blood, it was still intact. My second act was to nearly herniate myself, dragging Babar's body into the shadow of the loading platform. I covered him with a half-rotten roll of linoleum I found in the garbage, took off my blood-soaked shirt, turned it inside out and used the clean parts to wipe blood from my face and neck. After taking the straight razor from her hand, I removed Hattie's mandarin jacket, which had soaked up the blood like a blotter. Her small breasts heaved beneath a white silk blouse as she leaned against the fender of Rodeo Jim's Duster.

I wiped the blade, folded it back into its bone handle, which I also wiped before throwing it into the garbage. Better to let them find it here. I put our bloody clothes in the trunk, wrapped in a discarded *Daily News*, then tried to stop my mind from racing long enough to see if there was anything I'd left undone; there'd be no second chances. The only thing that occurred to me was getting away.

Half in a trance, Hattie allowed me to lead her to the passenger side. When she was safely inside, I got behind the wheel and pulled out. We drove towards the Hudson on Canal, turning uptown on West Street.

"Thanks, Hattie."

She didn't reply, just stared ahead like a zombie. We drove under the shadow of the fallen West Side Highway with no particular destination in mind. I just wanted to put distance between ourselves and Babar's corpse. It was good to see the Jersey lights on the water. Finally, she broke her silence.

"What are you going to do?"

"You saved my life."

"Because of me, you almost lost it." I squeezed to the right to make room for a passing van. The breath caught in her throat. "And poor Ponce!"

"What happened, Hattie?"

She shook her head, leaned against the dashboard as if to relive thirty nightmare seconds on Avenue B, then fell back against the seat and started to explain.

"It was a sweet deal, Pablo. We could've retired on it. We had it all. A new source, stuff as good and cheap as any I ever brought back and a buyer ready to pay top dollar."

Passing the docks at midtown on the elevated highway, I repeated her words to myself. We approached the *Leonardo da Vinci,* her white hull as snug in her berth as a foot in a shoe. Ships and shoes, those Italians had a way with both. I'd always loved the *Leonardo*'s lines. They reminded me of another ship, one I'd been on not too long ago, and something clicked.

"Your new source . . . Danny Mac?"

"You knew?"

"I should have. It was no coincidence, running into him. I should've guessed."

"We wanted to know how much Ponce had told you. Setting you up with Danny Mac was a way of finding out."

"And if he'd told me everything?"

She shrugged.

What would've happened? Indeed. Would they have sent

me on a pleasure cruise—first-class on the *Leonardo da Vinci*? Perhaps Danny Mac would've kidnapped me, forced me to fuck and fish my way around the Grenadines until things had blown over? *Fat chance.*

"Here it was, right in my lap ... no need for me to look another customs man in the eye. All we had to do was come up with front money, eighty grand."

"Jesus!"

"Ponce did thirty-five, and I came up with the rest. It was big, Pablo. Over half a mill just for taking it uptown."

I tried to whistle, but couldn't pucker. Hattie didn't notice I was blowing air.

"It was a piece of cake. A room had been reserved for Mr. and Mrs. Ortega at the Americana. . . ."

"Room fifteen-oh-one."

"How did ..."

"Making one of the pieces fit. The number was written in Ponce's date book."

She rubbed her eyes with the backs of her hands, then grew pensive for a minute before continuing.

"Ponce and I were to check in at nine, wait for an hour, make the exchange and split."

"Simple enough."

"No simple fu'we, mon," creoled Hattie.

"Who was the driver?"

"Crahs de road be one nice spot fu sleep. . . ." She gazed vacantly out the window.

"Hattie ..."

"That's what we used to say when we were kids on our way to the market in town. We lived on the outskirts of Kingston, you know, shacks with outhouses."

"Who was driving, Hattie?"

She returned to the present with a jerk of her head in my direction. For an instant she seemed to be waiting for a lost part of herself to catch up.

"A simple enough job, right? Not for Rodolfo."

"Colon!"

"All he had to do was take us there, wait downstairs until we came out. He wasn't my choice, Pablo."

She turned to watch us passing those baroque stone buildings that rise along Riverside starting at Seventy-second Street. I waited. No reason to rush.

"I would never have used Rodolfo on a deal. He was all right for a drop. I kept his nose cold and he took my messages. But Ponce wanted him in. Ponce was a gambler, and including a dealer like Colon was for him the same as piecing off Lady Luck."

"What happened?"

"*Lady Luck, mon, she wiggle her raggedy ahss an blowaht de cold faht.* The night before the deal goes down, Ponce spots Colon coming out of the Vanguard with his little drummer friend. . . ."

"Julie?"

"Herself. He sees them sucking each other's lips in a doorway, follows them to her crib, waits outside half the night while Rodolfo's up there fucking her. By the time I saw him the next day, Ponce was crazed, threatening to kill Colon. I told him the deal was off and he calmed down, begged me to see it through."

"Ponce could've handled it."

"You think? Sometimes when things start falling apart, man, there's no way of stopping it. There was all this blow hanging around, you know? I told them both not to do it while we were doing business. Do you think they listened?"

"I saw Ponce every day. Where were my eyes?"

"He was OK. It was Rodolfo who started going to pieces. Snorted himself right into the jitters, insisted on taking his piece along. I told him we didn't need it for a sweet deal like this, but, Jesus! Pablo, those macho Latinos! He did everything I asked him not to because he'd be damned if he would listen to a woman. When the fuzz stopped us, he freaked like a five-year-old!"

"I think I know the rest, Hattie."

She shook her head, let it drop forward again as if it had suddenly become too heavy to hold upright.

"He was staring at me, opening and closing his mouth. He wanted to tell me something, only he couldn't get enough air to make the words. It kept leaking out. I grabbed those bags and ran for my life!"

Black Hattie sat up, took a deep breath, let it out slowly. When she faced me, her tearstained face nearly made me lose control of the car. I let the speed drop from seventy to fifty-five.

"Where did Babar fit in?"

"Poor stupid baby." She swallowed. "I kept him as far away from the deal as I could, but Colon used him, psyched him up to do his dirty work. Rodolfo was scared you were going to find out the whole story, turn him in or ice him yourself."

"He played it very cool with me."

"Why not? He used Babar to keep the heat on you, told him that if you knew too much, you would hurt me."

"All right, that makes sense."

"And after you started worrying his chick, he drove Babar over the edge. . . ."

When she scowled, her face became an ebony Kabuki mask. Her baby elephant was dead; she, the mama, had been forced to put him out of his lumbering misery. Just minutes earlier, Caviar Henry had assured me that my troubles were over, that the answers to my questions had been taken care of. He'd known about Colon, but not about Babar.

"Who pulled the plug on Rodolfo?"

Hattie played with a button on her silk shirt.

"He wasn't so slick. I saw what he was doing. I would have pulled it myself."

"Did you?"

She shook her head.

"Then who?"

Lights winked at me from the Jersey Palisades; they seemed to be making fun of my questions. But when Hattie showed no sign of answering me, I asked her again, louder this time, more insistent.

"Who, Hattie?"

"I discussed it with Henry," came her slow reply. "He's an old friend, Pablo. Almost as old as you and Ponce."

"Did he arrange it?"

I waited. She continued without confirming or denying the obvious.

"When you started breathing down my neck, he agreed to talk to you. I didn't want to get him more involved than he already was, but Henry insisted on it, said there was more to the whole thing than met the eye."

"What did he mean by that?"

"I didn't ask. There are some things, Pablo, you leave alone."

"Why am I still alive, Hattie?"

"What do you think I am!"

Outrage burned in her face.

"You could've had two for the price of one. I mean, without me, maybe . . ."

Her hand whipped out. I felt my cheek sting and turn to fire for a second before I realized I had been slapped. After what she'd just done for me, perhaps I deserved it. We were passing the park along the right side of the drive. The night-lights were on and two teams were playing softball.

"Would you give Caviar Henry a message for me?"

She nodded.

"Tell him that on second thought I've decided to accept his offer, if it's still good."

"Does that mean it's over?"

"Yes."

"And you forgive me, Pablo?"

"For a good slap in the face?"

"No, man. For everything else."

"I'm not a priest."

We turned off Ninety-sixth and made a sharp right after the stop sign up the hill to Claremont Avenue. Black Hattie sat there shivering.

"A priest wouldn't do me any good."

I tried to say it, to frame the words. It was simple. There were only three of them, but they wouldn't come.

A shock wave washed over me as a cop car, with its roof light revolving silently, crept up behind us. My passenger remained unmoved. I held my breath until it passed us, on its way to some emergency requiring stealth.

"Another time, Hattie. Later."

INSIDE THE BODY OF EVIDENCE

Blue Monday

I attempted to burn the bloody clothes in my bathtub on a bed of tinfoil. They hissed, stank and scorched the tiles. It took the better part of an hour and a can of Ajax to clean the place. I ended up throwing the charred articles in a double garbage bag secured with a wire, which I put in my can on the landing. Let the city burn them. Then I fell asleep. It was deep and dreamless. By the time I woke, a pink sunset was being reflected in the project windows along First Avenue. It was a few minutes before six. I had less than two hours to wash, dress and make it on time to Carlotta's reception.

In the shower I replayed last night's events. Distorted by my anxieties, they unfolded as images in the mirrors of a fun house. Whether a different course of action on my part would have changed the direction of events was impossible to say. All I had wanted was what a child wants, something to make it right. Not even the wrath of God can protect us from ourselves.

It wasn't until I stepped out on the street, heard traffic, saw people floating by in the balmy dusk of a May evening that my anxiety began to abate. I'd half expected a uniformed policeman to be waiting at the curb ready to cuff my wrists, but the only thing I found that vaguely resembled a brush with the law was a ticket on the windshield of Rodeo Jim's Duster. I had parked it in a metered zone.

Leaving the car, I caught a cab to the funeral home on Queens Boulevard. Zach, Bertie and I were led up a carpeted stair to a room on the second floor, where we waited to receive the condolences of family, friends and the more curious of her acquaintances.

Carlotta was where she should've been, just as she had requested: unembalmed, in a closed coffin surrounded by massive flower arrangements—sunbursts, fireworks, waterfalls. The room was Miami Beach: mauve carpet, mirrors and chandeliers. In the middle of it all, the coffin was a very small object. It looked like a loaf of Russian pumpernickel.

Zach, Bertie and I took turns stepping out to swig from Bertie's new hip flask. We shook hands with neighbors who had ridden up and down on the elevator with Carlotta for over fifteen years. Most of them had never made it beyond her threshold, but they were one and all admirers of the glamorous woman who had made going up and down memorable for them.

A fat publicist who fed copy to most of the New York columnists congratulated me on having a mother who was way ahead of her time.

"Not anymore," I told him.

Client friends wove in and out. Steve was there, in his dark solo-violin suit. Lillian became dewy on my chest until I sat her down in the vestibule and told her Carlotta would have wanted her to be a warrior. An attractive middle-aged lady from central casting pinched my arm like a chicken inspector. A funeral home executive appeared to say they were closing soon. His timing couldn't have been better.

Zach and I brought up the rear. In addition to cat hair, there was a fine spray of dandruff on his black crewneck. His eyes were lined with red and his cheeks were waxy pale. My concern for brother Zach disappeared instantaneously when I noticed Bertie, who'd lain back until everyone else had exited. Zach and I could hardly believe our eyes when he did what he'd been waiting to do all night.

Certain that he was alone with Carlotta at last, he rushed over to the coffin and raised the lid. Then he took out a packet of letters wrapped in a green ribbon and put them under her head. For a second, I thought he was about to crawl inside with her. Flashes of the red satin interior shot out like devouring lips and gums. They swallowed the correspondence when he closed the box. As we walked out the door, I was sure I heard Carlotta's voice.

"For God's sake," she said. *"Even here, can't I get any privacy!"*

Services and burial followed the next morning. Both were brief and to the point. A rabbi at the chapel gave a sermon in which he decried the fact that we could send men to the moon, pour billions of dollars into nuclear arms, but could not yet immobilize the scourge of our time, cancer. A radio talk-show host, whom she had known for many years, gave a eulogy. He recalled the first time he'd met her, after a concert, when she was a young musician. It was in Saint John the Divine, where he had been so captivated by her rendering of *The Meditations of Thais* that he had gone over and introduced himself.

By the grave, the rabbi instructed us all that while there was a period of grieving, after that we were expressly instructed not to mourn. I repeated the words of the kaddish as though I'd been saying them all my life. I said them for Carlotta and Ponce, for the Five Spot, and Joe and Iggy, too.

Afterward, I went home, changed and started walking east, where I found Christ in front of the schoolyard. He was talking to a pretty young woman with a small brown dog. I would have been content to continue on my way, but he broke off his conversation and came over.

"Sorry about your mother."

I nodded, even though there were no tears in me. Observing a personality being dismantled was like discovering there was only empty space at the center of the atom, a sadness beyond grief.

"Thanks. Looks like you're doing fine."

I smiled in the direction of the young woman, whose eyes were still on him.

"Not bad, considering the business I'm in. A cop's view of the world can get pretty grim."

"Would you rather sell insurance?"

"No." Christ chuckled into his beard. "But they're transferring me out, Pablo, taking me off the street."

"Why?"

"Because the Lower East Side is changing. They want the mavericks out to let in the boy scouts."

I nodded. It was true. This area had been a refuge for those who didn't run with the herd, on both sides of the law, for over a decade; they had been the last wave of immigrants from a society that had no place for them. In a world that aspired to clean verticals and horizontals, the Lower East Side had been a net for those crazy vectors that shoot off on a bias or carom back at their source with an urgency that sets the sirens blaring, the flames licking at the sky. Now, civilization, with its real-estate developers, was mustering an army of boutiques, co-ops and condominiums at our borders.

"Where are they putting you?"

"They've attached me to this new elite force on organized crime out of the DA's office."

"Sounds like a promotion. They giving you a gold shield?"

He shook his head, then lowered it so that I couldn't see his lips move.

"It's not the gold shield. I don't need the status, though I've paid my dues. But I can do some good on the street."

"Well, now you'll be able to go after the big guys."

"Not exactly. Oh, Pablo"—he heaved a sigh—"sometimes the objectives are so shabby, I forget why I ever went into police work. Certainly not to bust a few loan sharks and card games to make the pols look good. We'll never come close to the big guys."

"I'm sorry."

"Hey, don't get me wrong." He touched my shoulder briefly. "I've done all right for a man who swings between Saint Francis and Oliver Cromwell."

"You'll be missed."

He paused long enough to give me a dry smile which was barely visible under his shaggy beard and mustache.

"For a while. By the way, they're still working on a theory about Ponce, Colon and whoever else was in the car—they think Colon was the shooter. The theory is that they were tied in with Ali running guns."

"You believe that?"

"The FBI has been watching Ali for some time. They believe it. Don't be surprised if two men in blue suits ring your doorbell and want to talk about it."

"Ali has lymphoma."

"Terrorists get cancer. We can't find a trace of him. Who knows, he might be getting a hero's welcome this minute from Arafat."

I doubted it. Ali may have fooled me in some ways, but not in others. He was a private person. My hunch was that he knew he was being watched and with the impeccable timing of a master arsonist had gone somewhere, alone, to die. I was grateful. I couldn't bare to see another familiar corpse.

"I have my own theory," continued Christ.

"What's that?"

"It was a drug deal that went sour." He took a deep breath. "It was also a setup."

His words took me by surprise. I felt like a somnambulist

who had been shocked awake to find himself standing at the edge of a precipice.

"Setup! How do you figure that?"

"I started nosing around Narcotics. They move so slowly over there, things get lost. They're used to building a case a little at a time, so when something comes in quickly, they usually yawn."

"OK. So what?"

"On the day of the shooting, an anonymous tip was called in on two different occasions. It's right there in the files. The caller left no name but stated that a large quantity of drugs was going to change hands that night. The tip was specific; gave the name of the hotel, room number, description of the couple carrying the drugs."

"What happened?"

"Like I said, Narcotics yawned, sent over a couple of men. They staked out the room; nobody showed. There was the usual bureaucratic shuffle. No one connected the tip with what happened on Avenue B that night. The incident was logged, and everything got lost in the files."

"What happens now?"

"Nothing, probably. It's not my concern anymore, and the boy scouts won't want to draw it out. There aren't any merit badges to be won. But the way I figure it, Pablo, someone was trying to set up one, or all, of the individuals in that car. Except that through an act of God it went sour: a taillight didn't blink, and four people are dead."

Five, I thought. Five, and let's hope it stops there.

"An act of God," he repeated. "Eddie and Bill, they got caught in it. It doesn't matter. It cancels itself out. There's no way to make the pieces fit."

I nodded my agreement but looked away, at the kids playing in the schoolyard.

"Except for this, Pablo. Whoever was responsible for the setup is still out there."

"Have any ideas?"

"Nothing I'd move on."

"So you're going to drop it?"

"Like I said"—he scratched his head—"it doesn't matter anymore. It's academic."

I shuffled, gazing at the pavement as if it were a screen, an oracle, feeling like a child who avoids stepping on the cracks. But there were no answers at my feet, just the encrusted cement of East Fifth Street.

"Hey, Pablo, what's Black Hattie been up to these days?"

"Who?"

"Hattie," he repeated. "Have you seen her?"

Another shock. I was sure it had registered, and Christ had seen it. He was toying with me.

"She drops by every so often."

"Do me a favor. When you see her, give her my love."

I left him with the pretty lady who had waited patiently in front of the schoolyard, and headed back to my apartment. Christ knew. He had made a few of the pieces fit for himself. Colon was the shooter; the shooter was dead. Black Hattie had been the lady in the middle. It had been a drug deal, meant to be a setup, gone sour. Behind the facts was a pyramid of rivalries and jealousies—and one unanswered question. Who was still out there, perched at the top?

Sticks and Stones

At first Heather Moore expressed extreme reluctance to meet me. That's putting it mildly. She called me names and made threats in a most convincing way. I assured her I understood her situation, that she was on the threshold of a new marriage, a new life. But, I told her, she couldn't shed the old one without paying some attention to a few details. A very large detail being my readiness to link her husband-to-be to

Ponce's death in a way that would at the very least prove embarrassing, if not more. Reluctantly, she agreed to meet me at eight at Bradley's on University Place.

I had known guys like Matt Rosen, grown up with them in the Brooklyn of the fifties. They were the tough Jews, and sons and nephews of Murder Incorporated and the Amboy Dukes. They were the heirs of Bugsy Siegel and Meyer Lansky. When the Chassids along Eastern Parkway had been terrorized by the Irish, they'd driven up in carloads, mopped the streets and restored a wary armistice. I had known them; they were among the thickest-skinned toughs on the planet. Even the *capos* worked hand in hand with them. And the younger ones, the Matt Rosens, had acquired a certain veneer, a semblance of education, an astuteness in the legitimate business world, an acceptability in society unknown to their forebears.

Even so, when there was a problem to be handled, they did it with great dispatch.

Matt Rosen, as Bertie had told me, had his fingers in a lot of pies; chiefly gambling. He was a puppeteer who pulled strings from somewhere in heaven. When he did, people jumped here on earth. He'd worked Colon as Colon had worked Babar, and like Jehovah on the mountain, had finally shown the Latin dealer his ass!

No doubt Rosen was also in drugs up to his signet ring. He was captain of the big boat Caviar Henry warned me not to rock. Sure, that scanned. Rosen probably put the deal together, but, again, from a place on high, offstage. Hattie, of course, hadn't known it was a setup. She was to be busted along with Ponce. And Danny Mac? Now, *there* was an interesting consideration. Except, after a little thought, it seemed clear Danny hadn't known, either. It had been his coke, and he had taken a heavy loss. Maybe Rosen had found Danny as disposable as the others, but the descendant of Robert Bruce was not a man to play with. Well, for every Caesar, there was a Cassius, and a Brutus, too.

Don't rock the boat, Caviar Henry had warned. No, I

didn't think he had been in on it, at least not from the beginning. Hattie's protector, he had also been able to do Rosen a favor. Knocking off Colon couldn't have been a pleasant task for the king of salmon eggs. It meant that there were strings attached to his limbs, no matter how nearly invisible they were. When the puppeteer jerked them, Caviar had found himself doing his own dance of death.

Maybe I didn't have it all a hundred percent right, but the major parts fit. I understood how the machine had been set in motion. What I didn't know was *why.*

Bradley's was empty at eight, its dark-paneled walls sheltering under soft, indirect light. I chose a table in the rear, away from the bar, facing a piano and bass that waited for the touch, tonight, of Tommy Flannigan and Major Holly.

She was a few minutes late, which gave me time to compose myself, rehearse my assault. When she finally arrived, her lips were compressed in anger. She brushed her short blond hair back from her forehead, leaned towards me and said: "Waitz, you're a son of a bitch!"

It was a deep, throaty whisper.

"Now that you've said it, please sit down."

I ordered a Budweiser, and she asked for a Lillet on the rocks. As far as anyone else was concerned, we were adulterous lovers having a tête-à-tête. Our postures spoke of furtive meetings, whispered endearments.

"I mean it. You're a rotten bastard to pull me into this. And Garret, too."

"You're already in it, up to your eyeballs."

"How dare you!"

"You know it. Otherwise, you wouldn't have come."

"All right, Mr. Waitz. I don't have endless time. Matt will be expecting me back at ten. I had to lie to him, something I've never done. He thinks I'm meeting an old school friend for a drink."

"Are you sure he hasn't had you followed?"

"Just who do you think you're dealing with!"

She made as though she were about to get up if I didn't retract the horrible insult. I didn't retract the horrible insult.

"I know precisely who I'm dealing with. Do you? Do you know what your fiancé does for a living?"

"He's a loyal, generous, tender man, I don't pry into his business."

"He's a gangster who controls a complex of gambling establishments and drug traffic. He also dispatches people to the happy hunting grounds with a flick of his finger."

"I don't have to listen . . ."

"Yes, you do. Because if you don't know already, and I believe you do, you should. Moreover, I think you should know that he tried to set up Miguel Ponce in a drug deal."

"Are you saying he hired two cops to pull them over and shoot it out?"

"No, my dear. That was accidental. He had planned something far more civilized. Ponce and one other person were to be caught with a quantity of cocaine that would have taken them out of circulation for years."

"Why? Why would Matt do a thing like that?"

Her voice flared with indignation, but a shadow of doubt flickered in her clear blue eyes.

"You tell me. What did Matt know about Miguel Ponce?"

"You have me at a disadvantage, Mr. Waitz. What if I terminated this discussion right now?"

"I'd rock the boat until it tipped."

"Would you dare?"

"You bet. And I have the evidence to do it."

"You're bluffing."

"You told Rosen that Ponce was Garret's father, but did you let him know Miguel had been sending you support for years?"

"As I said before, I'm not in the habit of lying to Matt."

Of course she'd told him. My files had been shredded, my account books torn and scattered on the basement floor.

"I have two years' worth of canceled checks. A brief inquiry would produce more. You're the link, Heather. Together with the attempted setup, it's enough to establish a possible motive."

"You're a son of a bitch!"

"My first move would be to talk to a friend of mine, a cop in the gambling unit. He already knows your fiancé. Then I'd photocopy the checks and send him a love letter. I have a hunch that investigation of his personal life would blow Matt wide open."

The air went out of her before my eyes; a long sigh came from her throat, her shoulders caved in and her strong jaw dropped.

"Now it's your turn," I told her.

"He went crazy."

"Rosen?"

"No, Miguel. About a year ago he started showing up without calling, wanted to take Garret here, spend time with him there. All these demands. He never even cared before. Out of the clear blue, suddenly, just like that, Miguel Ponce wants to be a father?"

A tear ran down the ridge of her nose and her lips quivered. I recalled Mensch at the Hip Bartenders' Consciousness-Raising Group saying that Ponce wanted to know about his child; Mensch had explained to the group what he had said to his son, that to him the boy was a blessing. Ponce wanted his blessing. In this whole crazy world of misspent passions, it was the child he had come to want.

"He was timid at first. I told him he couldn't come barging in after all these years and demand a relationship. I had built a world for Garret and me, carefully, with great consideration for the child's feelings; he couldn't walk right in and shatter it to bits because he felt paternal for a second!"

"Was it Garret's world you were worried about or your own?"

"Both, Mr. Waitz. The two are synonymous. My world holds Garret's no less today than when I carried him in my belly."

"Go on."

"I finally had to discuss it with Matt. Ponce wouldn't stop. He even started talking about custody! Can you imagine, wanting joint custody of a child you never acknowledged?"

So there it was; at the center of everything, deep inside the body of evidence, a child.

No, I told her, I couldn't imagine how it had felt to be Ponce.

She was silent.

"Thank you for answering my question."

"And now, what do you want from me, Mr. Waitz? Blood? Money?"

"Neither one."

"Do you want to punish me?"

She scowled. By her tone I gathered that it would make her happy to be punished.

"No, I don't think so. I think you're a victim, too, Heather Moore. I also think that there's no greater punishment for you and your fiancé than to be locked into this together, never being able to look each other in the eye."

"I'm going."

"Wait! Just one thing more. I don't want to lose track of the child. No, don't get worried. All I want is for you to call me, say, once a year, on February twenty-third—OK? Call me on that day and tell me how he is, how you both are."

"You want to be our fairy godmother, Mr. Waitz?"

"I'm not your enemy, Miss Moore. Not unless you want it that way. Will you humor me?"

She gave me a very long appraising stare, tried to gaze right through my eyes down into the depths of a darkness that felt, for the first time in months, clear and unconfused. With great effort, she gave me a couple of nods. Then, unexpectedly, a very touching smile.

"You have my word on it. Do I owe you anything?"

"No, the drinks are on me."

At the Tin Angel I called Maria, to tell her I was a bit numb, which wasn't surprising for a man who had buried his mother that morning; but Carlotta was out of her misery, and I was ready to start with a clean slate. Would she join me for dinner? In an hour, she said.

No sooner did I give the phone back to Diamond Jim than I spotted Frankie Palermo in a light blue gabardine suit, with a dark blue shirt open at the collar. Beside him was a squatter version of a young Italian manhood, with contrasting suit and shirt in brown and tan.

"This is Carmine," Frankie introduced him to me. "He's in the funeral business, too, but he's looking to diversify."

Carmine shook my hand with something that felt like eight ounces of chopped chuck. He eyeballed the room.

"How much you want for it?"

"Let's sit down and talk."

I led them to the Second Street Café.

"Last time I saw you, Frankie, you were about to transport an army of winos to City Hall by wheelbarrow. How did it work out?"

"You know that Schwartzkoph who owns the hardware store? At the last minute he decides to make a profit on the wheelbarrows. It would have cost us . . ."

Bleeeep, bleeeeep.

I heard a long whine coming from a small walkie-talkie attached to Carmine's belt.

"It's so we can keep in touch with our people. You know, in the funeral business we're on constant call, like doctors."

"Sometimes it just don't stop," elaborated Frankie.

"When business gets real heavy, you gotta sleep with a squawk box."

Carmine nodded gravely, then picked up his train of thought.

"We're kinda like physicians. Someone could call at any time and say, for instance, we gotta pick up a stiff at St. Vincent's, or be ready for a stiff coming in on such and such a flight from Montreal. And you gotta be there 'cause that's your business and stiffs don't keep."

"Sometimes you get a stiff ready, and on the way to the reception somebody drops it or bangs it by mistake or smears the makeup," chimed in Frankie.

"Anything can happen," Carmine agreed. "Sometimes a stiff falls off a truck on the way to the parlor."

Stiffs and radar ranges.

Carmine's finger shook like a meat hook when he stuck it in his ear. "It's heavy work," he chorused. "I mean, you're familiar with the term, 'deadweight,' aren't you? No joke! You should try jockeying around a few stiffs."

Carmine paused to take a breath. If just talking winded him, I could understand his desire to diversify. He shook his head.

"Stiffs. They're breaking my back and ruining my marriage. I get into bed at night and all I want to do is sleep. My wife asks me when we're going to have a baby. Before I can answer her, my eyes are closed. I think maybe if I open a restaurant . . ."

"This isn't exactly a mom-and-pop operation," I told him.

"Skip the mom-and-pop stuff. What are you asking?"

"A hundred thousand. It's a steal at that figure."

"You gotta be kiddin'." Carmine knit his brow.

"Absolutely not."

"What kinda people come here, anyway?"

Bleeeeeeeep, bleeeeeeeep.

Jazz people, I told him. The Tin Angel was a jazz club.

Carmine leaned back in his chair. A hundred thousand and death were no longer awesome to him, but jazz still held all the terrors of the unknown. It was alive, spontaneous.

"Jazz! Is that what happens here?"

"Yes, Carmine," I nodded.

I wanted to explain to him that a Parker solo always had breath in it, that you couldn't get away from the man breathing; no matter how high the music soared, you could feel the heart pounding beneath the notes, the Bird metabolizing his own weight.

"Hey, Frankie, you didn't tell me that's what happens here."

It sure did. Seven nights a week the air crackled with improvisation, that whispered freedom. It whispered that there was a life within the life we seemed to live, where everything is expressed without reservation. I considered myself blessed to have heard it.

Bleeeeeeep, bleeeeeeep.

Frankie picked up his walkie-talkie and dispatched a hearse to St. Claire's for a stiff.

Carmine got up, wandered into the main room. Joe Lee Wilson was onstage with his quartet, featuring Monty on sax. Carmine couldn't have recoiled faster from *il bache d'morte,* but curiosity overcame him, and he stood in the door of the café staring out. It was as though he were trying to understand the two bearded black men at the front of the stage who loomed like Elders of Zion speaking in musical tongues.

"Carmine." Frankie walked over, tapped his colleague on the shoulder. "You ready to go?"

"In a minute, Frankie. A minute. I wanna see what goes on here."

Jazz goes on here, I wanted to tell him. It's a music made out of fingernail parings as well as the heart's blood, out of vague ancestral memories and a yearning for freedom coupled with a profound acceptance of the world.

Bleeeep, bleeeep.

"Carmine, are you comin'?"

"Shhh."

Joe Lee was singing the blues. Carmine stood transfixed, listening to the words.

> If it wasn't for the blues
> I'd a spent my whole life in jail,
> but I sang 'em so good
> that the judge he went my bail. . . .